LUCY PLAYS PANPIPES FOR PEACE

a novel

by Lynette Yetter

*For Larry –
keep shining your
light + illuminating
humanity!*

Lynete Yetter and MusicAndes.com

Los Angeles, 2010

Published by Lynette Yetter and MusicAndes.com
Los Angeles, CA, 90041
(323) 284-5595 • Lynette@musicandes.com
© 2009, 2010 by Lynette Yetter
Printed in the United States of America.

Photo and illustration credits in Appendix A

Library of Congress Control Number: 2010903023

Yetter, Lynette, 1959-

Lucy Plays Panpipes for Peace : a novel

/ by Lynette Yetter.--First U.S. ed.

p. cm. -

"Lynette Yetter and MusicAndes.com"

Includes bibliographical references (p.)

Includes glossary

ISBN-10 0-9843756-0-0 (pbk. : alk. paper)

ISBN-13 978-0-9843756-0-8

1. Travel - South America - Andes - Bolivia - Peru - Quechua - Aymara - Music - Fiction.
2. Indigenous Peoples - Andes - Autochthonous music - Fiction. 3. Globalization - Spiritual
aspects - Bolivia - Peru - Fiction. 4. Globalization - Human rights aspects - Bolivia - Peru -
Fiction. 5. Globalization - Economic aspects - Bolivia - Peru - Fiction. 6. Buddhism - Soka
Gakkai - Fiction. 7. Gay - Lesbian - Fiction. 8. Music - Panpipes - Fiction. 9. Ethnology -
Miscellanea - Fiction. I. Title.

First U.S. Edition, paperback 2010

For
BRUS SORIA
Musician, miner, husband and father
(May 13, 1942 - September 5, 1982)
and
LEONCIO HERRERA TORRICO
Miner, husband and father
and
all people who died suspiciously during CIA Operation Condor

Table of Contents

ACKNOWLEDGMENTS

Thank you to my mom, Alta Gale, who provided the love and financial support for me to complete this project. Thank you to Ron Rivera and Potters for Peace for being my Third World mentors. Thank you to everyone I worked with in Gotham Writers' Workshop. Thank you to Jean Pauline who is the best editor I could ever have hoped for. Thank you to all of my sikuri friends who continue to share life and music with me. Thank you to my brother, Eric Yetter, for being there through everything. Thank you to my stepmother, Voni Yetter, for teaching me that I could do anything I put my mind to. Thank you to my father, Don Yetter, for loving me when I felt unlovable. Thank you to my stepfather, H. Rodney Gale, for loving my mother and welcoming us into your family; without you this book would not have been written. Thank you to Angel Yasmani Mestas Quispe of "Asociación Cultural del Arte Milenario, Los Heraldos, Sangre Aymara (¡Q'ory Wayra!)" and José Domingo Calisaya Mamani of "Organización Cultural Armonia de Vientos Huj'Maya" for reading portions of earlier drafts (in rough Spanish translation) and giving your thoughtful feedback on sections dealing with sikuris. Thank you to Dave Tourje, founder of the Chouinard Foundation and the New Chouinard School of Art, for Chouinard fact checking. Thank you to Deirdre Smith, R.N. for medical fact checking. Thank you to Jean Monte for feedback on many of the chapters. Thank you to countless people, whose names are too numerous to list, for your support and inspiration.

Finally and continually, thank you to my mentor in life, Daisaku Ikeda, for teaching me to dream big and that nothing is impossible.

CHAPTER ONE
LUCY

A great human revolution in the heart of a single individual can change the course of human history.
- Daisaku Ikeda (paraphrase)

Hurtling through space and time, the blue orb was rapidly self-destructing. Vital fluids pumped out of its innards burned in orgies of greed. The vapors ate away its luminous ozone skin.

Indigenous Elders, you might call them brain cells of wisdom, were ignored.

New synapses of fiber optic cable and satellite rays rationalized the destruction as "progress".

Chaos surged like a flooding river.

You had only to pause for a moment in that raging current to feel the sadness and despair pounding against you. Your feet (firm on rock riverbed) kept you from being swept away. In that solid stance you felt something deeper than the swirling chaos. That, of course, was hope -- hope that the life of the blue orb could be saved; that you could be saved -- that Hell could be transformed into the Land of Eternally Tranquil Light.

But when?

And how?

It could happen in a moment.

And with the subtlest of incidents, like a single breath.

Lucy, a 40-something California free spirit who laughed and loved easily (and cried just as easily), encountered that single breath one smoggy summer day in, of all places, Disneyland.

She heard a sound that stirred her soul like a gentle breeze blowing away the cacophony of crowds and the worries of paying rent and health insurance bills. She felt like she was floating above a mountain peak, white glaciers all around. The air so pure. In her vision she saw a valley, hand-tilled in green and brown lopsided squares like a crazy quilt. In one of those squares an ox plodded. Behind him a small brown man gripped a hand-hewn wooden plow and steered its point in the Earth. Every muscle of the man's body focused on his cherished task like a master dancer at the height of his craft. A woman in long handspun skirts twirled around and around, just for the fun of it. Her calloused feet in tire tread sandals, patted the cool freshly tilled earth. The man paused in his work and smiled at his wife. She threw her head back and laughed in pure joy of life. They hooked elbows and spun each other around in the warm sunlight. Grasses in a neighboring square danced with the breeze as a condor pirouetted overhead. Such was the world that Lucy was transported to by that sound.

How different was that sound from the whines of those Ritalin-dosed kids over there in line for Space Mountain, complaining to their boob-enhanced mom about an ache, a hunger for something that money could not buy.

And how different was that sound from the melancholy drone of loneliness that orchestrated Lucy's days. She often felt lonely, even in the midst of a crowd. Sometimes that lonely song in her head got so strong, she yearned for the silence of death.

But, this new sound sang of life and sunlight, of living in harmony with the earth. It sang of a soulmate for Lucy. The music was a pied piper pulling her to happiness.

Lucy gazed into the eyes of her elderly bohemian Aunt Bert.

Aunt Bert had her own private sorrows, but she dealt with them in a different way. Today she was trying to cheer Lucy up by cashing in the two free Disneyland passes she received in barter for some carpentry work she had done.

Lucy took Aunt Bert's sinewy sculptor's hand into her own and said, "Wanna see where that sound is coming from?"

"Here goes Lucy, again," thought Aunt Bert with an affectionate smile as she let Lucy lead her into the crowd, "I wonder what she'll get herself into this time."

Like a person mesmerized, or a person waking up from a dream, Lucy searched for the source of that mystical sound.

There it was. Just past a fast food restaurant filled with people with distracted eyes - their teeth munching food that was guaranteed not to rot or to give much nutrition - was a group of musicians. They were short brown men, their feet planted like tree roots that tapped into the churning molten core of the Earth. They were playing music that sang primal energy, with only their breath vibrating hollow cane tubes.

"Oh those tubes!" Lucy thought, "Who knew that bamboo could sing and cry?"

Tears birthed from Lucy's eyes. She was home. At last, she was home.

"Yes," she thought, "This is my life! This beauty and harmony! Millions of years of Earth Wisdom in my bones, bones like fragments of the mountains that I once was!"

And then, the sound stopped.

Lucy's home disappeared.

The song was over.

Yet, Lucy now knew she had a home - if only while the panpipes played. It was like a parallel universe she had caught a glimpse of. In that place people lived in harmony with each other, the earth and the infinite. There, she would encounter her Inka soulmate who would dance with her in a fresh plowed field.

She set out to find or create that ideal world of which the panpipes sang.

CHAPTER TWO
DANCING AT THE BLOCKADE

When you bow to the Buddha nature in another person, just like in a perfect mirror, the Buddha in that person bows back to you.
- Nichiren Daishonin (paraphrase)

Lake Titicaca, Puma rock. Glacier melt from ages turned, filled the basin on earth crest thrust high from night marine depths like cupped hands raised with offering to the heavens.

Tendril of lake in shape of claw of Puma - liquid lapis someone named "border."

I

The Peruvian bus driver threw up his hands and shouted at the passengers, "You all need to take your luggage and carry it across to Bolivia and get on a different bus because of the emergency."

"He must have a mechanical problem with his bus," Lucy thought.

Her heart pounded in the 12,000 foot altitude as she arrived at the door of her dreams - Bolivia. Finally, she would attend the yearly Anata Andino festival, where she would meet the indigenous people who play the music she had been studying and performing with increasing intensity for years. She had applied for a Fulbright as an independent ethnomusicologist, not affiliated with any university. Also, she applied to the MA/PhD program at UCLA's school of World Arts and Cultures. She was waiting to hear from these two programs. In her essays she wrote that she would travel to Peru and Bolivia in February 2002 to attend specific festivals and lay the groundwork for future fieldwork.

Lucy picked up her worn North Face backpack from the bus luggage bay. The backpack, which she bought for five dollars at a garage sale, was stained with oily blotches from some other traveler's meal and brown mud from an unknown foreign land.

When hoisting the bag on her back, the strap yanked on Lucy's ponytail of sandy blonde hair. She hadn't cut her hair for over 20 years to be in solidarity with indigenous peoples. She flipped her ponytail free and headed across the Peru/Bolivia border along with the other bus passengers.

One of the passengers was a stout Swiss-German man who had more suitcases than children. A wiry porter with a cart hauled his family's luggage. The children held hands and looked with big eyes at the money changers holding fistfuls of bills.

Lucy felt a twinge of superiority as she carried her own stuff and didn't need a servant. Little did she know that in future crossings she would be so over-laden, she would make that Swiss-German man look like Gandhian simplicity.

A middle-aged passenger from Bolivia maneuvered her small black suitcase on wheels around puddles on the cobble-stones, never splattering its fabric even once.

All the passengers lined up at Immigration on the Bolivia side of the river that drains Lake Titicaca, the lake from which the Inka culture sprang. Fluffy clouds roamed like contented alpaca above the green and brown hills that embraced the sacred lake.

In front of Lucy, in line, was a willowy backpacker from Switzerland. He said to her, "The Beatles have the answer, you know. All you need is love. It's so easy!"

Lucy smiled in agreement.

II

The Bolivian woman with the small suitcase, the German man with all the children and luggage, the Beatle's fan, Lucy and all the other passengers got on a bus on jack stands. The bald tires were being replaced by somewhat less bald tires.

Soon, they were on their way.

Just out of town the bus turned off the highway onto a farm road. The dirt road, slick with mud, ran along the top of a raised embankment that snaked through fields of potatoes and quinoa. The bus fishtailed back and forth, dangerously skirting the embankment, first to one side, then the other. Everyone got real quiet. They stared out the windows at the scenery careening by like in a drunken nightmare.

Lucy thought, "Is this the day I die?"

She started chanting quietly with intensity as though grabbing onto a lifeline, "Nam-myoho-renge-kyo Nam-myoho-renge-kyo Nam-myoho-renge-kyo..."

Suddenly, deep in her heart, Lucy knew, "No, this isn't the day I die." Everything started to glow with an inner light.

"I know I'm going to die someday. But today is not that day. I have a lot more work to do in this life. I know I'm going to get to La Paz. I know that my story goes on."

Lucy settled into her seat. The bus continued to slide from side to side on the muddy embankment. She savored the luminescent landscape, clarity more alive than she had ever seen.

Poised in that moment in time and space, as if someone had stopped the clock, cranked up the lights and blew off the dust, Lucy appreciated the beauty of everything at her leisure.

The bus window seemed to disappear. No longer was there a wall separating Lucy from communing with that bee courting purple potato blossoms who fluttered their petals like unselfconscious children in laughing play. Potato plant leaves were limned in radiance; light of the sun that enters and dances. A dance of transformation; growth, vibrant ever-changing joyous life. Cumulous clouds brilliant as a silver smith's forge should have hurt Lucy's eyes, but didn't. Like that poem she'd written long ago.

Bright bright light / too bright for sight. / But just right / for those who are not as they seem.

Black moist soil whispered its lover's secrets to Lucy. She listened. Loamy earth was alive with energy that Lucy sensed as part of her own body. She felt as if her central nervous system had extended into the cool soil and impregnated the limitless sky.

The pulsing, flow, energy of plants she sensed as if she too was transforming sunlight and mud into roots, stems and leaves that danced in slow motion growth.

Distant mountains looked so close, so close. She could see every crevice and feel their ancient song reverberate in her bones. Her bones and that rocky spine on the horizon were one and the same. Sunlight, lover's warm breath, caressed her - even through the bus window safety glass.

"Nam-myoho-renge-kyo."

In a moment, her focus shifted to the other passengers grimly gazing out the windows.

"But, of course," she thought, "everyone else is scared they're going to die. How can I help reassure them?"

Lucy pulled her panpipes out of her chuspa knitted pouch.

"I'll play softly - to encourage the others."

After she played a few bars, the woman from Bolivia jerked her gaze away from the window. The woman's name was Martha.

She asked Lucy, "Aren't you afraid?"

"No. I know we're going to get there fine," Lucy said with a smile, her chubby face looking much younger than her 42 years.

"Good," Martha smiled back, sighed and relaxed her shoulders.

Lucy played her panpipes.

Martha sang along.

III

Between songs they chatted.

"You know why we're driving through the fields, don't you?" Martha asked Lucy.

"No. Why?"

"Because of the blockades."

"What blockades?"

"The indigenous farmers have blockaded all the roads to protest the U.S. War on Drugs. The U.S. wants to eradicate the coca crops."

"But coca is the sacred leaf in the Andean Cosmovision!" Lucy said, recalling what she had learned in Quechua class at UCLA.

"Of course."

Around the bend the bus came to a halt.

Blockade.

Rocks in a row, spaced like recently-thinned potato plants, spanned the muddy farm road.

Off to the right was a one-room adobe home. A five-foot-tall sinewy farmer stood alone in the middle of the road with his feet apart; arms folded across his narrow chest.

The bus assistant rose from his seat and headed for the door. The farmer could have been a cousin. They both had the same build, similar features. The bus assistant's grandmother lived in a house that looked a lot like this one. But, he didn't think about their commonalities. This was an Indio blocking his way; his way not only to La Paz, but his way to "success". In this racist society he was fighting for respect, for power. Although he understood Aymara, he didn't speak it. He was ashamed to. He would not be called an Indio or a campesino. He was becoming mestizo. One day, he too would drive a bus, his own bus. No one would look down on him as he sat high in the driver's seat of his huge shiny machine. Shiny, for he would wash it by hand down by the river; the river that sparkled in the sunlight. Those sparkles he would transfer to his chrome bumper. The river, deprived of its light, would run foamy away. But that he wouldn't see, as he turned his back on the river - the river that brought life to the people. He would admire his bus. His temple -- the temple in which he would be the god.

The bus assistant walked up and spoke to the farmer. Lucy couldn't hear what the bus assistant said, but she saw the farmer scowl, pick up a rock and throw it with all his strength at the bus assistant. The farmer's wife and child came running out of the house and threw rocks at the bus assistant and at the bus. The rocks bounced off the windows. Most of the passengers ducked way down low. The bus turned around and took off, swaying like a ship on stormy seas.

Martha, with courage strengthened from singing along with Lucy's panpipes, stood up. She grabbed the back of the seat in front of her and started yelling at the bus driver.

"What do you think you are doing? Let me off to go talk to the gentleman. You have to speak nice with the people. This is not our land. This is their land. You have to have respect!"

Lucy called out, "Yeah! It's better to talk."

The Swiss-German man in the seat ahead of Lucy said, "There's no use trying to talk to those people."

Lucy said, "Yes there is. When you don't talk, there's war. When you talk, there's friendship."

The bus driver didn't say anything. He just kept driving. His assistant ran behind calling out, "Wait for me!"

When the farmer was no longer in sight, the bus stopped. The bus assistant caught up. Panting, he climbed on board. The bus fishtailed down a different fork in the road. Around a bend, it lurched to a stop. There was another row of rocks. A quarter of a mile ahead Lucy saw a second row of rocks with a row of people. The assistant hopped off, headed towards the blockaders. Martha and Lucy stood up, propelled by a shared thought. We're going, too! We can't trust this guy to be our ambassador. As Lucy passed the seat of the Beatles fan, she lightly touched his arm, "Come on, let's go."

He stood up. Together they got off the bus and walked towards the row of people. The long-legged Beatles fan strode on ahead.

Martha stopped, turned to Lucy, and said, "Wait! I have an idea! Let's go back to the bus and collect a Boliviano from each passenger. We'll offer this money to the blockaders and request the right to pass!" She laid her hand on Lucy's arm, "Come with me so you can translate for the English speakers."

Back they went and announced the plan. Martha rummaged a couple of yellow wrinkled plastic bags out of her purse and gave one to Lucy. They worked both ends of the bus. Lucy held the baggie out to a young man from Israel slumped in his seat. Sad memories and worries weighted his face.

He looked at Lucy. His eyes conveyed yearning, yearning for peace.

"I came on holiday to get away from war," he said and dropped a coin in the bag.

A British university student clicked her tongue and whined, "I don't think we should give them anything. At the next blockade they'll just want more. It only encourages them."

"Come on. It's like 14 cents," Lucy said.

The young woman heaved a sigh and rolled her eyes as she dropped a Boliviano into the plastic bag.

The stout father whispered to his seatmate in German, "We should have killed them all when we had the chance. They just cause problems."

The collection complete, Lucy and Martha got back off the bus and headed for the blockaders.

Lucy strolled up playing the most traditional panpipe song she knew.

When she reached the blockade she saw half-a-dozen men and boys standing there. They were from about age 11 to a shriveled elder. Women with fresh scrubbed faces, whose hair was in long tight braids and wearing velvet skirts over layers of petticoats, all sat in a cluster on the side of the dirt road.

Calloused toes poked out of the men's worn tire-tread sandals. Many-times-patched clothes hung from their angular muscular bodies. In their broad work-hardened hands, each one held a whip, a stone or a stave.

Lucy thought, "These are the 'enemies' in Bush's War on Drugs? We in the U.S. are dropping multi-million-dollar bombs on the people of Afghanistan, and this tiny group of people is defending their culture from the U.S. military with sticks and stones."

A tense-jawed spokesperson of the group questioned the bus assistant, "What nationalities are on your bus?"

Lucy's adrenaline gave a squirt, but she kept playing her panpipes like serenading a lover.

"French, German, Australian, Canadians...," the assistant curtly replied, carefully not mentioning any Americans.

The Beatles fan stood-by with a hip flask in hand. The cap was off. He had offered the blockaders a drink. No one had drunk. Martha offered her little plastic bag of Bolivianos. The farmers ignored her.

"Ooo! Lots of tension here!" Lucy thought.

She finished the traditional song, then played the most gentle song she knew, sending a prayer with each note - we are one.

It was similar to when Lucy played in California on the Santa Monica Pier the Saturday after the World Trade Center was blown up. The pier was crowded with people, their emotions raw and huge on their faces. This river of humanity streamed past Lucy playing her panpipes while she stood against the splintery railing that kept them all from falling into the sea. The songs were Lucy's prayers, prayers for peace -- prayers honoring the magnificence of each precious life, each person passing. One guy hulked down the pier, his face red with rage. He looked like a bouncer at a biker bar. His fists curled and uncurled, hoping to throttle a terrorist. When he heard Lucy playing, he jerked his face towards her and beamed the most beautiful smile of appreciation. His whole face lit up. In that instant he was transformed to the purity of a three-year-old filled with wonder and awe.

At the blockade, Lucy played her panpipe prayer. The protestors' faces softened. Their shoulders relaxed. The elder - the one with the biggest stick - whispered to a companion. The companion listened then nodded. He turned and gestured to the women seated on the hump of dirt. One rose and came forward. Together they approached Martha. They peered into the bag of coins. They looked at each other, nodded and accepted the bag of money.

Lucy kept playing. Everyone started smiling. It started to feel like a party. The elder got a playful look in his eye and raised his stick, poised to hit the Beatles fan over the head. The Beatles fan, knowing that all you need is love, took off his hat and bowed as if to say, "My head is yours".

The elder laughed, still holding the stick high in the air. Lucy kept playing. The song shifted to a quick tempo dance section. The elder lowered the stick. Now, instead of a weapon, it was a dance prop. He started dancing over towards Lucy. He hooked his elbow through hers. Together they danced, side by side, with hopping steps, the wayño; a dance that celebrates the interconnection of men and women together with Mother Earth, Pachamama.

It was hard to play and dance at the same time, especially at that high altitude without much oxygen. Lucy dropped notes. Since the music was faltering, the elder let go of Lucy's arm and started another style of dance.

It was just like the folklore performance Lucy had seen in the theatre in Lima, Peru. She felt so lucky to see the original and actually to be participating in it! In the theatre performance back in Lima, one of the dancers wore a long beard and hunched over his long staff. He wandered among the groups of choreographed dancers and poked his stick at them as a prankster.

Well, this elder didn't have to put on a beard and pretend to be old. He was old. He danced with his stick with those same dance steps. Then he lifted his big staff horizontal and flirtingly poked Lucy in the belly with it like a giant penis. She shrieked and doubled over in laughter. He laughed, his face to the sky. The sacred sky, Janaq Pacha, so clean and blue. Celeste. Celestial air filled his lungs and his abdomen. His abdomen, strong from pushing the wooden plow, now pumped out mirth. Joy.

Lucy kept laughing almost to pee her pants.

Everyone was laughing. It was a chorus - a calloused foot choir singing snorts and guffaws, unrestrained enjoyment.

The laughter slowly wound itself down to giggles and chuckles. Wiping a tear from his eye, the elder gestured to the bus assistant and said, "You guys can go on through. But she," nodding in Lucy's direction, "she stays here with us."

CHAPTER THREE
AUNT BERT

Southern California February sunlight illuminated the homey kitchen with two old women at a table like a living Maxfield Parish painting. Bert held an onion-skin-thin letter in her 90-something-year-old hands and peered through her spectacles as she read Lucy's adventures at the blockade to her best-friend, Doro.

"... I was excited to stay with the blockaders and ran over and sat next to the women who smiled at me with the most open sincerity and a sparkle in their eyes..."

"Doro," Bert said, "It sounds like my niece Lucy stopped a war with her panpipes in Bolivia."

Aunt Bert built her house by hand during the Great Depression. She dragged driftwood up from the beach and scavenged lumber from a shipwreck that surfaced at low tide. Always a tomboy, Bert hung out with carpenters as a kid, read books and learned the trade. A library card didn't cost a nickel - a good thing, too, for Bert was broke her whole life long.

Some of those library books had photographs of sculptures. Bert didn't have bronze or marble or that sort of thing, but she had wood, her gauge, chisel and mallet, a file, and could get sandpaper and oil on occasion. She started carving and sculpting. Her little house was a sculpture in itself. It was like something Alice might find in Wonderland. Or a Van Gogh painting come to life. The house would have been a tourist attraction, except no one knew it was there. The cypresses that Bert planted when she was young had grown into a living wall that separated her home from the ever-noisier street that passed by out front.

The street had changed over the years. At first it was just shifting sand. Now the Gay Pride Parade danced and sang down the boulevard half a block away every June. Bert was happy for these youngsters. As for herself, she never had been in the closet or out of it. She just figured that what she did with whom in the privacy of her own bed was nobody's damn business.

Now, Doro (short for Dorothy) moved next door to Bert about 50 years ago. She was a photographer. So had been her late husband. He was moderately famous and mentioned here and there in the history books. However, artist friends agreed that Dorothy's work was stronger. Her black and white silver gelatin prints seemed more alive, had more depth and soul. Her technique was flawless. But, he was a man and she was a woman, so his work got more recognition. At least that was what Dorothy had resigned herself to believe. Dorothy had taught for a spell at Chouinard Art Institute until it ended with the death of Walt Disney. Although the founder, Nelbert Chouinard, lived on she had signed the school over to Disney. With Walt gone, the Board closed Chouinard in a tremendously complex and awkward way. Later the Board opened a new school with new instructors and called it California Institute of the Arts.

That was the end of Dorothy's teaching career, except for small classes she taught out of her home. Her husband secured a tenured position at Otis Art Institute. She lived on her widow's pension from Otis since he died.

Bert read aloud the end of Lucy's letter, "I wanted to stay, but the elder said he was just joking and for me to go with the bus. And that's how I got to La Paz. Love, Lucy."

Dorothy said, "I think Lucy learned her bravery from you!"

"I taught her a lot of things, but that bravery she just has inside somehow," Bert said.

"I remember the day you taught her to rebuild the carburetor on that little car she had when she was sixteen. You had muffin tins all over the place, each cup numbered and holding a nut or a screw in the order that it came out of the carburetor."

"Lucy learned quick. She had that thing purring down the road the next day."

Bert let a memory of her own life when she was sixteen peek into her mind. That memory she seldom visited.

Harsh words. Welts. The beating they gave her when they discovered her bare-breasted, kissing another girl. That day was the last time she saw her parents. She ran away. Although she didn't go very far, their paths never crossed again.

A tear formed. Bert inhaled, sucking the memory back into its hiding place. Sitting up straighter in her chair, she pressed her lips together.

Her glance fell to Lucy's letter. Lucy, who went to so many places Bert had never seen.

"I always wanted to travel," she said to Doro.

They both knew that Bert never had money. If it hadn't of been for Prop 13, rising property taxes would have driven Bert from her home. She lived on her Social Security payments supplemented by odd jobs of carpentry and occasionally bartering sculptures. Although Prop 13 kept her property taxes low, it closed her local branch library. Bert was over 90 years-old, but she never stopped working so she kept her sinewy muscles. Those yoga classes she took so many years ago from that nice Indian man who taught at the YMCA for a spell; she kept doing her own routine of stretches and poses every morning when the sun was somewhere East of the San Gabriels and the gulls were just starting to stir. Her joints still functioned and she could bend down to pick up a dropped nail, or climb a ladder to re-shingle her roof from shake she split herself. She believed in that adage, "Use it or lose it."

Doro and Bert sat in companionable silence for a few minutes. Their friendship was solid. It had endured trials that had forged out all the impurities and left only indestructible gold.

Once, long ago, Dorothy asked Bert exactly how Lucy was related to her; for Bert had no living relatives that she knew of. All Bert would say was, "It's kind of complicated."

Now Dorothy broke the silence, "How is your new sculpture coming along?"

"Let's take a look," Bert said.

She unsnagged her long gray braid from a rough spot on the back of the chair as she got up.

"I've got to sand that...," Bert thought.

She retrieved Dorothy's walker that was folded and leaning against the wall and set it in front of her. As she watched her friend grab the grips and concentrate on standing up, she felt sad. A year ago Doro was fine. First the cane. Now the walker. Dorothy jerked her way forward with a clank and a shuffle. Together they slowly walked out the back door.

Woodblock print, portrait of Aunt Bert

CHAPTER FOUR
ORURO

Lucy arrived in Oruro just in time to catch the tail end of the Anata Andino.

Brown women, short as hobbits, danced through the streets. Profusion of herbs and flowers harvested from their chajras adorned their felt-hat brims and burst cornucopia-like from the llijllay cloth bundle around their shoulders. The flowers and fresh herbs, bounced with each step.

Men danced in handmade tire-tread sandals, their splayed feet with interesting toes patted the cobblestones with soft "fwump fwump fwump". In gnarled hands they gently held bamboo flutes. Altiplano lungs breathed life of music into these humble cylinders, gifts of Mother Nature, of the Pachamama. Black fedora-topped heads bobbed with the "one, two" of the song. Homespun pants and shirts draped their bodies strong and healthy from hard work. Flowers and fresh herbs cascaded down their heads and shoulders, dancing in joy.

Each swirl of skirt and skipping of feet a "thank you". Thank you Pachamama. Thank you.

But, the word "you" in "thank you" implies an "other", someone separate. When we say "me and you" we are making distinctions, boundaries, fragmenting life into compartments. But, English doesn't seem to have a word for expressing gratitude of the grandness of our shared life that surpasses any limits of space or time. Pachamama. Space/Time continuum. Joy. Life.

Night fell.

One last group paraded down the street. The women all played charangos, sang in falsetto voices and danced in a light jog to the rhythm of their music. Men followed behind, dancing in silence.

On impulse, Lucy jumped in and started dancing the wayño with one of those men. Holding hands facing each other, they swung their arms like school children. Then they twirled around. Elbows linked they danced side-by-side with little hopping steps. They looked into each other's eyes with a joy of being alive and sharing that moment together.

Lucy was in heaven. This was a taste of the ideal society of which the panpipes sing. With this man she danced and danced, laughter and smiles as his calloused hand gently grasped her computer-soft hand and pulled her to him and away and around and around, all the way to the end of the parade route.

Panting and with a big smile on her face, she talked in Quechua with her dance partner. The other men gathered around and tried to push in to talk to Lucy, too. But a leader spoke with authority to back off. The first guy had dibs. The other guys backed off.

"Maybe he's my soulmate!" Lucy thought.

A fantasy sprung into existence in Lucy's mind. She would live forever with these people. She would become one of the community. Laughter and love would fill her days. A simple life they would share in the countryside, the campo. A dirt-floored adobe home, emanating the vibe of Mother Earth, would shelter her and her lover in calm tranquility. Never again would she feel the pain of loneliness.

Lucy craved intimacy so much she grabbed at every hint of possibility. Oh, to have someone with whom to share life! But, she was clueless how to do go about it. Even though she was in her 40's, in some ways she had frozen emotionally at That Day when she was eleven years old. That Day in 1971, in the kitchen, her parents announced their divorce. That Day Lucy's Captain Crunch dissolved into a formless mess just like her home and heart.

"The peaceful world of which the panpipes sing has to include a soulmate!" she thought.

Lucy and her Quechua dance partner chatted while the musicians and other dancers rested.

"Where are you staying?" he asked.

Lucy named the hotel and the street.

"Just ask for me at the front desk!" she said.

The group started to move off toward their lodging. The man said goodbye to Lucy and ran to catch up with his group.

With skipping feet Lucy returned to her hotel, as if she was still dancing with her partner around and around.

The next day, Carnaval started. Brass bands blared and boomed down the street. Costumed dancers pranced in sequined platform boots and giant psychedelic headdresses. Lucy took photos and filmed for her research. As the hours and days of Carnaval continued, Lucy's enthusiasm dwindled. Her "soulmate" never contacted her. The crowds were filled with boys attacking with water balloons, spray foam and Super Squirters. To protect her camera Lucy draped herself in plastic and poked her lens out. Even then the lens got squirted with foam. After 48 hours of being a lonely observer and target (and not a participant) Lucy was desperate for a friend.

"I'll never make any friends here in Carnaval," she thought, "Being a gringa with a camera makes me an outsider. I'll go to another part of town and walk up and down the streets playing my panpipes until I meet an indigenous musician to play with."

Down a wide dusty avenue she walked, devoid of crowds, playing her panpipes with her whole heart.

A man approached her.

"Hey! The kenista in my group composed that song you're playing!"

"Really? What do you play?"

"Charango."

"Let's play. Where's your charango?"

"It's at my house. The kenista is in a cafe, playing right now. Let's go!"

They walked to the cafe. Bamboo flute music greeted them. At song's end the charanguista introduced Lucy to the kena player, then left to get his charango.

"How do you do, beautiful lady?" the kena player slurred in Spanish. "Do you speak French?"

"No, I don't speak French. I speak Spanish, English and Quechua," Lucy replied, "Your friend told me that you wrote this song . . . "

She played a phrase on her panpipes.

"Ah, yes! That is one of my songs, one of my children! I wrote that many years ago. I have toured Europe, France. Do you speak French?" he asked again.

Her previous reply apparently had been stored in a brain cell that just died due to excess beer.

"Why don't we play music?" Lucy said.

The kenista dipped the kena mouthpiece into his glass of beer.

"It sounds better this way," he said, bringing the dripping cane up to his mouth.

He and Lucy played his composition through a couple of times. When they wound down, he raised his glass and tilted it to dribble some beer on the uneven wood plank floor, then drank the rest.

"For the Pachamama!" he said.

"For the Pachamama," Lucy said.

Some more beer he poured from the brown liter bottle into the chipped glass and handed it unsteadily to Lucy. Lucy drizzled some beer on the floor, then drank it down and handed the glass back.

"Very good!" he said.

The charanguista returned, charango in hand. After tuning up and another round of beer for the Pachamama, the three of them played a song.

The kenista started talking to Lucy in French.

"I don't understand French," she said.

He continued talking in French, as if he didn't hear her.

The charanguista scooted closer to Lucy. His arm slid around her. The metal button on the cuff of his jeans jacket yanked her long hair.

"Ouch!" Lucy said.

He leaned in closer. The hair-snagged button pulled harder.

Lucy stood up. Hairs ripped out from the roots.

"Thanks for the music. It's time for me to go. It's getting late. Thank you. Goodbye," Lucy said.

The charanguista looked like a lost puppy dog. Blonde Lucy hairs dangled from his cuff. Lucy strode out the door and walked back to her hotel, alone.

MANUEL

The next day Lucy strolled down a different street, playing her panpipes, seeking a true friend. On the sidewalk, a man sat on a blanket. Around him were arrayed panpipes and other musical instruments for sale.

"Hola!" he said to Lucy.

"Imanaylla kasanki?" Lucy said, hoping that he understood this Quechua greeting.

"Walejlla! Qanri?" he said that he was fine and how was she.

Lucy thought, "Oh my god! He's gorgeous! He speaks Quechua! He has all these instruments! Maybe he's my soulmate!"

"You play the zampoña well," he said in Quechua. "What's your name?"

"Lucy. What's yours?"

"Manuel. How long are you in Oruro for, Lucy-cha?"

"Just a week. Then I go to Cochabamba to practice Quechua."

"Why don't you stay here and practice Quechua with me? We can play music and record an album together."

Being a California Free-Spirit, of course Lucy took him up on his offer.

First they went to check out the recording studio in town.

"Here comes a cab now. You have money for cab fare, right?" Manuel asked.

Without waiting for an answer, he waved the cab over.

"To the bus terminal," he said to the driver.

Manuel and Lucy slid into the back seat of the four-door Toyota Celica. The seats were covered with hand-sewn seat-covers of low plush texture; brown flowers and vines twined over beige background. Lace doilies draped over the headrests. Lucy felt like she was sitting in her grandmother's living room. The taxi meandered through back streets to avoid Carnaval crowds. During the cab ride, Manuel told Lucy a bit about himself.

"I live with my mom, older brother and my little sister. Dad died when I was 15. Then mom became an Evangelical Christian and forbade our Andean ways. So, I'm kind of the black sheep. My uncle, though, is very traditional and I spend a lot of time with him. Also I travel. The power of the siku pulls me to sacred lake Titicaca, Cuzco, all over. We sikuris are one big family."

One big family. Lucy liked the sound of that. She felt like she was coming home.

At the terminal, Manuel leapt out. Lucy paid the driver and followed Manuel down the street.

"It's down here, I think," Manuel said.

Around and around they walked. Eventually, Manuel asked a little boy in the street where number 36 was. Just then a green metal door opened next to them. Out walked a group of pony-tailed men carrying guitar cases, black square cases for wind instruments, and a bombo drum.

The door was swinging shut. Manuel caught the door. Lucy followed him inside.

SONQOY RECORDS

"Can I help you?" an Inka princess in tight jeans and lots of makeup asked.

"We're going to record an album!" Manuel said with a smile that made his cheekbones even more prominent.

Hip-hugger Inka Princess turned to Lucy and said, "I'll let Vladimir know you're here."

As she left the room, Lucy and Manuel both stared at her swaying rump.

Vladimir entered, greeted them and sat at the desk. Behind him on the wall was a poster of a bedroom-eyed pouty woman holding her charango. "Fani Mamani," the poster read, "Exclusive Artist of SONQOY Records".

Lucy and Manuel plopped side by side onto a low loveseat.

Vladimir looked only at Lucy, since she obviously was the one who would be shelling out the dollars. Manuel he recognized as a mediocre musician who drifted around town, drank too much, owed money to almost everyone and wasn't going anywhere musically.

"I lived in Canada for 20 years. Where are you from?" Vladimir said.

"California," Lucy said.

"Were you here for Carnaval?"

"Yes, and the Anata Andino. I play the zampoñas and I'm laying the groundwork for further field studies here as an ethnomusicologist."

"And you want to record an album? Wonderful! Please consider our studio as your home. You are welcome here anytime. You'll have the opportunity to meet lots of musicians. They are always coming here to record."

Just then, in walked the woman from the poster. She wore dark eyeliner, red lipstick and walked with the gait of a diva.

"This is my wife, Fani," Vladimir made introductions, then excused himself to return to a mixing session.

Fani tilted her head, peered at Lucy out of the corner of her eyes and in a tone of voice as if she was interrogating a criminal suspect said, "How did you get so involved playing the panpipes, being a gringa and all?"

Lucy felt nervous. She didn't want people to think she was like so many U.S. tourists that act like they own a culture just because they can afford to visit it. And of course she didn't want them to think that she was a flag-waving "patriot" who supported the recent invasion of Afghanistan. There she was on this quest to find the peaceful world of the panpipes and her white skin and accent labeled her as an imperialist or worse, as "enemy." Little did Lucy know that many people, Fani in particular, wondered if she was a spy. Fani had family "disappear" during CIA Operation Condor. It was suspicious, this gringa speaking Quechua and playing the panpipes. Interesting cover...

Feeling like a defendant under cross-examination, Lucy told her about the alienation growing up in Southern California and about that day at Disneyland.

"I know what you mean about the sound resonating in your soul," Fani said.

But, still Fani had that guarded look on her face, like Lucy wasn't even close to being trusted. What was Lucy like through and through? This question drilled deep into Lucy from Fani's eyes.

All of Lucy's life experiences, feelings and thoughts had been accumulating deep within her like water. She was like absorbent sandstone beyond saturation. She had felt compressed by society's expectations of what a woman should be, like being squashed between layers of impermeable rock. When Fani's unspoken question drilled into Lucy, all those experiences, thoughts and emotions gushed like the first-magnitude artesian spring cascading down the slope of the Island of the Sun, that birthed the Inka Empire. Lucy's artesian spring was of words in one long sentence.

"I bought this cassette of Andean music and listened to it over and over and then I went to Mexico to see the total eclipse of the sun and there I felt a different spirit in the people, once we got South of Ensenada and I wanted to spend time in Latin America and learn more about the indigenous spirit, so, I traveled through Mexico to Guatemala, then I went to Nicaragua with Potters for Peace, and when I got back from Nicaragua it seemed so shallow to keep teaching pottery classes to rich white people so I got rid of most of my possessions and quit my pottery teaching job and took what would have been the down-payment for a house in the Bay Area and got ready to return to Latin America and write, then my car was broken into and everything stolen, except for the tape deck with the spaghetti-wire dangling equalizer and the single tape of Andean music, so I drove alone, the wind blowing in the broken window, with that tape as the soundtrack, to my mom's house in L.A. from SF to start life fresh, but just then, my dad took a turn for the worse in New Mexico and I went to his side and helped care for him the last two weeks of his life and when he died of Leukemia I felt so sad and ripped apart because I was no longer my father's daughter, or a San Franciscan or a pottery teacher and then mom took a turn for the worse and my grandparents clung to me to take care of them and I felt like I was drowning so I chanted Nam-myoho-renge-kyo that a new mountain range of happiness would rise up out of the plains of suffering of my family and I made the decision, the determination, that in 30 days my mom would be emotionally stable, my grandparents would have reliable live in affordable care that they liked, and that I could follow through on my plan to go to Guatemala to language school then to Nicaragua to live with a potter family in the roadless mountains near the Honduran border to do cultural exchange and sure enough, in that 30 days, I hooked my mom up with a grief therapist who she said, 'Saved her life,' live-in care for her grandparents got taken care of (it was even cheaper than the 40 hour a week woman who had been helping them out) and grandma loved the attention and affection that she was getting, and when I flew to Guatemala, there in the plaza I heard the sound of the panpipes once again and it felt like coming home and I asked the guys if they would teach me to play and they did and every day I learned another couple of bars of a song and in the afternoons I studied Spanish and I started learning all I could about this instrument and the people who make this music that stirs my soul, and then on September 11, 2001, when I found out about the World Trade Center, my first response was, 'Damn Bush!' for I was sure that people had gotten frustrated with him that he had stopped listening to the rest of the world and ignored the Kyoto Protocol and didn't attend the U.N. Conference on Human Rights in South Africa and was ignoring the ban on nuclear weapons testing, so of course I figured that some people did the attack to get his attention so that he would listen, and my first action was to call my Congress people and to tell them not to retaliate, but to dialog and most important of all, to listen, for as long as it takes to work things out, then I put on my performance outfit and took my panpipes and bombo out into the streets and walked all over my neighborhood playing and I sent the prayer with each note, 'We are one. Cherish humanity. Don't hate. Shine your light, Illuminate humanity,' and the following Saturday I was scheduled to perform at a Peace event at USC for 10,000 people, but the event was cancelled by the police because it was too dangerous for large groups to gather, so, that day I took my instruments down to where I usually performed on the Santa Monica Pier and when I got there, there was this temporary stadium set up on the sand and it was ringed with about a hundred American flags flapping in the ocean wind and this roar of the crowd came out of the stadium and I got afraid because I thought that someone was giving hyper-patriotic speeches there and rousing the crowd to hatred, I was afraid that when that hyped-up crowd came out and saw this panpipe musician playing for peace, that they would beat me up or worse, and not only that, the pier was packed with people and if I went out on the pier I would be trapped and what if there was another attack and it happened here, I would die, so I chanted nam-myoho-renge-kyo and a little voice inside told me that even if I died that day, that I must go out and play for peace, so I did play for peace, and as I played on that crowded pier I saw how the sound of the panpipes brought joy to people, even to this huge guy whose face was red with rage, but when he passed me and heard the music, he turned and smiled the purest joyful smile like a three-year-old filled with wonder, and then I played to the setting sun over the Pacific for the sun to carry this melody of peace to Afghanistan and to the world, and as my song traveled, I waited for the terrorists to issue their manifesto, their list of demands, of what they wanted Bush to hear, and when there was no manifesto, I started to question, 'Why was the government cracking down on talk of peace and dialog? Why was the media all of a sudden on the same page of spreading fear and hatred?' and how convenient it was that the anthrax scare closed down the House of Representatives and quarantined all their mail from their constituents while they voted to push through the Patriot Act to change the constitution to make it easy for the President to declare war, then I thought about how Bush Sr. had been head of the CIA and the School of the Americas that trains terrorists, including Bin Laden and I imagined Bush Sr. and his cronies sitting around one night drinking and talking and saying, 'You know, that Constitution ties our hands. What would it take for the U.S. people to willingly let us change the constitution to give us unlimited power? Only if they felt attacked,' and at that moment, I realized that it was totally possible that the Bush administration had engineered the attack on the Twin Towers in order to have an excuse to invade countries and I keep looking for evidence to contradict that, but I haven't seen any at all. . . "

All talked out, Lucy took a deep breath and slumped into the love seat. She looked at Fani to see what her reaction was.

Fani had a different look on her face.

"It's obvious that's what happened," Fani said, "Here, we call that State Terrorism."

Fani believed Lucy. She trusted her. She liked her.

She said, "Lucy, I'm giving a concert later this month. I invite you to play a few songs as an opening act."

MARTES DE CH'ALLA

Leaving the studio Manuel said to Lucy, "Tomorrow is martes de ch'alla. Why don't you come celebrate with me at my uncle's house?"

"What's martes de ch'alla?"

"It's the Tuesday after Carnaval when we ch'alla, bless, our homes and workplaces."

"Cool! I'd love to go! Can I video?"

"Of course! And make me a copy."

The next day, Lucy met Manuel at the spot on the sidewalk where he sold his instruments. He sprinkled multicolored confetti (mistura) in a ring around his sidewalk spot (no blanket of instruments, he was closed today. A holiday). Then he uncoiled long paper streamers (serpentina) and arranged the paper coils around his work space. Next, he pulled a liter brown glass bottle of local beer out of his chuspa shoulderbag and popped the lid with his teeth. He put his thumb over the opening and shook the bottle vigorously. Then he let go with his thumb and sprayed the erupting fountain of foam over the mistura and serpentina in sweeping arcs.

Serpentina he wrapped around the neck of Lucy, like a giant lei. He handed the package to her so she wrap around serpentina around his neck. He opened a second bottle of beer and poured some into a glass. He drizzled some beer in the four corners of his workspace, then drank down the rest of the beer, throwing the last bit onto the ground as an offering for the Pachamama.

He refilled the glass and handed it to Lucy.

"It's your turn," he smiled, pointing with his pursed lips to the sodden coils and colored shreds on the ground.

"Which corner do I start with?"

"There," he pointed.

Lucy solemnly drizzled beer in the four corners, while praying silently for the success of Manuel's business.

Then she drank the rest of the beer in the glass and drizzled the last few drops as an offering.

"Let's take this mini," Manuel flagged down a passing Nissan mini van.

They climbed in, bowed low, and passed to the back past the school children in pressed uniforms and an elderly woman with her qhepi bulging with purchases to take home, and sat on a tiny hand-welded seat with handmade seat covers. The front windshield held the destination cards in a contraption involving suction cups and plastic straws.

"It's a Boliviano each," Manuel told Lucy, as he motioned for her to pay the driver.

She handed two coins to the woman in front of her who passed them up to the driver who placed them in a wooden coin holder wedged onto the dashboard with a stuffed animal.

The van bounced down a dirt road that led to a ramshackle barrio on the edge of town.

"On the corner, Maestro!" Manuel said to the driver.
The van stopped. Manuel slid the door open and they got out. He shut the door firmly with a thud. The van rattled away.

Manuel rapped a coin on the rusted corrugated metal door set into the crumbling adobe wall. A little girl, barefoot and grimy, opened the door. Her hair was uncombed and sticking out every which way.

"Hola Tio!" she squealed in delight. Manuel bent down and thrust out his chin for her to kiss his two cheeks.

"This is una amiga! Give her a kiss," Manuel said.
Lucy bent down and the girl kissed her two cheeks, leaving wet smooches. They crossed the hard-packed earthen courtyard and stooped to enter the blue painted wooden door of the adobe house.

Manuel's uncle, aunt and their three adult sons with their wives lounged in the small room. Manuel greeted each in turn with elaborate stylized hugs for the men and kisses on each cheek with his hand on her shoulder for the women.

Lucy followed behind Manuel and greeted each person with, "Mucho gusto (good to meet you)," as they embraced.

The day stretched long. First everyone sat around the adobe room. A radio blared U.S. pop tunes from over 20 years before: Village People, Disco Man, Hotel California. People sat on the bed, mismatched chairs, a wooden bench, or stood. One of the wives left the room then returned with flower patterned ceramic bowls (made in China) of hearty homemade soup, a big spoon poking out of each bowl. There was no table, so people supported their soup bowl on a knee or held it in one hand as they ate.

Another wife collected the empty soup bowls and returned with enameled plates heaped with boiled potatoes, corn on the cob, oqa (a type of Andean sweet potato), and topped with a fried steak. Everyone ate with his or her fingers.

After lunch they drank beer and chewed coca leaves. The family talked in Quechua. Lucy filmed with her second-hand RCA VHS-C camcorder. Spontaneously, the uncle stood up, cheek puffed out with a wad of coca leaves, a glass of beer in one hand and a lit cigarette in the other and began a speech in Quechua.

"I am a miner!" he began. He expounded on what it was like to go into the mines day after day and why the miners offer coca leaves, alcohol and cigarettes to the Pachamama and the Tios.

The Tios, Lucy learned, were the Earth spirits that live in the mines. If the miners make offerings to the Tios and the Pachamama, they will be protected by them in the mines. They will not have accidents.

Lucy filmed this monologue with her eyes wide open, amazed to be catching this moment on film.

"Can I make a song using your words?" She asked.

"Sure," the Uncle, the miner, said.

In mid-afternoon they all moved outside into the courtyard and sat on haunches or stood while the beer was passed around (one glass refilled over and over and shared by all).

Someone placed a plaster-of-Paris frog on the ground. The frog had been spray painted gold and was about as big as a misshapen cantaloupe.

"What's the frog mean?" Lucy whispered to Manuel.

"Good fortune. Money. That kind of thing," he answered.

Manuel's uncle wrapped serpentina around and around the frog's neck, poked a lumpy lit cigarette in its mouth and ch'alla-d the frog with pure alcohol from a plastic squirt bottle, then a squirt of alcohol into the uncle's mouth. Everyone ch'alla-ed the frog in turn, in order of importance in the family. Lucy was last. The children didn't ch'alla. They just ran around playing.

The cousins lit firecrackers and threw them on the corrugated tin roof where they exploded with sharp pop pop pops, scaring away any negative spirits.

The uncle offered coca leaves to each person. He stood in front of the person and reached his hand into the green translucent bag and lifted out a handful of dried green leaves. The recipient cupped both hands to accept the sacred leaves with respect.

Manuel taught Lucy to nip the stem off with her teeth and to spit it on the ground. Then to insert the leaf in her mouth and slide it over to her left cheek with her tongue. Leaf after leaf she put in her left cheek and held them there for a few minutes, lightly chewing with her molars. He handed her a hunk of gray ashes of burnt peach wood. He taught her to scrape it against her incisors and let it mix with the coca leaf juice in her mouth. He told her to think good thoughts for everyone there. Then, to move the wad to her right cheek and think good thoughts for her own desires. Then to divide the wad with her tongue and have it be even in both cheeks and think good thoughts for her and everyone together.

KALLAWALLA

A cousin's wife with long braids was dressed in the traditional clothes of the region of Cochabamba. She wore layered skirts and a white painted wire mesh hat bedecked with flowered ribbons. She was nursing a baby, chewing coca, and chatting with Lucy.

"When my oldest was five years old, he stopped making piss and swelled up. I took him to the hospital and the doctors said he had kidney failure and that he would have to live in the hospital for a year. I stayed right with him. I slept on the floor next to his bed. After a week I told the doctor, 'I see what kind of food you feed him. I can cook that food at home. Every day you give him a pill. I can give him that pill at home. Every now and then you examine him. I can bring him in every now and then for you to examine him. I want to take my baby home.' Well, the doctors got really upset at me and said that I was refusing treatment and that I would have to sign a document saying that I was refusing treatment and that they weren't responsible for him once I took him home. I signed the paper and took him home. I cooked his food. I gave him his pill. And I went to visit a Kallawalla," she said.

"What's a Kallawalla?" Lucy asked.

"A Kallawalla is a wise man, a healer. They're from a pueblo near Lake Titicaca. Well, this Kallawalla read the coca leaves and told me what to do for my little boy. I bought the herbs he told me to buy and I made the tea and gave it to my baby and the next day he made his piss with no problem," she sighed with relief at the memory.

"That's great!" Lucy said.

"When I took him to the hospital for his exam, the doctors said that he was fine. He didn't need special food. He didn't need the little pill. And he didn't need to be in the hospital for a year," she said.

"Wow! That's amazing!" Lucy said. "How can I find a Kallawalla?"

"In the Sagarnaga in La Paz. They sit there on little stools," she turned turned to the boisterous boy who was chasing a little girl and said, "Come here papito."

He came over, panting and rosy cheeked.

"See how strong he is? He's been healthy ever since," she said, hugging him close.

The next day Lucy bought a bag of coca leaves. The coca vendor chatted with her a bit in Quechua. Lucy went back to her hotel room and wrote a poem.

COCA VENDOR

High in the Andes,
Lina the coca vendor sits
in her tiny market-stall
like a regal matriarch ,
like a meditating Buddha,
or a sentient landform.

Aware.
Serene.
At-one
with her surroundings.

The hard wooden plank bench
padded
with a folded hand-woven llijllay
that once carried
her nursing baby

The sky-blue metal walls
of her stand open out
to display an overflowing cornucopia
of coca.

It all is an extension
of her body,
of her spirit.
For here is

her life.

Everyday,
she inhales
the rust
of the oxidizing stall
which reddens her blood,
pulsing with every heartbeat.
Every exhale,
her coca-moistened breathe
ch'allas, or blesses, the environment.

In.
Out.
Breath after breath,
moment after moment,
for days,
weeks,
years,
decades,
a lifetime.

Till there ceases to be
a separation
between the coca vendor
and her coca stand.

Naked light bulb dangles, illuminating her
like a sacred relic,
like an enshrined deity
surrounded by offerings.

But her offerings
are to the people.
Glistening green translucent bags
of buoyant coca leaves.
A bounty
of sacred plant
that connects the generations
and the land.

I approach.
The coca vendor smiles,
revealing a wad of coca leaves

stored guinea pig-like
in one cheek.
A knowing twinkle dances in her ancient eyes
as she adds a couple more handfuls of leaves
to the two peso bag
and snaps off
a hunk of ashes.

Coins exchange hands.
Molecules mingle.
Transformation occurs
in the coca vendor stand
in Oruro, Bolivia.

Lucy showed the poem to Manuel that next night, at their rehearsal for recording their album.

"What do you think?" she asked.

Manuel read it, smiled and said, "You understand! Pretty good for an ethnomusicologist!"

ETHNOMUSICOLOGY

Lucy had applied for a Fulbright as an independent-scholar ethnomusicologist. But she didn't really want to be an ethnomusicologist.

Once before she had applied for a Fulbright as an artist. She proposed to be in the Andes, play panpipes with the people and write about it. Fulbright was not interested. The next year she was advised her chances would be better if she applied as an ethnomusicologist.

An ethnomusicologist. She would have to analyze and measure and document. She wasn't into analyzing, measuring or documenting, but more into participating and intuiting.

Intuition was what led her to follow the sound of the panpipes to find a world of harmonious interconnection. What Buddhism calls "dependent origination". She wanted to be immersed in that world and to help others be aware of it, too. She wanted to change the world. For everyone to wake up to this sad happy buzz that joins us all - all people, all life.

The mountains have voices, Lucy knew. The trees talk. Animals are our siblings. One family of life, ever changing life.

Not solitary computer games and plastic pink Barbie back-packs. Not road rage and office politics and competitive materialism. No, that wasn't life. That felt more like a type of slow death.

Although Lucy didn't want to be an ethnomusicologist, it was the closest fit to who she was. Lucy didn't fit in any box.

But who does?

We try to squash our unique individuality into a box. Like ill-fitting shoes, none of the boxes fit. So we numb our pain with Paxil and wine in order to not self-reflect. Or we yell at the driver who cut us off in traffic. Or we yell at the kids. Or we hang the kids by their necks in the closet of our double-wide. Or we take a shotgun to work, or to school, and blow everyone away - including ourselves.

It was sort of like that line from one of Lucy's favorite movies, Shirley Valentine - "We say we're fine. An' we carry on an' on an' on until we die. An' most of us die... long before we're dead. An' what kills us is the terrible weight of all this unused life that we carry round."

Lucy didn't want to die from unused-life-poisoning. Somehow she would find a way to stay in the Andes and live her dream. This trip was just for three months. She wanted to stay there a lifetime.

If being an ethnomusicologist would make it possible to live in the Andes and play panpipes with the guys and create that ideal society of which the panpipes sing, so be it. She read a pile of dissertations and designed her Fulbright project proposal: "Mountains of Sound - Confluence of Ethical, Political, and Aesthetic Dimensions of Autochthonous Music Forming and Maintaining Relationships in a Bolivian Quechua Community."

Lucy also applied to UCLA's graduate program in World Arts and Cultures - Performance. She was waiting to hear if she had been accepted, hoping that one of these programs would provide funding for her to live with the people who made the music that stirred her soul.

LA PAZ
Manuel and Lucy went to La Paz for a few days to do some research for their album. Lucy stayed in the apartment that the recording studio owned. Manuel stayed in a residential hotel. House rules. No men overnight.

When Lucy thought about Manuel, she got all trembly inside.

Manuel. Manuel who knew how a smile and a laugh could smooth over any situation. Even though he never spoke of it, Lucy knew that he deeply felt the mystical, which cannot be explained in words. Lucy felt that, too, that glorious universe that is just a glance away.

Manuel who lived in the moment and didn't worry about the future. Although Lucy worried about the future. She worried that this mutual attraction with Manuel was ephemeral, like dew on a spiderweb soon to disappear. That worry created an ache. That ache made her trembly attraction to him all the more acute. Every night, as she slept alone, Lucy fantasized about Manuel.

And every night as Manuel slept alone, he worried that Lucy was falling in love with him. He felt pushed by her. She got this judgmental look on her face and a harshness in her voice when he was an hour or two late for rehearsals, or when he didn't show up at all the night before because he was drunk. A man had to be a man. It wasn't right to have a woman bossing you around. If he was going to fall in love with anyone, it would be a woman who knew how to be a woman. She would be quiet and follow his lead. She would make sure he was comfortable and had a blanket when he passed-out drunk. She would understand that a man has to have his freedom and be with his compañeros, sometimes all night or days at a time. His true love wouldn't push him to be a "success", she would love him just the way he was. If she wanted to change him, she didn't really love him. It was tempting to act like he loved Lucy and let her pay for their trips here and there and buy a case of beer for his friends. But, that time when he chanted nam-myoho-renge-kyo for an hour with her, well, the nam-myoho-renge-kyo told him not to sleep with her unless he really loved her and was going to be her compañero. Powerful stuff, that nam-myoho-renge-kyo. He believed in karma. That was one heavy message that he wasn't going to mess with. Better to set her straight, not let her keep going with those stars in her eyes, like one day they would get married or something. Better set her straight.

The next day, after leaving a café Manuel and Lucy were crossing a street and Manuel said, "You drink a lot of coca tea. It's really strong stuff. Maybe that's why you can't control your emotions."

Emotions roiled in Lucy. Maybe it was being PMS. Maybe it was the altitude. Maybe it was her basic nature to have quick emotions. Maybe it was genetic family karma. She hunched her shoulders and didn't say anything, but made a point of brushing against Manuel as they walked. She wanted to feel him close to her.

He didn't look at Lucy, but jammed his broad fists into his jacket pockets. His shoulders were tense in the cold that slipped off of Mount Illimani's glaciers and crept like tendrils through the cobblestone streets of La Paz. His voice was quiet and determined.

"So, why me? Why are you so infatuated with me?" Manuel asked.

"Because the first time I heard the panpipes I felt like I was in the arms of my soulmate. I wrote a list of attributes of this soulmate - he would be a musician and speak Quechua and chant nam myoho renge kyo with me and …"

"What? It sounds like a shopping list! You thought you could come here with your dollars and buy a soulmate? I'm not a souvenir for export. Take your list somewhere else," Manuel said, "I don't love you."

Lucy froze in her tracks in the middle of the street.

"He doesn't love me," she thought.

She watched his muscular back and stubby black ponytail as he walked away without a backwards glance, each step light as a fleeing llama.

Gone.

Pain like a sharp knife sliced into her sternum and slit all the way down her abdomen to her pubic bone. She was a living human sacrifice. She felt her heart and vital organs spill out. Empty. Pulsing viscera strewn at her feet clung to loose grit in the crevices of the cold round paving stones.

A blue Mercedes stake-bed truck full of battered five-gallon propane tanks barreled down the hill towards Lucy.

"Go ahead! Run me down!" she thought, "I can't possible feel any more miserable than I am already."

A distant promise stirred in her pulsating heart there on the ground. She recalled a night in 1978 in her alcoholic dad and step-mom's non-descript tract home in a Los Angeles suburb. Lucy was then 18-years-old and had decided to commit suicide.

"It's all a lie, that you can live your life how you want. Forget it! I'll just gulp down a bunch of those Valiums and Percodans that are in the medicine cabinet," Lucy had decided. "But wait! What if reincarnation is true? What if we are here to learn a lesson? If I kill myself to end this suffering and then get reborn into the exact same situation because I didn't learn the lesson this time around, I would be a hundred times more miserable. So, I'll stick it out and learn whatever I'm supposed to learn."

Air horn blare shocked Lucy back to the present. The heavy truck gathered downhill momentum, heading straight for Lucy. She sucked in her guts and sprang. Her llama wool poncho streamed behind her like the raised flag of a charging army. The white-painted cast iron bumper snagged only poncho fringe.

Manuel was gone. Alone she walked along the broken sidewalk, tears streaming down her face, back to her rented room. The cold key seared her fingers as she unlocked the deadbolt.

Her footsteps echoed on the warped hardwood floor in the unheated and empty third-floor hollow brick apartment built on a crumbling cliff edge.

"Sensei, help me!" she silently cried.

Lucy opened a Buddhist book at random and read some words of her teacher, Daisaku Ikeda, "We determine our own happiness; it is not something outside of us. For instance, getting married doesn't necessarily guarantee happiness. Some people find marriage a source of suffering and frustration. There's no need to panic or rush into such things. It is important to lead your life by staying true to your personal mission, do your very best in the realm of kosen-rufu (world peace through individual happiness) and become a strong and resilient person. That's the key to a life of supreme happiness."

Lucy sighed deeply and blew her nose on flimsy pink toilet paper that dissolved with the moisture of her sadness. She sat down at her makeshift altar. Her two-inch tall traveler's gohonzon perched on top of a towel draped over the TV. Bell, a brass bowl the size of cupped hands, rested on a cushion nearby. Ivy twig curled out of a vase she made by cutting a two-liter plastic bottle with her Swiss Army knife. Three lumpy Bolivian red speckled apples sat on a napkin. She struck a match and lavender smoke twirled up from incense she bought from an Argentinean hippie in the street, its stick held between the closed pages of a book.

"Nam-myoho-renge-kyo Nam-myoho-renge-kyo Nam-myoho-renge-kyo . . . " Lucy chanted.

A crack of light she detected in the dead-end wall of her life. The crack spread to reveal a door. She leaned into that heavy groaning door of her life and kept on chanting it open.

She thought about that line, "It is important to lead your life by staying true to your personal mission."

"What is my mission for this three-month trip?" She thought. "I wrote it down. I better read it over as I chant."

Lucy dug into her backpack and pulled out a folded piece of paper. She unfolded it and propped it against the front of the towel-covered TV.

Lucy read: I am determined to become a world class musician, artist, writer and scholar of Andean music and culture in order to contribute to the flow of kosen rufu.

I am in Bolivia to:
- Lay the groundwork for future fieldwork
- Research autochthonous music and dances
- Collect books, musical instruments and associated material Andean culture
- Practice Quechua
- Make friends and colleagues with shared interests
- Learn how I can reciprocate

She hadn't written down that she hoped to meet her soulmate. That was engraved in her heart and needed no paper to remind her.

CONCERT

The day of Fani's concert in Oruro arrived. Lucy was sick with a bad cold and hacking cough. All she wanted to do was stay in bed. But, if she failed this invitation to perform, she would be just another flaky American dilettante tourist. A memory stirred in the murkiness of her virus-addled brain.

The voice of Mary, who she considered her "Buddhist mom," was again telling her about teachings of Nichiren Daishonin, "When you make the determination to do something great, obstacles arise. It's like demons vying with each other to trip you up. Don't be afraid. It's a sign that you are on the right path. Keep going, chant Nam-myoho-renge-kyo like the roar of a lion and you will triumph."

A lion was not what Lucy felt like; more like a slug who nibbled too many Valerian blossoms and passed out.

She chanted till lion life force welled up. She chanted to have the wisdom to say the most appropriate words to the audience, to form a bridge of friendship and mutual understanding.

Grabbing a thermos of herbal tea (to still her hacking cough) and her instruments, she went to the theatre. Backstage she guzzled a couple cups of tea and glanced over the program. There was her name in black and white, "Lucy Powell - Zampoñista from the United States".

At that moment, she was the face of America.

Alone, she walked onstage and faced the audience of about three hundred people. People who had suffered, directly or indirectly, violence of the U.S. government.

Boom she hit her bombo. The momentum of the song carried her like running down hill, each note like a step catapulting her.

The song finished with a long held panpipe note and bombo rumble. The audience politely applauded.

Searching for words, true words, sincere words, words that would make friends, like Daisaku Ikeda who, as an ordinary citizen, apologized to the head of China for the atrocities committed against the Chinese people by the Japanese back during World War II and opened the door for normalizing international relations; Lucy's intuition led her to say into the mic, "This is the song I played when I entered Bolivia on February 6, during the blockades. The blockaders danced with me and let us pass. Toquemos, bailemos, pasemos. We played. We danced. We passed."

She paused. Three hundred faces waited expectantly for her next words.

"The next day, on the road from La Paz to Oruro, army tanks cleared the blockades," her voice strained with sadness at the thought of military force.

Bowing her head, memories flashed of seeing those tanks from the bus window.

Standing tall, feet apart, facing full to the audience, like a martyr bravely embracing her fate, Lucy said, "I wish that my government can learn to communicate with music and culture instead of weapons and violence."

Leaping to their feet, three hundred people applauded till their palms stung, yet they kept applauding as they shouted, "Bravo! Bravo! Bravo!"

Coca Vendor

INTERLUDE

LETTER TO AUNT BERT - GUIDEBOOK

Dear Aunt Bert,

What kind of guidebook one uses sure makes all the difference in how the journey goes. For example, I accidentally tucked my Lonely Planet Bolivia guide up on the overhead rack when I got off the bus to dance with the bloqueros.

And there it stayed.

Upon arriving in Oruro, I was immediately swept up in the activity of Carnaval and had no time to miss having the guidebook. Later, when I searched for a copy to buy, I was told that there were none in this city and also that I was the only American that anyone had met during all of Carnaval.

My only reading material in English was "The Wisdom of the Lotus Sutra, Volume One." Everyday I read more of it, making notes in the margins and underlining favorite parts, such as: "We are the life of the universe itself. And that life causes changes." p.30

Also, "The vibrant spirituality and dynamic, creative cultural force of the Lotus Sutra are revealed in its capacity to manifest the vibrant pulse of the eternity of life in society and, in doing so, transform the world." p.103

And, that the body of the Buddha is life itself.

"Life is also free and unfettered. It is an open entity in constant communication with the external world, always exchanging matter and energy and information. Yet while open, it maintains its autonomy. Life is characterized by this harmonious freedom and an openness to the entire universe." p.24

For the next month or so, I ventured forth into the city from my hotel, making friends, sharing sacred ceremonies and music.

Then one day, a traveler from Holland checked into my hotel. She had a copy of the English language Lonely Planet Bolivia guide. She loaned it to me and I photocopied part of it.

Among the maps and points of interest I found:
"For women travelers - 'The machismo mid-set remains and the mere fact that you appear to be unmarried and far from your home and family may cause you to appear suspiciously disreputable.

Because many South American men have become acquainted with foreign women through such reliable media as girlie magazines and North American films and TV, the concept of gringa facil (loose foreign woman) has developed. Many men consider foreign women -especially those traveling alone - to be fair and willing game.'"

After reading that, I walked out of my hotel, just as I had everyday for the previous month, but all of a sudden the street seemed filled with lecherous men. Instead of returning greetings with joy and appreciation of our shared humanity, I was tangled in the web of differences. Every smile from a man directed my way became an insult. My gait sped up and my gaze narrowed directly ahead; my face, expressionless. I felt like I'd just arrived in a foreign dangerous place, even though I'd already happily lived here a month.

It took most of the day for this shell of fear to wear off. At lunch I read more of the "Wisdom of the Lotus Sutra".

"The bodhisattva is in no position to criticize or revile people... because those states of being exist within the life of the bodhisattva as well." p. 147

In the afternoon, I wandered into a part of the market where I hadn't been before, and met a Quechua speaking pottery vendor. I bought a candlestick holder for my altar from her and played a song on the panpipes. She and the other vendors applauded. I sat down among them and proceeded to play song after song, interspersed with conversation in Quechua. The ceramic vendor treated me to a glass of the local peach drink and the thread vendor next door bought me an ice cream bar and invited me to dinner.

Back at the hotel, I wrote this song in Quechua, "Waj Warmi Kani" - "I'm a different sort of woman".

Waj warmi kani	I'm a different sort of woman
Qhari jina kawsayta munani	I love to live like a man
Sikusta kenatawan takikuni	I play the sikus and the kena
Mana wawasniyojchu	I don't have any children
Kay musika wawayqa	This music is my child
Ari	Yes it is.

And this different sort of woman was really glad to have had a different sort of guidebook to introduce me to Oruro.

Love, Lucy

P.S. I got the news from UCLA and Fulbright. They both said, "No". So, I bought some handcrafts and musical instruments and I'll go into the import/wholesale distribution business so I can spend as much time as possible here in the Andes.

CHAPTER FIVE
CALIFORNIA GIFT SHOW

SET UP

     Teamsters perched like roosters on forklifts that whirred around the loading dock of the South Hall of the Los Angeles Convention Center, carrying pallets loaded high with furniture, clothes and handcrafts from around the world. One by one, they disappeared through a opening in the far wall.

     Lucy found an empty pallet between a Ryder rent-a-truck and an 18-wheeler. She dragged it over to her friend's van she'd borrowed. Not wearing gloves, she was careful to not get a sliver from the rough-cut wood slats. The day laborer she picked up at Home Depot helped her unload the van. He heaped the pallet high with an old trunk, side-table, shelves, chair, TV/VCR and boxes of Andean musical instruments, textiles and handcrafts. Lucy un-piled it and piled it again the way she preferred. Sweat marked her cotton tanktop under her arms, breasts and on her back. She had pulled her hair up in a quick ponytail on top of her head, out of the way and off her overheated neck.

     July in Southern California. Time and temperature flashed 103 degrees at 3:14 on the bank building across the way.

     The Teamsters were too busy to forklift her pallet of stuff, so Lucy loaded up a little handtruck and hauled it all, bit by bit, to her booth.

     In the cavernous underground hall of the Los Angeles Convention Center the air was stale with propane exhaust, sweaty bodies and synthetic carpet. Hot. The management would turn on the air-conditioning the next day when the paying customers arrived and the loading dock doors weren't gaping open. But not today.

     Tooting horns echoed. Passing forklifts hummed a drone that rose and fell like the sound of a mechanized ocean on a nightmare planet. Bubble wrap popped as it tangled around a wheel. Drills whirred. Hammers banged. Then came a shouted cuss word from behind a portable wall, the next aisle over and the strangled cry of packing tape ripping off of its roll.

     Every booth was a pile of chaos. Importers single-mindedly unpacked and set up their booths, oblivious to anything else going on around them. They talked in the language of the country whose treasures surrounded them - peaking out of boxes, plastic bags and crates.

     Lucy hadn't had much luck going store to store to sell her merchandise. So she rented this booth. It was 10'x10' and cost her almost $2,500 on her Visa for the long weekend.

     Sales better be good.

     The convention center's floor was covered with drab grey industrial carpeting unrolled over concrete. Canvas walls hung from aluminum tubing. A black cord, thick as a boa constrictor, snaked under the back wall and ended in a square head with multiple three-prong outlets. The booth was provided with a beige plastic folding chair, trashcan and a white posterboard sign, "Booth 1321, Orqo Warmi (Mountain Woman)."

Speaking Spanish, Lucy directed the day laborer to help her hang the rolls of bamboo she had purchased with her Visa at Ikea. They took turns standing on the rickety folding chair, to hook the heavy wall covering. On the back wall she hung a rainbow wiphala, the flag of the Quechua and Aymara peoples. Over it she hung toyo sikus (panpipes as long as she was tall) in an X pattern. Finally, she draped Aguayo fabrics on either side of the wiphala and toyo sikus.

A fire Marshall came by to inspect. Lucy held her breath. The thick rule book had said that fabrics or other inflammables used in booth display would need to be treated with fire retardant, unless it was a sample product from the catalog. Fire retardant cost per square foot. Lucy was in debt and didn't want any extra expenses.

"Is that flag in your catalog?" The fire Marshall asked.

"Yes," Lucy said. No one would ever order this item, but it was truthfully listed in her catalog.

"Okay." He went to the next booth.

Lucy let out a sigh of relief that her big bamboo had passed inspection as well as all the fabrics.

She rolled an old barrel (that an ex-roommate had abandoned) into the center front of the booth. She filled it with woven chuspa bags. Next to the barrel she arranged big baskets (borrowed from several friends) overflowing with chullu crocheted pointy caps with ear flaps.

Then, she arranged on shelves and hung on the bamboo curtains panpipes of all sizes, bamboo flutes, wooden tarka flutes, kena end-notch flutes, all kinds of autochthonous instruments.

On a sidetable she set up a 13" TV/VCR and popped in a tape with some of her ethnographic footage. There she was, chewing coca in Manuel's uncle's house. Campesinas danced in the Anata Andino with bundles of plants and flowers on their backs. And there was the soccer stadium in Puno filled with indigenous communities playing and dancing on the field.

Glancing at the screen and hearing the music, she sighed.

"I'm coming back," she promised silently, "I'm coming back."

As the day laborer and Lucy worked, they snacked on dried mangos, pineapple slices and peanuts from Trader Joes. That was their meal. After awhile, Lucy took a break to find the bathroom and to fill up their water bottles. Passing by the other booths on the way there and back, she saw that most were now completely set up and the vendors had gone. Presumably, they had gone back to their hotels to sleep.

Instead of the earlier chaos, the other booths were like exquisite paintings; everything had been arranged with an eye to composition. Bright colors, the whole range of textures and glittery sparkles saturated Lucy's senses even through the thin sheeting draped over the fronts of the booths that were there as a "keep out" sign.

On the other hand, Lucy's booth looked like a tornado had just passed through.

"Nothing to do but keep at it 'til I'm done," she thought.

Her feet ached from the hard concrete. She was exhausted from the unaccustomed physical labor. She was overwhelmed with the countless details to wrap up. She was tense with worry. She had never done this before. This was the big time. These were pros. She was jumping in and learning to swim-or-sink.

SHOWTIME

The next morning, Lucy shoved gel inserts into her shoes and nighttime feminine pads into her underwear and arrived in her booth an hour late.

She had misread the brochure.

Lucy had never been good at sales, so it took all of her concentration to develop the mindset to sell. She had crammed in preparation, reading books like, "How to Sell Anything to Anybody" and was appalled by the "white lies" the books suggested. She wouldn't tell white lies, but she took what she could from the books and adapted it to her way of being.

"The customers are my guests, and my booth is my living room," she thought.

She would give them a tour of the amazing things she had found in Bolivia and brought back - all lovingly displayed.

A bent grey-haired woman ambled into her booth and touched one of the backpacks and asked, "How much is it?"

Now, one of those books that Lucy had read said to never directly answer the question "How much is it?" First one should promote the positive attributes of the product.

So, Lucy took a deep breath and launched into the spiel she had practiced, "This one-of-a-kind llijllay was handmade by an indigenous woman in Bolivia. She carded the wool from her sheep, llama or alpaca, handspun it with a drop spindle; collected the plants to dye it, and hand wove it to carry her nursing baby on her back. When the baby grew up she sold it to a little old Quechua man who walks the mountainsides visiting remote homes to buy the llijllays. Then he carries the llijllays in a bundle on his back to town where the indigenous artisan family that I work with recycled it into these purses and backpacks."

"But how much is it?"

"$25"

The woman placed the minimum order of $100. She requested it to be shipped COD, then ambled away.

Next a young woman walked into the booth. Her gaze locked onto a bundle of brightly colored mini-ocarinas. Lucy's gaze locked on the woman's name badge. It read, "Buyer, Catalina Island Museum Store."

"Oh my god!" Lucy thought, "How many phone calls have I made to that very store! But I never got past the clerk. This is so great!"

"Of course, I have to talk to the board of trustees before placing an order. But I just love what you have here. Can I buy one of these little ocarinas right now?"

Lucy was just too happy to oblige. She started to untie the bundle of 50 ocarinas on cord necklaces. Eight buyers swarmed into her booth like flies. Lucy was flustered and kept trying to untie the bundle and untangle the strings until she got the red ocarina that had caught the museum store buyer's eye.

She handed over the ocarina, pocketed the dollar, then looked around. Those eight other buyers had fled her booth. She was alone.

"How do people balance so many things at once?" she thought, "How do they make the customer they are dealing with feel taken care of, and also for everyone that enters their booth to feel welcome and to stick around?"

Lucy tended to focus on the person in front of her, and on one thing at a time. These were not skills that translated well into staffing her booth alone at this high profile wholesale market.

Alone in her booth, she recalled a motivational tape she had listened to. It said to always look busy. If there were no buyers, dust your booth with a feather duster. Lucy gave her booth the once over with the duster. When she reached the TV/VCR, she turned on the tape. Panpipe music sang from the speaker. A man walked into her booth, drawn by the magnet of the TV.

"What's the score?" the buyer asked, staring at the screen with the look of a child in a candy store.

"This is an indigenous music and dance contest in the soccer stadium in Puno, Peru," Lucy said, feeling like a teacher sharing special tidbits of lore.

"Oh, it's not the game." he said. He left, without glancing at even one of Lucy's Andean treasures.

Lucy picked up a panpipe and played with her whole heart, to attract people to her booth. Lots of people smiled at her as they passed. But, they didn't come in.

The river of people passing in the aisle was dressed for show. One woman, on the arm of a man, was wearing a flat elastic sports bra backwards over her leotard. It could give new meaning to the phrase 'lift and separate'.

She pondered that the woman probably wore that risqué outfit only because she had a man on her arm to protect her from unwanted advances, and only in this elite environment where the panhandling alcoholics outside weren't allowed to enter.

And so the days passed.

On the last day of the show, two women paused at the edge of her booth. The older whispered something to the younger, gesturing towards items in Lucy's booth, then walked away.

The younger woman was the new Assistant to the Buyer for Men's Accessories at Suburban Provisioners. She picked up one of the chuspa bags from the barrel and said, "These are great! Let's write!"

Lucy pulled her Purchase Order book out of her big apron pocket and poised the pen at ready.

"We'll take 1,000 of these bags, to be packaged as per our instruction sheet that we'll fax you, terms net 30. And if they sell like we think they will, we'll be ordering this much every month."

Lucy scrawled out the order, her hand shaking with excitement, "Just sign here."

The young woman signed the Purchase Order and handed her card to Lucy.

"Oh, and I love these beanies!" The new Assistant to the Buyer picked up a chullu and tried it on. "How do I look? Well, we'll be ordering these, too. Soon. Just like the bags. Can I take this one with me?"

Of course Lucy gave her the chullu. The new Assistant to the Buyer of Men's Accessories for Suburban Provisioners put the pointy chullu with earflaps on her head and bounced out of the booth to see what else she could spend someone else's money on.

"Every month?" Lucy thought, "My god! That's like $7,000 a month! I don't need much to live on, so now I can afford to hire people to help me! I can delegate and live in the Andes and play the panpipes!"

After the Gift Show, Lucy took out cash advances on her Visa card and started hiring. She hired a North American Manager to set up a home office in her bedroom. Well, the bedroom was really a dining room but that is where Lucy slept. All the bedrooms were filled with roommates. The owner of the Craftsman Bungalow lived abroad. A property management company had leased the house to a friend of a friend of Lucy's at low rent. That friend of a friend got a big break and went to New York to perform on Broadway. But, since the house was so beautiful and the rent so cheap, she wanted to keep her options open in L.A. So, unknown to the property management company, she sublet to a friend. They had done so with the verbal agreement that if and when she decided to come back to Los Angeles, whoever was living there would move out and she would move back in. It had been 10 years now and the original person was still in New York. Over the years many different subletters had lived in the house. Lucy's housemates were actors and visual artists. Everyone worked weird hours and gave one another space to do their creative thing. So, nary an eyelash was batted when Lucy ushered in Clara, the new North American Manager, into her dining room/bedroom/home office.

The housemates didn't have a lot of personal possessions. The stuff that cluttered the garage were things that had been abandoned by previous subletters when they moved on. Lucy hired day laborers to clean out the garage and turn it into a warehouse. Then she hired someone from Craig's List to pack and ship the orders from the Gift Show.

The first job for Clara, Lucy's North American Manager, was to sort chaos into folders, and organize those folders in a filing cabinet. Lucy delegated all the phone calls to Clara to make, because Lucy didn't like chit-chat. Clara not only loved chit-chat, she adored organizing and making things tidy and pretty. Finally, Lucy scrawled out a priority To Do list and thumbtacked it over Clara's desk.

Lucy then bought a 1985 Toyota van for $1,300 in order to haul merchandise to the next Gift Show. It had a cracked windshield, oil leak, dents and the musty smell of the previous owner's dog. But it ran great.

Perfect.

The company set up as best she could, Lucy jetted down to Bolivia to stock up on merchandise, buy samples of new items, fill that big order from Suburban Provisioners and continue her quest to find or create the ideal world of which the panpipes sing.

Orqo Warmi Logo

CHAPTER SIX
DON JAIME

BOLIVIA

Don Jaime felt the hard mineral earth beneath his sit bones. The hole dug out of the rocky ground was a meter in front of him. How to get to it?

These old legs just don't work anymore.

Centimeter by centimeter he used his one good arm to propel himself across the arid ground in this dusty mining camp at the edge of Oruro. Rocking from one sit bone to the other, he could feel his fragile skin flopping in loose wrinkles beneath his frayed slacks. The sunlight, strong here at twelve thousand feet where the ozone layer thins out before it disappears altogether, heated the shaggy black hair covering his skull and darkened imperceptibly his leathery face. Feeling the rocks, he recalled his years working in the mine, in the bowels of the earth. Down in the heat. Why was the mine hot, he wondered. It must be the Tios, the demons that live there. Memories of offerings to the Tios flashed across his mind. Offering chicha corn beer and pure alcohol that scorches the throat, sacred coca leaves wadded in a cheek – guinea-pig-like, smoking a lumpy hand-rolled cigarette; all offerings to the Tios, so they would protect him from harm in the mines.

Maybe he wasn't sincere enough. Maybe his faith was weak. Maybe he was too drunk and he forgot one time to bless the Tios and the Pachamama (Mother Earth and space/time continuum). It was that accident which made his right arm dangle like the arm of the rag doll he would have given to his daughter - had he had a daughter. Or a son, for that matter. He had no children - that he knew of.

His drunken unions with a handful of women did produce a couple of children, but he didn't know about them. He didn't even remember the women themselves, what they looked like. Their long black braids that he tickled their breasts with, he did not recall. They were part of a drunken blur that was his life.

The women remembered, and were ashamed of him. One told her baby that his father was dead. The other told her daughter she was a gift from the wind - wayra. Wayra blew a tooth of corn into her vagina and from that seed grew her daughter, Sara. Sara is the word for corn in Quechua.

His children passed don Jaime in the street, but they didn't know each other.

Don Jaime heard footsteps scuffling along the stony road. Cold sober he looked up and saw a 80 kilo gringa approaching.

"Señora, help me!" he called.

Lucy took in the scene, a cripple on the ground, a stick nearby. Of course, she assumed, he must have fallen.

"Here, I'll help you up," Lucy reached out her hand.

"No! No!" don Jaime exclaimed. "My knees are no good. They don't work. I need help. I don't want the people pushing me again. You will help me?" he gazed up hopefully into Lucy's kind hazel eyes.

"I don't understand what help you need. My friend lives right here. I'll ask him to help, okay?"

"Thank you, thank you señora," don Jaime intoned.

Lucy strode up to the big black metal door of the artisan's home-workshop of one of the artisans working on the Suburban Provisioners' order, searched for and found a doorbell dangling from its wires twisted around a nail driven into the adobe wall. She pushed the button and heard a buzz inside the house. She waited. She fished her key chain out of the chest pocket of her homespun men's shirt and rapped on the door with a carved bone key fob. She waited. She rang. She knocked. Then she glanced over at the old man. Don Jaime was maneuvering himself closer to the hole in the ground, rocking on his bony hind. Lucy continued ringing and knocking at intervals. She could hear a little dog yapping inside the house.

She looked back at don Jaime. Don Jaime was pulling his pants down as he lay on the ground. Patiently tilting from one side to the other, he yanked his pants bit by bit lower with his one good hand to expose his bottom. Lucy averted her gaze to give him some privacy.

After ringing again and knocking, Lucy noticed a padlock on the front door – a sure sign that everyone had left the house. How was the Suburban Provisioners' order of chuspas coming along? That answer would have to wait until the artisan came home.

Lucy was now free to ponder what to do to help the cripple lying next to the road. On her way here she had passed a little store. She could ask there for someone to help the old man. Lucy turned and headed back down the road past the contorted elder.

"Are you going to help me?" don Jaime pleaded.

Lucy turned to him. He was covering his privates with a piece of cardboard. He had a sheepish look on his face.

"I don't understand very well," Lucy explained. "I'm going to look for help for you."

"Thank you! Thank you señora!" don Jaime gratefully cried out.

Around a bend in the road, Lucy encountered three girls in high school uniforms.

"Excuse me," Lucy approached them.

Two of the girls ran off giggling to the other side of the road. The third (her name was Matilda) looked Lucy straight in the eye, open to deal with anything this middle-aged gringa had to say.

"Around the bend I met a man lying on the ground and asking for help. I didn't understand exactly what help he needs," Lucy explained.

"I know that man. He can't walk. Everyday his family throws him out into the street in front of their house. In the night they bring him in," Matilda said.

"Can you see what kind of help he needs?" Lucy asked.

Matilda paused. "Okay," she said.

"Thank you!"

"Chao," said Matilda, heading up the road, the two giggling girls running to catch up.

"Chao," Lucy said, then thought, "Perhaps my friend Martha will know what to do? I'll ask her if there are laws here to protect old people from abuse from their families."

Don Jaime finally got his rump onto the edge of the hole. Oh, the release of this diarrhea!

Matilda came around the bend, saw the brown stain forming on the edge of the hole, turned around and headed home. Don Jaime was fine, the same as always.

Lucy's nose prickled with the negative ions of an approaching storm. She opened her umbrella, but felt just a few drops. When she arrived at Martha's house, she saw that a cloudburst had drenched this block. But all around was dry.

The street door was ajar. Lucy walked across the muddy courtyard to Martha's room. The door was open. Lucy tapped on the door, went in, and said, "Hola?"

"Hola," a man's voice responded from beyond the wardrobe. Peeking around, Lucy saw Martha's son, Bonito, and his baby daughter lying on Martha's bed watching TV.

"Have you seen Martha?"

"She went out to do some shopping."

"Perhaps, as a lawyer, you know the answer to this question."

Bonito got a serious look on his face. He hadn't expected to be working today, but he braced himself for the question.

"Are there laws here to protect old people from abuse from their family?" Lucy recounted her recent adventure to Bonito.

"Ah, yes," Bonito said in his wise lawyer voice. "You go to the police. Downtown in the plaza, in the Prefectura. There is an office for the protection of families. It is composed entirely of policewomen. They will interview the neighbors and decide if the elder should go to the old folks asylum."

"Thanks! I'll go right now," Lucy said, and walked out the door.

She caught a Toyota mini-van, that seats fourteen, to the Plaza. The driver sat erect in his starched and pressed white shirt, green monogrammed tie neatly knotted. Lucy opened the front passenger door and hoisted her bulk into the passenger seat. As she started to shut the door, it was caught by the burly hand of a man intent on boarding. Lucy hesitated between scooting over and being pinned between the driver and this hulk of a guy, or getting out and letting Mr. Burly sit in the center.

The driver called out to the man, "No room! No room!"

The man looked stunned, but obediently shut the door and stepped back. The driver pulled away muttering, "Drunks!"

Along the route, the driver passed up many people flagging him down, but then pulled over to pick up a lone young woman. A selective driver, he filled his van with who he wanted, not just anybody. And he carefully negotiated potholes.

Feeling like a precious egg being carried in a basket, Lucy arrived at the plaza and hopped out. After a few questions to various people she found the office of Family Protection. In the doorway two young policewomen lounged.

"An invalid elder is being abused by his family. Every day they toss him into the street," Lucy blurted out.

"Come inside," said the cute policewoman, her thick black hair pulled back in a tight bun from her meticulously made-up face.

Inside, the policewoman asked questions. Lucy described what she encountered in the mining camp at the edge of town.

"He is probably from a humble family," the pert policewoman surmised.

"Yes," said Lucy.

"Poverty causes a lot of problems," she said, glaring at Lucy.

Lucy stiffened.

Neither woman knew why they were being antagonistic with each other. They didn't know that in 1980 U.S. President Reagan and British Prime Minister Thatcher changed international policies. The effects of those policies trickled down to this very moment with the policewoman and Lucy. They didn't know that U.S. pressure on the IMF (International Monetary Fund) and the World Bank created new criteria for Third World countries to get loans. They required borrower countries to privatize their national resources. Those resources were then bought by transnational corporations. A U.S.-based transnational corporation purchased the mine where the policewoman's family had worked for generations. The mine wasn't making enough short term profits, so the corporation closed it. The mining community went to 100% unemployment in an instant. The policewoman (who was too small at the time to remember) and her parents moved to town to try and find work. But so had thousands of other people. To say that life was hard would be an understatement.

The policewoman grew up hearing how life used to be before the US company bought the mine. There had been a theatre with red velvet curtains where touring performers played music and presented plays. There was a radio station where her grandfather had a show every week of folklore music. On Saturday nights the family all used to go to the cinema and watch a double feature. Now the cinema, the radio station and the theatre were just humps of eroded adobe in a ghost town soon to be erased forever.

A US company closed the mine. This gringa in front of her – she was one of "those" people. And this gringa was now asking her to waste her time on some Quixotic adventure.

The young policewoman folded her arms across her chest and said, "What do you want me to do about it? Everyday people call us that their husband is beating them up. Then we go out there and they say, 'No, it's okay. I love him.' You want us to waste our time going out to the edge of town? Besides, there's not enough gas in the truck. Come back another day, like a week from now. Tell me, what do you want me to do?"

This was not what Lucy expected. She felt sad, defensive and confused. Sad that the U.S. had put the Third World in virtual slavery to fill First World insatiable consumer demands. She felt defensive that she was being blamed for all the suffering in the world caused by her government and its international policies; confused that an old cripple was tossed out on the ground every day by his family and the caring police women (who Lucy assumed would take over and make sure that everything was okay) turned out to be a bitter cynic who was refusing to do anything.

Near tears, Lucy said, "Why do you ask me what I want you to do? You're the officials who are supposed to help take care of people. We can't abandon this crippled old man who is pleading for help in the street. I was told that you would do an investigation and find out if he is being maltreated or not. You should know what to do. Isn't this the office of Family Protection?"

The policewoman relented to this sincere display of emotion. Not that long ago, she too had her own altruistic aspirations. But this work had embittered her, and she wasn't even twenty-five years old. A memory nudged, of how she once dreamed of helping people.

"Yes it is," she said in a different tone, "Maybe there's enough gas to get out there and back. Hop in the back of the truck."

Hop in the back of the truck? This was another surprise for Lucy. She had imagined making the report and they would take it from there, like the time she had to file a report back in the States of suspected child abuse. She filled out a form and that was that. Here, she would have to go and be part of the investigation, with the implication of the white woman butting into everyone's business. Oh well. Speaking up for what was right sometimes was inconvenient, but if she didn't do it, she knew she would be like all those silent good people who did nothing as Hitler rose to power. She hoped this wouldn't take too long, so she could get back to taking care of the myriad details of filling the order for Suburban Provisioners.

Storm clouds gathered overhead. A fat drop plopped on Lucy's cheek.

"Can't I sit inside the truck, up front?" Lucy asked.

"No. The driver and the policewoman who will accompany you will be up front. You sit in the bed of the truck." The policewoman turned and went inside the building.

Resigned to the unexpected, Lucy made the best of it. She blew towards the sky, wishing the clouds to hold their rain a little longer. She folded her sweater as a cushion and wedged herself into a corner near the cab so she wouldn't jolt around too much and would be protected somewhat from the rain.

A boyish policeman sat in the driver's seat. A more compassionate looking policewoman came out, radio in hand, and got in the passenger seat. Off they bounced.

In the cab, the radio squawked. A call came in of domestic violence on the other side of the tracks. The driver detoured from the route to the mining camp and bumped over the tracks.

In the bed of the truck, Lucy (who couldn't hear the radio) was alarmed that they were going in the wrong direction, and with little fuel. What if they ran out of gas before they got to the old cripple? She banged on the window and gestured towards the mining camp. The driver nodded and kept on ahead.

A few blocks later, a woman flagged them down. She was the abused spouse, accompanied by another woman.

"My husband hit me! We're separated. I don't want anything to do with him! He's drunk and he was hitting me!" she said.

"Yes! He was hitting her!" the companion agreed.

"Where is he?"

"In that stone house that says 'propane for sale'," the woman said.

The policeman grabbed a tear gas canister. The policewoman with him rapped on the weathered wooden doors. A wizened matron opened the door just enough to poke her head out.

"What do you want?" she demanded.

"We have a report of domestic violence at this address and we want to come in and check it out," the policewoman said.

"I don't know anything about this. I'm busy. Go away," the matron said, and started to close the door.

The policewoman wedged her foot in the doorway and kept the door from latching. Her foot was shod, not in steel-toed army boots, but in stilettos with pointy toes (possibly Italian leather) poking out of her baggy green pants' leg. Lucy, standing up in the bed of the truck in her sensible TEVAs, noted this unusual police footwear with surprise.

"It's like 'Barbie and Ken go on a domestic violence call,'" she thought.

The matron was more determined than "Barbie" and managed to squeeze out the fashionable foot, slam the door and slide the dead bolt.

Lucy and the police heard a shout through the door, "Come back with a search warrant if you want in! This is my house and no one comes in without a search warrant."

Soon, the sound of barking, snarling dogs could be heard coming from the building.

The policewoman turned to the abused woman and asked, "Do you live here?"

"No. It's my husband's home," she replied.

Her companion yelled at the abused woman, "What were you doing in his house?"

"It was Carnaval," she whimpered.

"If you are separated, you don't go visit him for Carnaval. You don't dance even one dance with him. Nothing!" the companion spat out, and stomped off in disgust.

Hanging her head, the abused woman wandered away. The officers headed back to the truck and invited Lucy to sit up front with them. She sat in the center, tilting her knees to the right to avoid colliding with the stick shift. On turns she grabbed the handle over the glove box, where the tear gas canister was hanging by its trigger.

They arrived at the mining camp without running out of gas.

Lucy glanced towards the artisan's house. The padlock was still locked in place. She looked to where the crippled old man had been.

"He was right here," said Lucy, pointing to the hole.
Damp brown stains dribbled down the edge. A piece of cardboard, flattened and curled in the shape of his rump, lay next to it.

The policewoman looked at the front door - a shred of corrugated tin tacked to a wood frame on hinges - and paused.

"Let's knock," Lucy said.

The policewoman knocked.

Inside, don Jaime heard the knock. He was lying on a scrap of cardboard on the concrete floor of what used to be a bathroom, but the fixtures had been removed. He watched his little niece head across the courtyard.

The child opened the door.

"Is your grandpa home?" the policewoman asked in a gentle tone.

"A visitor!" don Jaime thought. He struggled to raise himself up to greet his caller.

"Yes, he's home." the child stepped back to let them in.

The policewoman and Lucy entered a tiny dirt courtyard. The child gestured to an open door on the right. Lucy and the policewoman saw don Jaime sitting on the floor.

"Are you alright?" the policewoman asked.

"I'm fine, thank you," he responded with a grin.

Soon, a potbellied man came out of the house. He saw the policewoman, in his front yard, poking her head into don Jaime's room.

He bowed his head like a dog putting its tail between its legs and held one hand in the other. "Good afternoon," he said, "He's my brother-in-law. We take care of him."

"Don't you get cold in this room?" the policewoman asked don Jaime.

"No. It's warm!" he insisted, patting a pile of raggedy blankets stacked next to him.

"Do they bring you your lunch?"

"Si," he nodded, beaming in joy at this visit. "They bring me my lunch."

Inside the house, Maria was in the kitchen cutting an onion for the soup for supper. A toddler clung to her long apron. The round purple root was in her left hand, which stung raw from its juices. In her right hand was a knife. She had cut a myriad of tic-tac-toes across the flat face of the onion. When she sliced them, their bitty squares fell into the chipped enamel bowl on the wood plank counter. Her eyes stung. Maria heard strange voices in the courtyard.

"Now what's going on?" she muttered, tossing down the onion and knife and rushing out of the kitchen. The baby toddled after her.

Fists on hips and standing next to her husband, Maria demanded of the policewoman, "Alright, what's happening?"

Lucy felt embarrassed to be invading their home and said as gently as she could, "He asked me for help in the road awhile ago."

Maria relaxed. No one was attacking her. They wanted to help.

"He asks everyone for help," Maria said. "He's my brother. He drank all his life and was living in the streets. His arm went bad years ago in an accident in the mine. Then a car ran over his legs. I took him in. None of my other brothers or sisters are willing to help him at all."

"How difficult," Lucy sympathized.

"Si," Maria soaked up the sympathy. "It's not easy."

The policewoman asked don Jaime, "Do you like living here?"

"Si! I like living with my nephews," don Jaime said, looking around at the assembled group.

"Sometimes he talks good, like now. Other times he talks crazy. It's the alcohol. It ruined his brain," Maria said.

"Have you thought of taking him to the asylum? They can take good care of him. They have diapers for adults," the policewoman gently suggested, gesturing to the urine and excrement around a hole in the floor.

Maria and her husband exchange a glance, "Actually we have been talking about that."

"It's hard work for you to take care of him. In the asylum he'll be well cared for," the policewoman continued.

"We'll think about it. Thank you," responded Maria. She turned to don Jaime and yelled, "Why did you have to spend your life drinking? Look at you!"

Don Jaime gave the tiniest shrug. His cherubic face crinkled with joy.

Lucy saw that don Jaime didn't need her help after all. He was a king granting audience to his courtiers from a cardboard throne.

Adobe house in the mining camp

Dear Aunt Bert,

Quick postcard to let you know I'm thinking of you. I'm stressed out to get this big order finished and I miss playing the panpipes. But, it's all a learning experience. Give my love to Doro.

XXOO,
Lucy

CHAPTER SEVEN
CANDELARIA

Complaints erase good fortune.
Grateful prayer builds happiness for all eternity.
                                    - Daisaku and Kaneko Ikeda

Whereon the light, by me still undivined,
Out of its depths, whence rose its singing first,
Went on, as one whose joy is to be kind...
Joy doth in heaven splendour to shining add,
As smiles on Earth; but down below the shade
Outwardly darkens as the mind is sad.
                                    - Dante's Paradiso

"Hola amiga, why don't you come play panpipes with us in Puno for the Festival of the Candelaria? ;) - Manuel"

Lucy read the email with mixed feelings. She wanted to go, but was overwhelmed with tiredness from working on the Suburban Provisioners order and also with emotional stuff.

The emotional stuff was about Manuel. When she thought of him, she was flooded with images of how happy they would be if only they were together. How could she go to Puno, Peru and bear it, "just being friends"? She wanted to cling to him like lichen on a rock. But Manuel was like a phantom rock, a mirage. As she tried to cling to that rock, she only found herself tossed about by the changing winds of her feelings.

Emotional swings and dark thoughts were not new to Lucy. Generations of her family had struggled with them. An aunt was institutionalized and zapped with shock treatments. How many relatives had attempted suicide? Too many to list. Plus, peri-menopausal hormone imbalances added to Lucy's emotional tug-of-war. The causes of depression are vast. While her relatives numbed themselves with Paxil, Lucy explored the depths and heights of her emotions. After all, who else but Lucy had felt the call to follow the sound of the panpipes to the Andes? Her desire to play panpipes was stronger than just about anything, even a broken heart.

Nam-myoho-renge-kyo she chanted until she felt grounded. Some clothes and a couple of World Tribunes she threw in a daypack. She boarded a bus to Puno.

On the bus she read the World Tribunes and got inspired by an article about chanting appreciation. It said complaints erode good fortune and grateful prayer builds happiness for all eternity. Lucy didn't want to erode her good fortune, so she decided to focus on appreciating everything.

In Puno Lucy got herself a $3 hotel room. It was in an old colonial-style adobe building. A black iron padlock hung on the door. The hasp looked like it had been hand-forged. Inside was a twin bed with homemade sheets that almost, but not quite, covered the sagging mattress. It all smelled kinda musty, but Lucy didn't mind. In fact, she liked it.

"It's real," she thought, "It reminds me of root cellars."

Next to the bed was a brown-painted wooden writing-table covered with cigarette burns and stains of . . . Lucy preferred not to guess what made the stains. A straight-backed chair completed the furnishings. Hooks stuck out of the wall on which to hang clothes. Graffiti was scratched into the wooden door. Smack in the middle of the door, amidst etched names of couples in love was a big graffiti of a penis and testicles. Noticing that penis, Lucy frowned like she had just stepped in dog feces. She looked around for something to cover it up. On her hands and knees on the splintery floor, Lucy peered under the metal frame bed. Back in the corner she spotted a rolled up paper. She extended her arm its full length under the bed, holding her breath to not breath too much dust, and scissored her index and middle finger to grasp the edge of the roll.

Groaning a bit, she stood and unrolled the paper. It was a poster of the Virgin of the Candelaria. She glanced around the room and saw some old thumbtacks and nails of various sizes poking out, here and there, of the yellow painted plaster and adobe walls. Her fingers grew numb as she pried them out. The phallus she covered with the poster, hammering the nails with the heel of her hiking boot.

Standing back to admire her handiwork, Lucy observed that The Virgin resembled the phallus. The Virgin was erect. At her feet were a variety of objects, two of which were large and round, located on either side, similar to the testicles.

"I wonder if this is some hidden meaning of the Virgin being revealed," Lucy thought.

After getting settled in her room, she went to where Manuel said the rehearsal was going to be.

A sikuri named Carlos peered at Lucy through his wire-rimmed glasses, smiled and handed her a pamphlet about the group, a bombo drum and siku.

She glanced at the pamphlet. It read, "Every day we are losing our culture. It is invaded by cement and bricks. As musicians we must rescue our culture. For this reason we play the music of our ancestors on the sacred millennial siku ."

Strapping the bombo across her chest, feeling it's comforting weight against her body, holding the fragile cane tubes in her hand and thinking about the group's mission statement, Lucy felt like she was living a dream come true.

Carlos assigned Lucy a partner, Ayllu. Ayllu was a young man with a quick smile. Lucy smiled back then glanced at his hands.

He wore a wedding ring.

Together they rehearsed a song. A cool breeze from the lake ruffled hairs that had fallen loose from Lucy's ponytail. She concentrated on the joy in the music and forced herself to not think about Manuel, who showed up late then flirted with a female dancer.

During a break, a sikuri from another group walked over and said to Lucy, "Come play with us. Since you're from North America you can get us grant money to perform in the U.S.."

Lucy's thoughts started down the well-worn synapse superhighway of complaint. Her inner rant went something like this:

"Here I want to connect with people on a deep spiritual level, and they just see my white skin as a ticket for them to get money. As soon as someone tells me how they want to go to the U.S., I instantly close my heart to them. They don't care about their culture. They would bury it in an instant for money, like the Native Americans did in Palm Springs and built Casinos. Sure, they can get rich materially, but they sold their souls to do it."

With effort, Lucy recalled her vow.

"But, hey! Appreciate everything!"

As she concentrated with all her might on appreciation, she could feel and hear new synapse connections forming with slight crackles in her head.

"Not many sikuri groups allow women to play at all. I'm lucky to be playing with these guys. Nam-myoho-renge-kyo Nam-myoho-renge-kyo Nam-myoho-renge-kyo."

They all rehearsed until 11 PM.

Carlos announced, "Tomorrow we play at Alba. Everyone meet at 4 AM at Pablo's house."

"Where's Pablo's house?" Lucy asked.

Pablo wrote down vague directions in Lucy's notepad. The house had no number. His street had no name. So, he wrote the names of major streets near his house.

Seeing Lucy's perplexed expression, Manuel said, "Don't worry. I'll go by your hotel and pick you up."

The next morning Lucy awoke with a start. Booming noises echoed in the adobe passageways and courtyard of her hotel. She glanced at the clock. 4:15 AM.

"Oh no!" she thought, "Manuel's knocking at the front door of the hotel! Gotta run!"

Out of bed Lucy sprang. A poncho she threw on. Helter skelter she ran to the reception area. The 2x4 security bar she lifted from brackets. The heavy wooden door she dragged open.

"Manuel! Manuel!" She called into rainy darkness.

The night watchman roused up and came out of a side room to see what all the commotion was about.

"My friend is supposed to come pick me up for Alba!"

"No one came," he said with a look that said he was going back to bed.

Lucy returned to her room.

Again she heard, "boom boom boom."

It was fireworks someone was setting off.

Manuel or no Manuel, Lucy didn't want to be late. She grabbed the bombo and siku and rushed out.

A tricycle cab approached. Lucy climbed onto the bench seat in front under a fringed canopy. The sinewy man on the bicycle seat in back pedaled her across town. They arrived at the intersection Pablo had scribbled in her notepad. She got out and stood in the mud. Drunken people milled in the streets. Down the block a group huddled in a red-lit doorway. The air smelled like a horse stall.

No sikuris.

The cab pedaled away.

Alone, Lucy stood on the corner.

She pounded the bombo, hoping to draw the sikuris to her. A face looked out a lit window.

"Maybe that's his house!" she thought.å

Lucy went up to the door, waiting for someone to come open it.

No one did.

She pounded the bombo again.

The face looked out, again, with a curious expression. He had no idea who the gringa was pounding a bombo under his window at 4:30 in the morning.

No public phones were in sight.

Lucy thought, "Maybe they already left for the cathedral! I'll walk!"

She strode off through the mud, past the redlit group drinking, and headed in the direction she thought was towards the cathedral.

A couple of different drunks on different blocks yelled out to her as she passed, her bombo slung over her shoulder, "maricon!" (faggot)

Whether they both thought she was a feminine man carrying a bombo, or a masculine woman carrying a bombo, Lucy had no idea.

"Maybe they just yell that at anyone who walks by," she thought.

As she trudged alone through the mud and the rain in the night her mind clouded with dark thoughts.

"Nobody appreciates me. Manuel was going to pick me up, but I bet he passed out drunk. Here I am wandering around alone, after a late night rehearsal, for what? Maybe I should go join that other sikuri group that courted me. I have other places to go! I won't put up with this!"

Then she remembered her vow to appreciate everything. As she chanted nam-myoho-renge-kyo silently as she walked along, other thoughts surfaced.

"If I leave this group and join another, what example am I setting? I, who speak of world peace. If I stomp off in a tiff, I'm not setting any example at all."

She decided to follow through on what she had started. She had rehearsed. The group was expecting her to perform.

"I'll do it. I'll appreciate this opportunity to grow. I'll see it through to the end, no matter what."

Slogging through the mud, she got turned around. All the red brick buildings looked the same. There was no sun to orientate her. She stopped at an intersection and stared.

Like a drowning person slipping beneath the sea of despondency, Lucy struggled with her waves of emotions.

Just then, a voice said, "Can I help you?"

It was a cop.

"Which way to Parque Pino?" Lucy asked, grabbing onto this lifeline that appeared from nowhere.

"Go up the street a couple of blocks, then turn left for three blocks. It's right there."

"Thanks!"

Her faith in humanity tentatively restored, she plodded along.

In Parque Pino there were brass bands and police, but no sikuris.

"Maybe they're in the cathedral," she thought.

She went in. Mass was in session. She sat in the back. After awhile she felt the impulse to look outside again.

Crossing Parque Pino she encountered Sebastian, the president of Jaqe Runa.

"Where are they?" Sebastian asked.

"I have no idea," Lucy said.

Her dark thoughts started to cloud her mind again.

"Sebastian announced at last night's rehearsal that he would bring instruments to Parque Pino at 5 am for the late-comers. He has nothing with him. I can't trust anyone. What am I doing with this group of irresponsible drunks? Wait! Appreciate everything. I've found at least one other member of Jaqe Runa. This is progress," she thought.

"Maybe they're inside," Sebastian said.

"I didn't see them, but let's go look again," Lucy said.

In they went. The church was full. Standing room only. Lucy, carrying her bombo, followed Sebastian. They got as close as possible to the front of the assembly. A couple of marching bands with their tubas and bass drums crowded in behind them.

Not seeing any Jaqe Runa's, Sebastian wiggled his way back out of the press of humanity. He left Lucy behind.

"I woke up early to play panpipes with the group. Instead, I'm pinned in a group of strangers, enduring a mass," she thought.

After awhile, Lucy decided to leave, too.

Leaving a crowded church while carrying a giant bombo drum is no easy feat, but with determination and gentleness it can be accomplished, Lucy found.

"'Scuse me. 'Scuse me. Pardon me. 'Scuse me."

At the door she encountered Jaqe Runas entering at the tail end of the mass. Manuel was in the group.

"Sorry for not showing up, I overslept," he said, looking extremely hung over.

Pablo linked his arm through Lucy's and maneuvered her into their group of about eight sikuris. Each young man kissed her on the cheek in greeting. The guia smiled as he pulled a siku of six tubes out of his bag and handed it to her.

The ghosts of her sad lonely abandoned feelings flew away in an instant. She felt embraced in a family.

Mass ended. Together they left, playing their bombos and sikus with all their hearts, tromping through the muddy streets. As Lucy played her part intertwined with the others, she felt joy reverberate through her being.

"Ah! This is that feeling I came so far to experience. I am not alone. On a deep level we are one. Even the mud glomming onto my shoes is life embracing me."

The vibration of their shared music seemed to call forth the sun. In early morning light they arrived at the house of Pablo.

To celebrate their arrival, they played an energetic song outside of Pablo's house. A bent woman swung open the door and with a smile ushered them into the muddy yard, freshly strewn with dry sawdust. Benches of boards on bricks lined one side of the yard. A tarp stretched overhead to keep the rain off. More and more sikuris arrived till the yard was full with close to a hundred people there. They ate a warm breakfast then played sikus and bombos and danced all together.

The family feeling intensified. Lucy felt embarrassed about having had any dark thoughts earlier.

Gratitude flooded in.

She blinked back tears.

"What's with these extreme emotions?" she thought.

Off and on, for the next few hours of food, music and dancing, she choked up with tears. Tears of happiness. They finally spilled out when one of the founding sikuris of Jaqe Runa took her hand and gazed lovingly into her eyes and told her how beautifully she played the sikus and bombo.

"Thank you," Lucy said, the tears falling.

So much appreciation to be accepted into this group of guys in another land, another culture, another world.

A few minutes later that same sikuri told her that he was separated from his wife and why didn't they go off and screw.

Lucy politely declined his offer.

The dark thoughts hardly came in at all.

The gathering wound down. Rita, one of the dancers, invited Lucy and another sikuri, Dante, to visit her father in the hospital.

HOSPITAL

The man in the hospital bed reminded Lucy of her own dad. It hit her with a shock, like suddenly seeing someone come back from the grave. Dad was dead. She'd seen him die and lay limp. No more air coming out of his nostrils. Skin getting colder and colder. The mortician guys wrapping him in a sheet and carrying him away as her stepmom screamed that way only mourning wives can scream. All this she had seen, and cried over like she had never cried in her life.

Now here was Dad alive again. Or so it seemed.

Rita's Dad had that same bit of thinning black hair flopped up off his forehead as his head lay on the hospital pillow. Dad, if he had lived, would have been three years older than this 72-year-old Inka man who just had back surgery. Rita's dad, his eyes glassy from pain killers, cracked a joke, rolled over (morphine is amazing), pulled open the dented metal drawer on his bedside table and pulled out a professional harmonica in the key of G.

He lay back on the pillow and played the harmonica. The notes leapt and danced. For his coup de grace he pinched one nostril closed and did once-more-from-the-top inhaling and exhaling the notes with virtuosic precision through his open nostril sliding across the harp.

Lucy applauded, "Bravo! Bravo!"

"Papi," Rita said, "This is Lucy and Dante."

"Diente," her dad replied. "Diente Molares?" ("Tooth Molars" in English). "I had a friend, Dante Morales. He was a dentist. I always called him Diente Molares."

A nurse came in.

He hid the harmonica under the covers and put a forlorn expression on his face.

"How's the pain?"

"It hurts," he said, "Ooooh. I need more pain killers."

She injected morphine into his drip bag, then left.

He smiled, picked up his harmonica and set into playing a long set of sikuriadas, waynos and tangos.

"You should rest," Lucy said as she applauded the lengthy performance.

"I once played for 24 hours straight. In Lima. For the Guinness Book of World Records. And I never repeated a tune. 18 hours. 24. I don't look 72-years-old, do I? No one believes me."

He placed his harmonica against his lips to play another tune, just as the security guard came in to shoo Lucy, Rita and Dante out. Visiting hours had ended some 30 minutes before.

The other five patients in the room seemed relieved to have the party wind up. After all, they had just had surgery, too. By the pained looks on their faces, their morphine doses apparently weren't as high as Rita's dad's.

Walking down the corridor, Lucy thought about her own father. She hadn't thought about him in years. His little chuckle she'd forgotten, as he laughed at his own witticisms; his shoulders bouncing up and down with mirth - mischievous twinkle in his eyes.

Thirteen years he'd been dead. Her most recent memories of him were from letters. Letters he wrote while courting her mother. When Lucy found the letters in an old shoe box tied with a string, Lucy expected them to be poems or sonnets.

Instead, he wrote love letters to her mom that said, "I'm hung over again ... my drinking is nothing a good wife can't cure … I want you to lose twenty five pounds before the wedding next month ... I have a new roommate. We share a bed. She's real pretty. Just kidding. His name is George..."

"If some guy wrote me letters like that," Lucy thought, "I'd run away as fast as possible. I can't believe mom married such an egotistical judgmental jerk."

Little did she know that she was seeing some of her own character flaws. She, too, could be an egotistical judgmental jerk.

Rather than self reflect, Lucy had chosen to not think about those letters, nor about the drunken shouts and fists through walls of her childhood home. She had closed the door on all father/daughter memories, including the sound of her father's laughter.

That laughter with the Inka man - it was like sunlight flooding in to Lucy's heart. She felt a joy she hadn't felt since she was a child and snuggled up for bedtime stories, her ear warm on daddy's mountainous chest. His voice rumbled in that breathing mountain like from the Earth itself.

Walking out the hospital door, tears sprang to Lucy's eyes.

She cried as if she had just lost her dad all over again.

Was her dad in the sound of the panpipes? Somehow, yes. The happy family she'd wished she'd had. A peaceful world. All of that was in the sound of the panpipes, in the sound of the sikus, played together, bodies swaying and bouncing in unison, braiding notes to make melodies that wound around and around like a parent's arms to cradle you and let you know everything was okay.

REHEARSAL

Later that afternoon, on the way to the rehearsal, Lucy went to pick up her camcorder from the repair shop. As she wrestled her bombo into a taxi, the driver was courteous and respectful.

Obviously she was participating in the festival and wasn't just another tourist coming to gawk.

"What group do you play with?"

"Jaqe Runa."

"Wow. They're good."

Lucy felt better about being associated with her drunken comrades.

The repair shop was closed. But the accordion iron-gate was open, so she sat down to wait for the technician to return. Lucy sat on the front step for an hour with her bombo. On her head she wore the official Jaqe Runa chullu pointy beanie.

"Jaqe Runa! Did you see that gringa over there? She's playing with Jaqe Runa!" a passerby said with approval to his companion.

The technician never showed up and it was past time to get to rehearsal.

Lucy carried her bombo up the mountain to Huacsapata, a park that overlooked the city of Puno and lake Titicaca. Along the way she struggled with her negativity.

"The technician failed me. Now I can't film the festival or film interviews. No. Don't go there. Poison into medicine. I'm determined to be victorious. Like Nichiren says, 'Suffer what there is to suffer, enjoy what there is to enjoy. Regard both suffering and joy as facts of life, and continue chanting Nam-myoho-renge-kyo, no matter what happens. How could this be anything other than the boundless joy of the Law? Strengthen your power of faith more than ever.'" She chanted silently as she walked, "Nam-myoho-renge-kyo, nam-myoho-renge-kyo, nam-myoho-renge-kyo..."

At Huacsapata the rehearsal, which should have started two hours earlier, hadn't yet begun. A smashed liquor bottle littered the concrete where the group would be practicing choreography. Sikuris lounged around.

Lucy waited another hour before the President of Jaqe Runa arrived. She asked him about getting a broom so she could sweep up the glass. He looked irritated.

"Borrow a broom from that store."

She did, and began sweeping up the glass, thinking, "More glass over here. Oh, here's a pile of feces, right in the middle of the plaza where we will practice our choreography in the dark night."

Crinkling her nose, she swept that up, too.

It brought up memories of when she was a Byakuren at the SGI Culture Center in San Francisco. She recalled how the Byakuren would arrive early to clean up the place for the other members.

"How many toilets I scrubbed! And we chanted Nam-myoho-renge-kyo in our hearts that we were polishing our own lives with every effort we made to clean up the Center."

So, of course it was natural to clean up. Even the feces. Lucy chanted silently that she was scrubbing her life till it gleamed.

She dumped the glass and feces in a trashcan.

A dozen sikuris, strangers from another town, arrived. They stacked their bombos high. Lucy walked over, stuck out her hand, introduced herself and welcomed them. Their faces lit up with lust. After all, aren't all blonde white women ready to rip off their clothes and have immediate sex? That's what the TV and print ads show.

She turned away, sat on a rock and sewed rainbow fringe on her red poncho.

Not sure how to deal with this strange gringa who didn't fit in a box, the twelve gangly youths swayed from one foot to the other like tortora reeds in lapis waves of Lake Titicaca.

The guia arrived and rehearsal began. Some grumbled about why there weren't more people there. There were so few in fact, that they didn't practice the choreography at all, even though the competition was the next morning. They were short about ninety people. Lightening flashed in zigzags that curled in the sky. The city's lights went out. They kept playing without pause. The trance of the music carried them along in unity. The lights came back on.

The guia wrapped up the rehearsal early due to lack of participants.

The next morning was rainy. Lucy strode out of her $3-a-night hotel in her sikuri outfit of ojotas, wool socks, black pants, shirt of bayeta de la tierra, faja, red poncho with rainbow fringe, chullu, bombo and an umbrella into the rain-spattered streets.

Up the hill Lucy walked to the President's house. The rehearsal was supposed to start at 7 AM. Lucy was the first arrival.

Going on 8:30, more people came in. The women were dressed in long flowing skirts. Some were red, others yellow and the rest were green. All wore little red jackets. Two long braids hung down their backs. The braids originated at the occipital bony lumps at the back of the skull (not over the ears like Heidi). For women with short hair, they bought braids of human hair that country women had cut off their own heads and sold. Or else they braided in black yarn. Giant colorful pom poms decorated the ends of the braids.

"Thank you, jilata," the sikuri to Lucy's right said, as he accepted a plastic cup of Coca Cola. There were so many sikuris in the group that no one knew the name of every single person. So they addressed each other as "jilata", brother.

The sun came out. Lucy got hot and antsy. Manuel motioned for her to come over and talk to him. He was with a small circle of sikuris sharing a bottle of liquor, sipping out of the bottle cap.

"Lucy," Manuel said as he put his arm around her, smiled at her with adoration and alcohol breath, "I..."

When Manuel was drunk, he loved Lucy more than anyone. When he was sober, he didn't.

He wiped tears from his eyes.

"I'm too emotional", he said, and walked away.

Lucy wanted to cry, too.

"Shees! I wish he would make up his mind," she thought. "It's hard to be 'just friends' when he does stuff like this."

To distract herself, she looked around at the other people.

Some of the drummers were gathering in a circle. Lucy joined them and forced herself to concentrate on the music and not think about Manuel and the lump in her throat. She played, listening closely to not make too many mistakes, and looking intently at other panpipe players who were excellent guides and were playing her part of the melody to see what pipes they blew and when.

Silently she chanted appreciation and thought, "How wonderful to be here in the Andes playing the sikus with these guys."

After a couple of songs she felt content and complete.

Someone yelled, "The radio says that number 25 is up! We're number 27! We better get to the stadium!"

Without practicing the entire set, or even a little bit of the choreography, everyone took off at a run to get to the stadium across town. A lot of people had shown up just that morning and had yet to rehearse anything at all.

Lucy slung her bombo over her shoulder.

They trotted through traffic, weaving their way through pedestrians, tricycle cabs, taxis and buses, to get to the stadium in time.

Gathering outside, they heard the boom boom of the brass band inside playing a Morenada dance tune.

"Move ahead! Move ahead!" someone official commanded.

Jaqe Runa crowded into the stadium, picked their way over the mud puddles and positioned themselves at the goal line to enter as soon as the Morenada group finished.

"And now ... Jaqe Runa," the announcer's voice echoed over the loud speakers.

The guia raised his mallet and swung it down and up and down again and boom boom boom they began their hopping march dance, playing, onto the field. Jaqe Runa ran through their sequence, did the choreography. The dancers danced around Lucy and the other sikuris, swirling their skirts. Somehow it was all coming together, there at the last moment.

One guy dressed as a kusillo lit a torch as he danced and blew flames.

Kusillos are androgynous mythical beings who span our quotidian life and the unseen. They are windows between worlds - pranksters who remind us not to take ourselves too seriously. Elements of the traditional costume are furry sandals and a cloth mask that covers the head. Three soft horns protrude from the forehead. The nose is long and upturned. From there, each kusillo designs his or her costume as he or she wishes. The most dramatic was a husky guy who sewed layers and yards of videotape onto the back of his tweed coat, like a flowing cape.

It turned out that the group had broken a rule and were disqualified because of the fire-breathing kusillo.

Jaqe Runa took being disqualified in stride, "We'll improve for next year."

Out into the street they paraded. Through town they did the little hopping steps, playing bombos and sikus. The women dancers spun in their colorful pollera skirts high, like blooming flowers. A block or two ahead, Lucy saw their banner dancing and shimmering on its tall t-shaped pole. Squares of homespun wool fabric dyed the colors of the rainbow plus white in the opposing corners, like a wiphala, outlined a royal blue field of a satiny fabric called "wolf skin". On the satiny blue field, painted in cheap white house paint with liquid pigments, floated the planet Earth. South America was front and center in this worldview. North America sort of disappeared in a vague blur up at the top. In the center of South America was a smudge of white to mark sacred Lake Titicaca. Criss-crossed behind the Earth were two giant sikus in golden colored "wolf skin." Below, dangling like fringe, were the characters JAQE RUNA and the year; white outlined in black, hand sewn.

A dancer swooped the pole. The banner fluttered and glimmered in the Andean sunlight.

Lucy felt like that triumphant banner as she danced and played together with a hundred trilling sikus of all sizes and dozens of thundering bombos. She was glad that she had stuck it out and not abandoned the group in frustration that first day when she was lost in the dark.

"Suti Mama! Suti Mama!" the guia hollered over the pounding drums and siku music. The musician at Lucy's side took up the call and passed the word back, "Suti Mama! Suti Mama!"

When they finished playing the current song, they would launch into Suti Mama. Suti Mama was an appropriate choice since the Spanish and Quechua lyrics are a greeting to the Virgin of the Candelaria, whose cathedral they were now approaching. This was her festival. The mixture of Spanish and Quechua represented the syncretism of the Andean Cosmovision of the Pachamama and the superimposed Catholic Virgin.

"Suti Mama" was one of Lucy's favorites. "Suti" means "name," or "is called." "Mama" meant Virgin, Pachamama, Mother Earth. The lyrics were simple and repetitive - the melody happy and upbeat.

Buenos dias (tardes/noche) suti Mama
Suti Mama Candelaria
Buenos dias suti Mama
Suti Mama candelaria
Wai waiiiii waka waka
Wai waiiiii toro toro
Wai waiiiii waka waka
Wai waiiiii toro toro

After singing once through with bombo accompaniment, they launched into playing the melody on the sikus. Their abs got a work-out with each deep breath, blowing with their whole hearts across the cane tubes. Pounding bombos, each sikuri spun in a slow circle as they progressed down the avenue.

The Virgin of the Candelaria was a delicate doll perched on a giant poof cushion. Her cushion rested on a large wooden litter. Four men carried the liter, poof and Virgin down the street. Jaqe Runa followed behind the Virgin in procession, playing and dancing, song after song.

When Lucy looked at the Virgin statue, she chanted Nam-myoho-renge-kyo to honor the life-state of Buddhahood, the Pachamama - all of the shoten zenjin and apus of the universe, especially of this land. Lucy felt the vibe of the land. The vibe of the people being aware of the vibe. The vibe was everywhere in the world, of course, but Lucy thought that in the Andes, more people were aware of it. And that awareness made the vibe stronger.

Above, out of second story windows people leaned, with long handled implements, about ten feet long, to dump rose petals on the Virgin. Lucy and all of Jaqe Runa followed behind, traipsing on stray petals, playing for the Virgin/Pachamama; playing for each other; playing for the invisible that connects everyone.

Jaqe Runa paraded through the streets all day into the night and the rain.

Strangely, the more miles Lucy danced and played her bombo and siku (even though at one point she thought she was going to hallucinate from dehydration and sunstroke), the stronger she became.

By the end of the parade she felt better than when she had started.

The guias unstrapped their bombos. The other musicians followed suit, stacking them high on the side of the street. Everyone mingled and dispersed to drink and socialize.

Ayllu, Lucy's sikuri partner, was enjoying the temporary peace that playing the sikus together with others brought him - for Ayllu suffered greatly inside. The sound of the sikus was salvation for him - playing together this instrument that represents, is, the union of people with nature, of individuals with community. Played in pairs, in dialog, in community, the breath sounds in the hollow reeds. Reeds cut from the moist earth. Ayllu became the wind in the reeds.

When he played the sikus with the group, he felt complete, he felt loved, he felt part of the whole, not alone.

Alone. What loneliness haunted his soul. His girlfriend was pregnant. Her father took her away to live in a distant town, away from Ayllu, who he said was a bad influence.

Lucy. Ayllu had fallen in love with Lucy over the course of the festival. It didn't conflict with his love for his girlfriend. That was different.

Ayllu's feelings swelled and thoughts swirled, "Lucy stands solid on the ground, playing the bombo and sikus. She understands. I can see it in her eyes. She understands my pain. I love her. I want to give her something."

He invited Lucy to visit the Cathedral.

He taught Lucy to enter through the door on the right, to dip her fingers in the Holy water and tap her forehead, her sternum, her right shoulder, her left, then to hold her hand with the thumb vertical and the index finger horizontal behind it to make a cross and to kiss her thumb. Then he led her past the pews of praying people and up the steps to the Virgin. They stood in front of her, gazing.

As Lucy looked at the Virgin, open to sense her sacredness, she saw the Virgin's chest rise and fall in gentle breath and her face smile.

"Amazing," Lucy thought, "the life that the devotion of the people breathes into this statue."

Ayllu reached out and rubbed the gold fringe of the Virgin's garment and made the sign of the cross again. Lucy followed suit, chanting Nam-myoho-renge-kyo silently. A huge spray of American Beauty roses was arranged at the Virgin's feet. Ayllu reached down, bent a stem and snapped off a blossom. Lucy gasped. He held the perfect rose lovingly in his cupped hands, gazing down at it with pious adoration as he and Lucy walked back up the aisle, crossed themselves with Holy water from the other side of the doorway, and exited.

Outside, Ayllu paused and turned to Lucy, "This is for you," he said with a smile and handed her the rose.

Lucy accepted it with both hands cupped. She pulled a safety pin from her faja and attached the rose to her poncho, near her heart.

They smiled at each other, enjoying the moment.

Ayllu's cell phone buzzed a text message.

"It's my brother. I'll see you later." He kissed her on the cheek goodbye and walked away through the crowd.

As Lucy paused, thinking what to do, that cute guy that played in front of her the whole parade walked up and invited her to join him and his friends for a beer.

They went to a speak-easy. In an inner courtyard, through two doors, walls of woven mats divided the space into booths where locals sat and drank. There was no sign outside. No tourists inside.

The cute guy led them to a metal-legged table with a Formica top surrounded by molded plastic stackable stools. They all sat down. Someone ordered a round of beer.

Then the cute guy put his arm around the dancer nearest him and pulled her close.

"Isn't she beautiful? She's my princess! I love her!" he said.

Lucy's thoughts started to crank up the well worn record of complaint, with the accompanying chemical rush that filled her chest, clenched her throat and made tears spring from her eyes.

"No," she thought, "appreciate everything. Nam-myoho-renge-kyo."

Suddenly, everything changed. Each effort Lucy had made to appreciate everything formed a new synapse. Each synapse was like a fresh-water spring bubbling forth out of a crevices of her rock-hard mind. Underground streams and currents carved new pathways. Those streams converged one by one, accumulating force. Now they reached a critical mass. They erupted like a geyser. This spiritual geyser lifted Lucy up. She felt as if she were floating above the scene. She viewed herself from aloft.

"Look at me! I'm 40-something years old. That cute guy is 20-something. I'm old enough to be his mother. I've got a saggy chin, wrinkles, gray hairs. It would be absurd for me to cry over a lost love who's 20 years younger than me," she thought.

In that moment, Lucy matured. The lump in her throat disappeared. Her chest felt expansive with a love that had no room for adolescent angst. She felt herself as a mother-figure, or an auntie. The cute guy who played the sikus and bombo with his whole being was like her beloved nephew.

This transformation passed in the space between the cute guy saying, "Isn't she beautiful?' to Lucy nodding her head and sincerely saying, "Yes, she is."

After a few glasses of beer, Lucy excused herself to go to the bathroom.

The bathroom was a single roofless stall with a sheet draped across it. Concrete foot-pads flanked a hole. Lucy squatted, raising the fringe of her poncho, gathering it into her arms, so it wouldn't trail on the wet stinky ground. Lucy tried not to breath too deep as she took care of her necessities.

As she walked towards her booth, three of the visiting sikuris from another town, the very ones who had viewed Lucy with lust at the last rehearsal, approached. After parading together through the town, aching feet dancing in tire-tread ojota sandals, blowing their sikus till their bottom lips bled, striking bombos with long-handled mallets that blistered their hands, rainbow poncho fringe drawing squiggles of joy in the air; through sharing all of this, the visiting sikuris developed a respect for Lucy. She was no longer the blonde gringa. She was one of them. A sikuri.

They were ambassadors, diplomats on a hallowed mission.

"We present you with this chullu of our group as a symbol of your promise that you will play with us in our Festival of San Miguel."

Lucy bowed her head as she accepted the long-tasseled knit cap with both hands and agreed to play in their festival.

"Have you heard of our town, Ilave?" a sikuri asked her.

"No."

"We're the ones who stoned our mayor to death," the shortest sikuri said with a grin.

"He was corrupt," the middle one said.

"Oh!" Lucy said with surprise, but going with the flow. She gazed at each sikuri, "What did you do during this? Did you have a big knife?"

"I had a sling shot," the third sikuri said, miming taking aim.

The three sikuris, bony as Inka super models, stood erect, to their full five-foot-two, or three or four. Their teenage eyes glistened with pride. They did not have killer eyes like some gang members in Lucy's hometown of Los Angeles. No. That was what was so striking. Their eyes shone with altruisim. They were youth with ideals, with hope.

"We're warriors!" they said.

Meanwhile, in another straw booth, Ayllu was drinking hard with companions. So sad, Ayllu was.

"Help me!," he silently cried.

His brother said something rude. Ayllu grabbed an empty beer bottle by the neck and hit it against a rock. He waved the broken bottle at his brother. His brother just laughed.

Ayllu paused, hung his head. Looked at his own tender skin. He cut himself.

Once. Twice. Three times.

Watching the lines turn red, he saw the blood well up drip, drip dripping like the pain in his heart that wouldn't go away.

Lucy was on her way back to her booth after her meeting with the sikuris from Ilave. Ayllu spotted her and ran up crying, "My brother was fighting with me and he cut me!" Ayllu thrust out his arm to show Lucy the three slashes on the tender flesh of his left inner forearm, dripping red.

Shocked, Lucy quickly assessed the gravity of the wounds. They weren't deep. The blood would quickly coagulate.

Ayllu picked at one of the wounds and pulled out a tiny sliver, beer-bottle-glass brown.

"He did that to himself," Lucy realized.

All of Ayllu's misery gathered in his chest and throat and exploded into a round of sobbing. He tried to embrace Lucy as he cried. Lucy wrestled him around to avoid touching his blood.

Together they plopped onto a wooden bench, side by side. Lucy put her arm around him, like a protective mother. Ayllu bowed his head and cried.

"So much suffering," Lucy thought, "His pain is so much deeper than my puny complaints."

All at once Lucy's mind saw the pain of everyone. The technician who didn't fix her camera - what shame he felt that he seldom completed his promises. The frustration of the Jaqe Runa president who saw so clearly how things could be better, but he didn't know how to lead people to make it so. Poor Manuel who felt uncomfortable in his own skin when he wasn't drinking. And Ayllu, slashing himself.

"How can I help Ayllu?" she thought.

How could she help all of the people who suffered?

She said quietly into Ayllu's ear, "I have something very special for you."

"Wha' ?" he said, looking at his feet through his tears.

"Repeat after me. Nam."

Ayllu repeated each syllable, one at a time, after Lucy, of nam-myoho-renge-kyo.

"Now together with me."

Lucy and Ayllu chanted Nam-myoho-renge-kyo Nam-myoho-renge-kyo Nam-myoho-renge-kyo over and over.

At first Ayllu's chanting was in gulps with his sobs. Gradually his voice steadied like an off-balance spinning top finding its center. As he calmed, he sighed deep and relaxed.

He laid his head on Lucy's shoulder.

She rocked him. Like a parent her arms cradled Ayllu, letting him know everything was okay. They looked somewhat like a living Pieta, as her lips brushed his coarse black hair, smelling of sweat and she chanted - appreciating everything.

Portrait of Lucy

INTERLUDE
NOTE TO AUNT BERT

Dear Aunt Bert,

Even though we don't talk about it much, you know how my parents' divorce when I was a kid ripped me apart. Well, I feel like I took a tiny step, or maybe better to say "a tiny stitch," in healing my heart. As I was chanting I realized that me and Dad are the same person. That sounds kind of weird. But it's true. I'm not sure how else to say it. I can be just as much of an egotistical judgmental jerk. And I can also be a loving parent.

In Puno I just played panpipes with a bunch of guys in a festival and learned a bit about appreciation.

Appreciate the sun - it's where our life comes from.

Appreciate the night - a time to rest.

Appreciate your mom - without her you wouldn't be here.

Appreciate your dad - ditto as above.

Appreciate when someone is a jerk - you are learning self-control.

Appreciate the harsh weather - you are learning endurance.

Appreciate not having everything you want - you are learning to value what you do have.

Appreciate everything - for everything is part of your very life itself.

Love, Lucy

P.S. I got an invitation to play sikus in a festival later this year in Warrior Town (Ilave). And Manuel invited me to another festival coming up soon, in Conima.

CHAPTER EIGHT
CONIMA

Conima. The community of sikuris on the North Shore of Lake Titicaca. This is where Lucy had dreamt of visiting ever since reading Tom Turino's book "Moving Away From Silence." Now, Lucy felt strong enough to not be swayed by her emotions for Manuel. The Suburban Provisioners order was moving along nicely. She could go away for the weekend to fulfill a dream.

Sitting with Manuel on the lakeshore in Conima, leaning against a whitened weathered log on grass cropped close with llama nibbles, they both watched the lowering sun cast crystalline jewels across the undulating blue water that went down1000 feet deep and guarded an ancient city and other secrets. The sound of distant panpipe groups warming-up mingled with lapping wavelets and the contented grunts of a pig tied to a stake as he rooted around the Alpine meadow starred with miniature sunflowers.

Paradise grew a shadow when Manuel announced, "Everyone here works with contraband or drug trafficking."

Yet, a splay of rays danced watery reflections as the sun disappeared in cumulus horizon. Manuel and Lucy ambled up the stone path. Stones had been laid with such care that they could date back to the Inka Empire. They walked past a handmade adobe house with sky-blue wood window frames like two eyes over weathered slat door. The door, a celestial blue, merged with the universe molecule by molecule.

Passing laden llamas with dreadlocked fur, they hurried up to the plaza for the start of the music festival. People milled around, a few sitting down. On side-streets unseen musicians rehearsed. Buses and trucks drove into the plaza. Then out again. One bus driver waved and smiled to Manuel.

"That's my friend!" Manuel waved back. His friend parked his bus. They gathered to drink cups of steaming alcoholic punch in the plaza.

The friend, Ruben, had an open round face with an easy smile and joy of life twinkling in his 20-something-year-old eyes. He told stories of driving a bus all over Peru. The tales quickly turned to the occupation of just about everyone in town - contraband.

"That big truck over there is hauling eggs from Bolivia," Ruben said as a blue and white stake-bed truck belched black plume against twilight sky.

"Aren't there chickens in Peru?" Lucy asked rhetorically.

Manuel rolled his eyes.

"Eggs from Bolivia are a lot cheaper, almost half price!" Ruben said. "Taxes are at 38%, so we sneak the eggs in."

Drink followed drink and Ruben went into more detail of the life of a contraband driver. Ostensibly he drove a passenger bus. But, when he neared this remote border-crossing, well, he hauled contraband.

With a proud smile he mentioned his recent accomplishment of crossing over with a load of shoes in a bus empty of passengers.

Lucy shared some of her bus driving stories. As they swapped tales, they drank more cups of warm punch in the plaza. Manuel was an attentive audience to their shoptalk.

But this young indigenous man's driving experience went far beyond Lucy's.

"And then there's rolling your bus, when needed," he said.

"What?" Lucy asked, not sure she had heard him right.

"Well, when you're hauling contraband you face a five year jail sentence if you are caught. But in order to not get caught, here's what you do. You see, the police try and stop you on the road. But they only have little cars or maybe a pick-up truck, and you've got this big vehicle FULL of contraband. All that contraband won't fit in their tiny cars. If you pull over and stop like they want you to, they will arrest you, along with all the contraband, and drive your vehicle to an impound yard. To avoid this you learn how to roll your bus over. But not over and over – that's too dangerous. Just on its side."

Lucy gestured to show a slowly tilting bus and said, "Tranquilo."

"Sí, tranquilo!" he smiled.

They clinked glasses and drank.

Ruben continued his bus-rolling story, "You jerk the wheel this way then back that way, but not too much. Once the bus is on its side you take off running and escape. The local folks come running out of their houses to loot the abandoned contraband. Then there is hardly anything for the police to confiscate! No evidence! A while back the police shot out my tires, but I kept driving and got away! But you never know," Ruben paused.

The expression on his face shifted. The boasting, the joy, was gone. Shoulders slumped, his voice grew quiet.

"Last week," he said, "the police shot at a truck hauling contraband. They killed the driver. He was only seventeen-years-old. The bullet went in here," he pointed to his forehead over his left eye, "and came out here," he pointed to the back of his head on the right side. "Seventeen-years-old."

He shook his head.

They sat in silence.

Manuel fidgeted against this seriousness.

"Hey," he said in a loud cheery voice, "the festival should be starting soon," and slapped Ruben on the back.

They drank up.

Ruben bid them goodnight and went to nap in his bus.

Manuel and Lucy walked to the other side of the plaza, to where a bright light was set up in the night for TV cameras. Nearby, people mounted a stack of building materials. Lucy and Manuel followed. The pebbly cement of the narrow concrete T-shaped columns poked into their sit bones. They wiggled to adjust. It was a fine bleacher.

Soon, the parade started.

Rhythmic pounding of big drums resonated in everyone, filling their beings.

The contest had two categories: Negritos and Sikuris. Negritos was a style with blackface, drums, bells tied to the clothing in various places to jingle with the jumping dance steps, a leader in olive drab fatigues blowing a whistle in time to direct the group, and a youth playing a ribbed scratch instrument.

For the scratch instrument, most groups used a long hollow bamboo with ridges cut in it and rubbed a large plastic comb over it to make the scratching rhythm. But one group had two boys with tin cans and a little stick each, rubbing the natural ridges of the tin can. The drums were Andean bombos hit with a homemade softheaded mallet; except for one where the guy hit it with his open palm. Whether this was to be more African or because he lost his mallet, Lucy didn't know.

Homemade masks covered their faces. Huge pink tongues lolled out of giant lips beneath bulging eyes.

Lucy snapped a photo, yet felt disturbed by these racist images. She was a tiny girl when the local pancake house changed its name and took down the images of Little Black Sambo chasing a tiger into butter. Or was it the tiger chasing Little Black Sambo? In any event, that was when her dad taught her that making fun of a culture was racism. This lesson was part of Lucy's knee jerk reaction to the world.

Ruben's contraband stories didn't phase her. He was a good guy making do in a bad situation.

But these black-face Negritos ridiculing African slaves brought to the Andes -- why? Lucy could understand costumed dances parodying the Conquistadores. That was like reclaiming your power from people who had enslaved you. But why parody other people who were also enslaved?

The idealism that her parents had instilled in her often ran into these quandaries. Like that day long ago when Lucy drove a bus full of inner-city black kids in San Francisco past the Castro District. An African American boy screamed out the window, "Faggot! Faggot! Faggot!" Lucy had assumed that oppressed people would sympathize with other oppressed people.

In Conima, as the Negritos pounded their bombos and jumped around, tongues flopping, Lucy looked around at the crowd.

Everyone was out for this event - the whole town plus musicians from as far away as Lima and family members who had moved away and returned to their pueblo for the festival. There were approximately 500 people with performers and audience. Everyone fit easily into the plaza. In the center of the plaza, sculptures of giant sikus overshadowed the nearby modernistic concrete Cathedral as a focal point of importance in the community. The flower beds in the plaza around an illuminated fountain bloomed like a nursery catalogue with roses, begonias and lots of other flowers whose names Lucy did not know. Also, artistically arranged in the plantings were gnarled cactus and cornstalks in full ripe tassel; stalks thick and sturdy, broad green leaves tinged with a hearty red. The plants gleamed with life, exuding a freshly washed purity even in this dusty town.

After awhile Lucy wanted a different camera angle, so she left the bleacher seats, which were immediately filled by a family wrapped in blankets, and headed over to stand in a pool of bright light where there were guys with tripods and cameras of every shape imaginable.

Another group paraded in. An elderly local told Lucy, "This dance is in extinction. It's called Loqhe Palla Palla."

Tom Turino's book stated that Loqhe Palla Palla was a style for school children just learning to play the sikus. Lucy had read this, but had forgotten. What with learning to be an international entrepreneur, the ethnomusicology cramming she did when applying for the Fulbright and UCLA got pushed out of the way in her brain by economic necessity.

If she had remembered that Loqhe Palla Palla was supposedly played by children, she might have taken more pictures, to document it. For these were definitely not school children. They were five or six elderly men with giant arca sikus - that is, just the female or following row. Half the notes of the scale. They wore costumes like Lucy had never seen before. On their heads perched giant newspaper hats, the kind she had learned to fold as a child. But these were oversized. Huge. Each musician wore a giant cardboard tail as if he were Tyrannosaurus Rex. The tails swooped up behind them, ruffling their scales of layers of cut newspapers. As the old men played they bowed and turned with the flow of melody and rhythm. The tails swept up, each musician dancing with his own inspiration. A tail almost knocked the camera out of Lucy's hands. She laughed and jumped back just in time. Then a tail swept the other onlookers, who squealed in amusement as they darted out of range. The scale-like layers of cut newspaper also covered the musicians pants and suit jackets.

Loqhe Palla Palla passed around the corner. Their music faded into the distance.

Huge trucks rumbled onto the narrow street along the plaza. "Why are there so many big trucks here in this tiny town?" Lucy asked Manuel.

"I told you, it's the contraband. The border to Bolivia is just down the road," he said, irritated at having to repeat what appeared to be so obvious.

Lucy was distracted from getting miffed by the sound of Sikuris entering the plaza. This what Lucy had come for!

"Wow," she thought, "They're good!"

The sikuris played a style of music called Palla Palla. Lucy had learned a tune or two of the Palla Palla genre some time ago from an elderly siku Professor in Lima, but this was her first time seeing it performed. The Profe had explained to her that Palla Palla was a dance mocking the military draft imposed by the Spanish conquistadores, and later the Peruvian government. Military authorities would come to their tiny town and round up all the young men, tie them in a line with a rope and lead them away to "Die for Their Country."

These Palla Pallas were dressed in mock officer uniforms with cardboard or wooden swords and marched in an individualistic parody of military order. When the Profe explained this to Lucy back in Lima, she was not interested in Palla Palla. After all, she had been a pacifist since she was old enough to pronounce the word. Now, here she was in an idyllic Andean pueblo at a panpipe festival, and literally every single siku group (with the exception of the Loqhe in extinction) was playing Palla Palla! She was disappointed to be immersed in military uniforms when what she wanted was indigenous spirituality blessing the Pachamama.

The military -- over the years, Lucy noticed that many people who joined the military seemed to have given up on themselves.

"The only hope some people see is for someone else to tell them what to do, just as long as they are paid well, "Lucy thought, "Like Shirley, my old best friend from college."

Shirley had given up the Bohemian life in order to work for a defense contractor writing top secret bombing manuals. She told Lucy she did it in order to have health insurance, buy a house and drink a bottle of fine Merlot every night.

Others joined the military because society presented them few other options, like the situation of so many Latino and African American youth in the U.S.

There was so much discrimination. So much injustice.

It isn't like the Andean Cosmovision, as expressed through panpipe playing, where everyone is equal. All is shared for the good of the community.

Lucy's mind wandered, mixing memories together in new combinations.

She wondered if the Conima contrabandistas could be likened, in a way, to Gandhi's Salt March or to the Bus Boycott in Montgomery, Alabama. When Lucy was little and just learning to read and reason, her mom taught her that a person must become strong and wise in order to discern if a law was just, or not. If it was not just, then breaking it was the right thing to do.

"But," Lucy thought, "people in the military blindly follow orders, allowing themselves to degenerate into the realm of evil. From Auschwitz to Afghanistan, people committed atrocities and shrugged them off, saying, 'I was just following orders.' Panpipe players in military outfits. How bizarre! But wait! ..."

As Lucy watched and listened to the musicians, she started to feel happy.

Why?

Her favorite Palla Palla sikuri was a round-shouldered old old man, blowing the sikus with his whole heart, shuffling along. His costume was minimal. A cardboard cap topped his head, a quickly made cardboard white sword tucked in his waistband and tiny irregular epaulets cut from a white piece of note paper safety pinned to his shoulders.

"The indigenous people have triumphed!" Lucy thought. "The wiggle-butt marching is a proclamation of freedom: freedom of the human spirit; a joyous victory of the continuity of humanity in all our rich ways to express who we are! Perhaps that is what 'culture' is."

After the contest, all of the musical groups crowded together in the streets around the plaza and played - all at the same time, all night long. Behind a string of blue tables, sober mothers with propane tanks and large tin tea kettles served up cup after cup of steaming punch (alcoholic or not) to warm the innards and keep the spirit going. The public bathroom locked up around 10 pm, so rivers of urine ran off shadowy abobe walls and collected in cobblestone side streets and streamed along the plaza. Lucy's eyes grew large at this sight. No one else seemed concerned, so Lucy hitched up her jeans and stepped gingerly across the yellow manmade river. She was too interested in people to be censorious. On the other side of the urine current she joined in a circle dance around a sikuri group.

The cold night made bones shiver. Everyone drank and danced and reveled in the music for hours.

The next morning, the sun warmed the plaza. Everyone was exhausted to contentment. Musicians, dancers, film crews with their TV cameras, punch vendors with their gear, and Lucy and Manuel staggered onto a bus. It was standing-room-only for flattened sardines. But, incredibly enough a man offered Lucy his seat so "the drunks wouldn't bother" her. Lucy nodded off as they passed volcanic rock that looked like sculptures, fertile fields, and autumn ripe stalks of purple and hot-pink quinoa. Past the lake they followed a feeder river up into a gash in the rocky mountain.

Lucy's dreams hummed with the happy military jest of the Palla Palla marathon as the bus roared down the road.

A jolt woke her up. The bus braked hard. It stopped. She looked out the window. A huge armored tank blocked the road. It looked like something out of Mad Max. Helmeted police swarmed the bus. They shouted. Big black guns clenched at ready.

"Are those flame-throwers? Machine guns?" Lucy didn't know.

She started to chant silently, "Nam-myoho-renge-kyo. Everything will be okay. What's going on? I don't know. But everything will be okay. Nam-myoho-renge-kyo."

"Where are your license plates!?!!!!" a cop yelled to the driver.

"Great," Lucy thought. "I got on a bus that has no license plates. Nam-myoho-renge-kyo nam-myoho-renge-kyo."

"Who is the owner of these propane tanks!?!!!!" the cop jerked his gun towards the roof rack.

"Nam-myoho-renge-kyo."

"Everyone off the bus!!!!"

"Nam-myoho-renge-kyo."

"Show me your tickets!!!! Show me your documents!!!!"

A passenger straddling a 100-pound sack of sugar in the aisle yelled back, "Leave us alone! This is a passenger vehicle!"

"Sí," yelled a middle-aged woman in the back of the bus, sacks of rice bulged from under her seat and into the aisle. "Let us get on with our journey! You're holding us up!"

"Nam-myoho-renge-kyo."

Lucy's feet rested on another 100-pound sack. Bulging sacks poked out from under every single seat. They filled the aisle.

"This bus is packed with contraband!" Lucy realized.

"Everyone off the bus!!!!"

"Nam-myoho-renge-kyo."

Police climbed up the side ladder to the roof rack.

"Get out of the bus! I want the owner of these propane tanks!!!!!" screamed another cop. Spittle spattered his face shield. Neck tendons tightened. Knuckles paled on gun grip.

"We're in a hurry! Let us get on our way!" A passenger challenged the angry armed policemen outside the glass windows and door.

"Yeah! We have no documents! There is nothing here! Let us get on our way!" shouted the middle-aged woman.

The police opened the luggage bays. They climbed up to the roof rack. The handed down all of the round squat propane tanks.

"I said," the police kept shouting, "Everyone! Off! The! Bus!"

The driver did not open the door. He leaned out his little window.

"Hijo de puta," he spat at the cop below in riot gear.

The cop tensed. He unsnapped the leather strap on his holster. He pulled out a stainless steel canister.

"Tear gas," Lucy observed. "Nam-myoho-renge-kyo nam-myoho-renge-kyo nam-myoho-renge-kyo," she chanted with even more quiet intensity; chanting as if to steer the heavens and reverse the tides.

The cop slid the canister back into his holster. He glared at the driver.

The driver produced no license plates. No one 'fessed up to owning the dozen or more shiny new yellow 5-gallon propane tanks. No one got off the bus. The door never opened. The police never saw the sacks of sugar and grains protruding from under every seat and blocking the aisles.

A cop loaded all the propane tanks into the Mad Max vehicle.

Another black-clad cop waved his big weapon, its shoulder strap flapping.

They were dismissed.

The bus driver backed up and swung around the black armored Mad Max obstacle. Everyone sighed relief as the bus shifted gears. Once again they were on their way.

A man who had been yelling at the cops, now chuckled in victory and said, "And this bus is packed full of contraband!"

Lucy heard panpipes playing on the radio, or was it still reverberating in her head from the night before?

Suddenly, Lucy realized that this encounter was like a continuation of the Palla Palla. It was in-your-face disrespect for military authority that oppresses the people.

But the main difference was that these guns were real.

Lake Titicaca

CHAPTER NINE
WARRIOR TOWN

I found my master had taken a seat
Already on that dread creature's haunches bare.
"Be bold," he said, "and think not of retreat.
...Mount thou in front..."

- Dante's Inferno

ILAVE
Bus headlights barely cut through the torrential downpour.
Lightening and thunder rolled on top of each other booming like the chaos of
the big bang. Bus doors rattled open. Lucy and other sikuris stumbled out
into a turbulent puddle in the darkness of Warrior Town. The bus sped away,
taking its lights with it.

FEAR
Of course Lucy was nervous about arriving in Ilave, Warrior Town.
Violence was against her grain. It would be a challenge to her pacifist ideals.
But, she thought of Daisaku Ikeda, the SGI Buddhist leader traveling to the
Soviet Union. Someone asked him, "why are you, a religious leader, going to
a country that has no religion?"

"Because there are people there who want peace," he answered.

So, Lucy, committed to embracing everyone's shared humanity,
strove to overcome her fears; such as fears for her personal safety.

FLASHBACK
After all, she could end up like that American woman who was
stoned to death in a village in Guatemala. The people thought she had come
to steal their children. That happened around the time when Lucy was going
to Guatemala to study Spanish back in the '90s.

"You're going to die," friends in Los Angeles warned Lucy. That was
even before it became fashionable to fear foreigners (especially those in
turbans).

Lucy got scared, but she had gone anyway.

It was fine.

In Guatemala Lucy met a couple from Amsterdam who were
traveling all over Central America with just their guidebook and nary a word
of Spanish.

"We're having a great time!" they said, "We went to visit Mayan
ruins in Honduras. The beaches in El Salvador are lovely! What lush scenery

on the bus ride to Guatemala! And the people are so kind and beautiful! I especially admire the women's glittery turbans."

"But, weren't you afraid to come to Central America all alone, without even speaking the language?" Lucy asked.

"No. Why be afraid? By the way, where are you from?"

"Los Angeles."

"Oh! We would never go there! It's far too dangerous!"

ILAVE, CONTINUED

On that dark and rainy corner in Ilave, one of the sikuris who got off the bus with Lucy turned on his cell phone. The glow of the screen illuminated their path through the rivers on the cobblestone street. Cold wind whipped the rain through their clothes. Lightening struck so close they feared they would be knocked down dead.

By the light of the cell they found the house where they were going. The sikuri rapped on the metal door with a heavy golden coin, a sol. The door opened. A man hunched over in a black overcoat admitted them into the rainy inner patio. A dog, hidden by darkness, barked close by.

"Quiet, Cerebus!" the bent man said. He led the wet sikuris up some slippery cement stairs into an unlit room.

"Welcome to Ilave..." the man said.

"Cell phones! Cell phones!" the sikuris hollered. Folks whipped out their phones and spotlighted them on the face of the host.

"Welcome to our town of Ilave," he began again. "It is a great honor that you have traveled so far, to honor our archangel, San Miguel, to play together with our group, Awkinaka. Together we will play our sikus and bombos, the sacred instruments of our people the Aymara. Together we will honor our archangel San Miguel. Welcome to our humble home."

After the reciprocal speech by the president of the visiting sikuris, people started milling about to settle in.

Lucy approached the host and said, "Excuse me. I was invited by another sikuri group to play with them in the festival, but I don't know how to contact them. I emailed them, but emails frequently get lost in South America. These sikuris were kind enough to let me travel with them. I feel so awkward accepting your hospitality when I'm not playing with Awkinaka."

Sikuri groups compete with each other. They try to keep things secret before a contest. Lucy was an infiltrator from another group!

"You're welcome to stay here with us until you can find your group. If you want, you can stay and perform with Awkinaka. We're all one, we sikuris."

"Thank you!" Lucy said.

More members of Awkinaka trickled in. Everyone sat down in a circle in the dark room, illuminated by occasional flashes of lightening outside. Someone passed around a bottle of Anis liquor. The sikuris drank out of the bottle cap.

One of the Awkinakas, slightly drunk, said, "Ilave is Aymara. Ilave means 'the fertile land.' Awkinaka is full of old men. Sikuris age 75, 80, 85. This is our pride, that we carry this tradition. Of course we don't do fancy choreography and we don't win the contests because of this. How are you going to do choreography for men 75 years old? But we are proud that when we play we don't repeat a tune. We can play 150 songs, all our compositions, with out repeating a single one. The other groups they play four or five songs. Over and over. Songs they copy. And that's it. Ilave. I am Ilaveño. This is my land. We've never been conquered."

The bottle came to the speaker, he drank, passed it on and continued, "When the mayor was corrupt, we got rid of him. This current priest is heading for the same fate if he doesn't watch out. We're rebels. Our Santo Miguel had wings of silver. Solid silver. But those have been stolen. Now they are replaced with tiny cheap wings made from an old tin can. The priest stole the wings. He's your countryman," he said, turning to look at Lucy, her whiteness apparent in the gloom. "United States. He's from the United States."

Lucy sat still, like a deer caught in headlights.

Someone offered the speaker a cigarette. He looked at the cigarette and took it carefully between his stubby brown fingers.

The moment had passed. Lucy relaxed.

He struck a wooden match. The flame flared to spotlight his face, leathery and grooved as a hand-plowed potato field. He lit the loose-packed tobacco and puffed thoughtfully. He continued.

"I don't say, 'San Miguel', I say 'Archangel Miguel, Michael, Miki, Mikisito'."

"What do you mean 'Miki'? 'Mikisito'?" A voice in the darkness said. "Our San Miguel is not Mickey Mouse! Show some respect!"

Footsteps sounded from where the voice spoke, and left the room. In the quiet, a rustle as people shifted on the hard benches in the circle.

Ember glow with raspy drag of breath on the cigarette between stubby fingers, gnarled as oqa roots, of the slightly drunk Awkinaka. Cloud exhalation like a gentle wind scented with tobacco and brandy.

"As I was saying, saints are dead and in the ground. The saints are people. They are my comrades. But, our protector of Ilave isn't a saint. He's an angel. My guardian angel Mikisito. He protects us rebels. This is my pride. After all, in the end, we are the Apus, we are the gods."

We are the gods. Lucy agreed with that.

The host walked up to Lucy and said, "My son will show you and the other women to your room."

A child led Lucy and two other women through a swinging particleboard partition to a room with one big bed to share.

The guys all would sleep on folded blankets on the concrete floor in the main room.

After everyone got their stuff settled, the host trooped all the sikuris out again into the lightening, thunder and rain (no one had any rain gear at all). He led them a few blocks away to a room filled with bombos and sikus.

Lucy followed the sikuris as they carried the instruments across town, in the raging storm, to another house. They entered a passageway lined with serious-faced men. Lucy and the other sikuris greeted each man with a "Buenas noches." The men politely returned the greeting.

Inside, in the interior patio, it seemed to be raining even harder, as if Lucy and the sikuris had reached the bulls-eye of the storm. People huddled on wooden benches under an awning. A side room gleamed with light and the bustle of a large crowd of people. Awkinaka passed out the sikus to the group, including Lucy. They formed a circle in the rainy patio and played a song.

After a bit, they filed into the lit room.

Lucy, entered the door and saw to the left about a dozen cholitas seated on the floor. The floor was covered with black cloths. The women were dressed in all black, from their pointy patent-leather slip-on shoes to their voluminous black pollera skirts and multiple petticoats to their long-fringed shawls to their black tiny bowler hats topping their neatly braided black hair. They wailed and whimpered, mourning the death of a loved one. Coca, the sacred leaf, was set out in a pile on a separate little hand-woven cloth, a colorful tari, on top of the black cloths.

To the right, the room was filled with people; people sitting on benches lining the walls, people standing crowded in the center. Everyone faced an open coffin; brass handles gleaming, velvet lush. The wall at the head of the coffin was adorned as an altar to the patron saint of Ilave, Saint Michael, the Archangel.

The sikuris faced the coffin and crossed themselves. Lucy folded her hands in prayer at her chest and whispered "Nam-myoho-renge-kyo" three times. The sikuris filed through the throng of people to the head of the bench on the left of the coffin, shaking the hand of each person in turn. Lucy followed suit, saying "Buenas noches" in her most solemn voice and looking into each person's eyes with the utmost sympathy. At the end of the bench she was back by the wailing women, to whom she put her hands together and bowed her head in respect.

A man announced for everyone to join in prayer.

"We will miss our friend, who was so involved in our neighborhood. She always had a kind word for everyone and would smile and laugh. Just yesterday she was dancing. Today her children are orphans. We never know when God will call us home. This life is so full of suffering. We all have our cross to . . . "

Lucy's attention wandered and she missed some of his words praising the deceased. She tuned back in when he said, "...her last words were, 'my head hurts' then she died. Let us pray. Our Father . . . "

After the prayer, a circle of sikuris started playing outside. Lucy approached the circle and tried to follow along.

When the sikuris stopped playing, one turned to her and said, "Did you come with Awkinaka?"

"Yes."

Only then did she realize that this was a different sikuri group than the one she had come with. None of their faces were familiar.

The sikuri chatted a bit with Lucy.

"The señora died so suddenly," he said. "Just yesterday she was dancing the Morenada, rehearsing for the festival. And now she is dead. At the festival we will only be pretending to be happy as we play. We will be faking it. Because we are so sad that our neighbor has unexpectedly died."

His eyes were moist as he took Lucy's hand. She offered what words she could. Of course they came out all wrong, but she hoped that her sincerity was somehow conveyed.

"It is a great honor to be here with you to share this event. I am so sorry," she said as she spontaneously squeezed his hand.

He returned the hand-squeeze with gentle words.

Two men approached carrying a huge wooden serving tray between them filled with plastic cups of steaming drink. Lucy and the sikuri let go of each-other's hands and each took a sip of warm alcohol.

At an appropriate moment Lucy excused herself and threaded her way through the crowd back to where Awkinaka was playing.

After a number of somber dirges, the sikuris and Lucy prepared to leave. They filed back past the serious-faced men lining the passageway, with more "Buenas noches, buenas noches," and went outside into the stormy street.

Wet and cold with a warm dot in their bellies from the alcohol they all tromped through the town, passed a couple of plazas and different cathedrals, till they were back at the home of the host.

"2:30 AM we rehearse for Alba," the host said.

Changing into dry clothes, Lucy and the other two women crawled into the big bed under the multitudinous blankets in the dark unheated hollow-brick room and went to sleep.

ALBA

The next thing Lucy knew, the sikuris were in full tilt on the other side of the particle-board partition. At the sound of the bombos, like Pavlov's dog, Lucy leapt to her feet ready to play. Her chest reverberated with the pulse of the bombos and her beating heart.

Everyone gathered up instruments and streamed out into the street into the now clear night. They climbed a hill. The city stretched out below. Dark silhouettes of mountain humps dozed on the horizon. Above unfamiliar constellations danced across the sky of Warrior Town.

Descending the other side of the hill, they encountered another group of sikuris rehearsing.

One of them called out, "Lucy! You came!"

Excusing herself from Awkinaka, Lucy joined Moqor Puriña, who had invited her.

"But later, come back and play with us in the funeral procession," the Awkinaka host said.

Lucy looked to the bony Inka model from Moqor Puriña for guidance.

"Sure, go ahead. After breakfast!" he said.

Awkinaka and Lucy parted.

The guia for Moqor Puriña handed Lucy a bombo and siku of six tubes. He started up the rehearsal again. After running through the songs a few times, the guia signaled to stop by setting down his bombo.

Everyone set down their bombos, too, and was attentive to what the guia would say.

In the darkness, the guia quietly acknowledged the contributions of people who made this possible, especially since most of the sikuris were young or still in high school and were dependent on others for their sustenance. He also acknowledged that they were many different sikuri groups coming together. He named each group. He acknowledged that each group had its own style and that now all were going to harmonize into one style for the festival. He was very eloquent and respectful.

Wearing everyday clothes (and Lucy in every sweater she owned to keep from getting chilled in the near-freezing night) they walked/danced in formation, playing their bombos and sikus. As they approached the plaza they started some choreography. The lines split in the middle, each sikuri turning to the outside, dancing away from each other as they played. Then turned and headed back towards each other. Then away again and back, as they moved forward down the street. Lucy stumbled over a big reflector glued to the road.

The Plaza was filled with crowds of people lining the streets watching. Their spirits perked up with such an audience. Lucy jumped a little higher with each step. Everyone played with more exuberance - bending low, arching back, throwing their whole beings into the joy of this communal music.

Other sikuri groups had already arrived and were playing in the streets framing the plaza. Moqor Puriña filled into an empty spot in front of the Cathedral that was reserved for them and played a few songs.

During a break a bottle of peach brandy got passed around the circle.

Warmed up, they played until dawn.

The sun rose. The priest said mass in the street. Santo Miguel with his tin can wings was set up behind the priest who stood on a platform under the entrance arch of the cathedral. A table in front of him was draped in white. On it sat mass paraphernalia and a big bible. The priest was gray-haired with a double chin and paunch. Bespectacled. And very white.

Lucy often felt embarrassed when she encountered folks from the U.S. in the Andes. When she only looked at brown faces, she felt like she was looking in a mirror and she must be indigenous, too. But, seeing a tight-jawed white face and hearing a too-loud voice with a strong North American accent was like looking at herself and not liking what she saw. Did she sound like that? Did she look like that? It wasn't rational, but Lucy felt like no one would notice she was North American if she was left alone to blend in. When another North American was around, especially one who seemed to be looking down on the Andean people from an attitude of superiority, Lucy felt societal guilt for any and all suffering her countrymen had caused to indigenous peoples. She felt this guilt and embarrassment whether it was tourists who acted like, just because they could afford to travel to the Andes that they somehow owned the culture; to U.S. politicians who funded Project Condor - training and supporting military dictators and terrorists who killed indigenous people.

The peach brandy did little to calm Lucy's ire.

Looking down from his platform, the American priest said Mass. His slow and heavily accented Spanish was amplified and projected from giant black speakers.

"After this celebration, I invite all of the sikuri groups to come together in weekly prayer and study of the scriptures. There are people willing to help you."

Lucy felt insulted by his condescending words.

"Help?" she thought. "How about respect the indigenous culture that has lived in a sustainable way for thousands of years? How about try and learn from this culture? Help?"

"Now I invite anyone from the sikuri groups to come up and lead a prayer..."

No one stirred.

"The music is our prayer," Lucy whispered to the sikuri on her right.

The priest cleared his throat and continued with the next part of his mass.

"Moqor Puriña will now play a song."

Playing the sikus and bombo with Moqor Puriña calmed Lucy.

It was truly a prayer. Lucy prayed and played with her whole being. She was one with the Pachamama, one with the sikuris. She was participating in the ideal society they created while they played bombo and siku, a society of mutual respect and dialog.

94

The song ended.

The feeling of camaraderie stayed.

Moqor Puriña moved to the back of the plaza to make room for the next group to be up front. A bottle passed around the circle. The sikuris talked.

"Why are so many priests from the United States?" one sikuri asked Lucy.

"They are?" she asked.

"Yes. And other religions too, the priests are from the United States. They forbid the Andean ways. Why is that?"

A couple of other sikuris drifted over to listen.

"Like the Mormons?"

"Sí."

"The Seventh Day Adventists?"

A pause to consider, then, "Yeah, them too! Why are so many from the United States?"

"Well, in the States I hear a lot of churches saying that they want to send missionaries in order to 'save' people."

The sikuris burst into laughter at the concept that they needed saving.

Lucy paused to think, then said, "I think it's a type of cultural imperialism."

The sikuri absorbed this and pronounced, "It's okay to have different religions, but leave our culture alone. It has its good and bad points, but it is ours. Our culture."

Lucy said, "I read a biography of this young priest from Canada. He came to lead a parish in a mining town in Bolivia. I think it was Siglo XX. Well, when he first arrived he forbade the consumption of alcohol during fiestas."

The sikuris burst out in laughter. Alcohol and fiestas go together like men and women, seed and soil, the sun and moon in the sky. It is impossible to have a fiesta without alcohol.

"That was how he started out, trying to change everybody. But bit by bit he listened to the people and learned about their sufferings and their struggles. He started working alongside the people. When the government started attacking the people, he sided with his parishioners. He wasn't going to shoot a gun, no. He was a pacifist. He volunteered with the Red Cross and helped the wounded indigenous people. A government soldier shot him dead as he was helping a wounded man, even though he was clearly with the Red Cross. This was in 1971, during CIA Operation Condor."

"The government killed him because he was on the side of the people," the guia said.

"Looks that way."

"What was this priest's name?"

"Father Mauricio Lefebvre"

"There isn't a single priest in Peru who is like him, who is on the side of the people. We need priests like him."

"Well, he had to learn. He needed time to listen to the people. This priest here is new, you say. Maybe he'll learn, too."

Lucy sincerely hoped that this U.S. priest, who was rumored to have stolen Mikisito's wings, would learn. She wondered if she should seek him out to try and teach him.

No.

That might risk her acceptance with the sikuris, if she was seen hanging out with him. Lucy's loyalty to the peaceful world of which the panpipes sing came before just about everything.

The priest would have to learn on his own.

It did not occur to Lucy that she was being equally condescending in her thoughts of "helping" the priest as he was of "helping" the sikuris.

The mass ended. The guia picked up his bombo, a symbol for the rest of the sikuris to scurry over and strap on their bombos, pull their sikus out of their chuspa shoulder pouches and have a maso mallet in hand. The guia raised his maso high, swung it down with bent knee so it swung behind him, then up again (a symbol to play "caida de bombos" 'falling drums'). On the downbeat they all pounded in unison an ever-increasing rapid rhythm that peaked in volume than fell off into silence, like a landslide that had passed.

On the next upswing they started the song.

Blowing across the bamboo tubes, Lucy looked at the guia who played the six-tube siku like she did, to see which tubes to blow and when in this unfamiliar tune. The thunder of the music transported the sikuris into a single unit of life, as they played in concentric circles, facing each other.

Lucy thought about how this music forms community. The point isn't to be an egotistical star in front of an audience. On a stage musicians face the audience and not each other. Sikuris, when not parading through the streets or doing a choreographed performance for competition, face each other, face the center. Lucy felt the energy flow out of each musician into the center. The center grew stronger and fed the spirit of each musician.

At the end of the song, the guia took off his bombo. The circle of sikuris relaxed.

A man from the crowd came up to Lucy and introduced himself in a formal respectful manner, "I am from the countryside. Thank you for playing our music. This is the first time that I have seen a foreigner playing our music. This memory I will always carry here," he placed his hand over his heart.

"Thank you," Lucy said with much emotion, putting her hand over her heart, too. "It is a great honor to play here in Ilave. I will always remember Ilave and your kind words."

After Alba, Lucy and Moqor Puriña trooped off, in a boom and trill of music, to a house.

The house was the home of doña Antonia and her family. She had four sons, three of whom were sikuris. Lino, the oldest, was one of the guias. He played the seven-tube siku and was a sober polite responsible person, from what Lucy saw. Their house was the center for Moqor Puriña. The family made their living selling aluminum cookware in the open-air market. Doña Antonia bought the pots and pans in Desaguadero and sold them in Ilave. Everyday, around dawn, they loaded up their bicycle cart and wheeled the merchandise to their market stall.

Their home was made of hollow red bricks, like almost all the new constructions in the Altiplano of Peru and Bolivia. It was a large house with several rooms in separate but attached buildings. That is, they shared a wall. To go from one room to another one had to cross the earthen courtyard. The kitchen was a separate building butted against the exterior wall of their little compound. It, too, was earthen floored. A five-gallon propane tank powered the free-standing tubular burners. A small Formica kitchen table nestled in one corner with a couple of mismatched chairs. A tiny black and white TV was perched up in the corner above the table, to keep everyone company with its folklore variety shows brought to you by Magica Blanca, the laundry detergent that is pretty magical in the whiteness it brings and the marital bliss that it creates.

The sikuris filed into the courtyard and quietly sat in a circle on chairs, benches and cement steps. Soon people appeared with another one of those giant wooden trays with a handle carved on each side for two people to carry. It was full of enameled bowls of steaming soup with a big spoon sticking out of each one. It took several trips to serve a bowl to each sikuri. Lucy and the other sikuris began spooning the steaming nutrition into their mouths as soon as the bowls were in their hands.

Afterwards, the soup bowls were gathered up and plates of the "segundo" or main course were passed out. White rice, steak, boiled and peeled potatoes and chuñu. Lucy always skipped the white rice because it made her constipated.

After filling their bellies with the delicious substantial meal, the plates were gathered up. The sikuris strapped on bombos. Lucy did, too. They formed a circle in the middle of the courtyard. They began to play for themselves and the host family for about two hours. Lucy felt like she was in heaven.

With the last maso fall on the bombos, filled with contentment, the sikuris smiled at each other with soft chuckles of joy.

People started saying their goodbyes with handshakes all around. Lucy kissed everyone on the cheek, shook their hand, said goodbye and left to find Awkinaka, to play with them in the funeral procession.

FUNERAL

The coffin carrying the deceased señora swayed down the street with the heavy steps of six pallbearers. A crowd of black-clad mourners carried flowers. Flowers bursting in profusion from a plastic bucket. Flowers intricately arranged on a standing arrangement with a name card and covered with plastic. Flowers carried in arms with stems wrapped in newspaper.

At the plaza, the procession paused. Women unfolded two ornate metal stands in the center of the plaza. The pallbearers placed the coffin on top of the stands. People gathered around the coffin as someone spoke sad words. The sikuris stayed close together in the street. Someone motioned for the procession to proceed. New pall-bearers hefted the coffin on their shoulders and off everyone trudged through the streets; booming drum and droning panpipes, to the cathedral of San Miguel. Under the white stone arch they filed, blue painting of the patron saint on the keystone. Down the stone open-air corridor towards the building they shuffled. At the open doors of the cathedral, the two sikuri groups turned aside, flanking the entrance. They took turns playing a song as the procession entered. The crowd had grown. As the surging flow of mourners passed the lintel of the doorway, stepping down into the sanctuary, men removed their black fedoras and women removed their black bowlers. The hats lifting looked like ripples on a black stream as it passed rocky rapids. The coffin dipped at the door. A man rushed forward to replace the fatigued pall-bearer.

The sikuri groups stood outside, in two circles, during mass. The sikuri next to Lucy, Paco, handed her a two-liter bottle of Sprite - its sides collapsed in for easy handling, and a plastic cup. She filled the cup then passed the bottle to the next person in the circle. As Lucy drizzled the first drops to the ground as an offering for Pachamama (Mother Earth and space/time continuum), Paco exclaimed, "You know how to do it!" The sikuris smiled and nodded in appreciation of the gringa honoring Andean religion. Lucy drank her Sprite, shook out the last drops for the Pachamama and handed the cup to the sikuri on her right. He repeated the ritual.

A bottle of apricot brandy made the rounds in the same way. Paco chatted away with Lucy.

"My parents were so embarrassed when I started to play the sikus," he said.

"Why?"

"Well, there's a lot of racism here in Peru. We indigenous people are looked down on by the mestizos. My parents have worked so hard to be accepted into the mestizo world and to give me an education, and here I go, joining a sikuri group at the university. Sikuris. Playing the music that was forbidden in the city not that long ago. It was the noise that the peasants made. Peasants who were really not people at all, but little more than animals."

"But your parents should be proud! The world needs the message of harmonious interconnection that sikuris communicate through their breath in the reeds and the throbbing of the bombos," Lucy said, chest out like a preacher.

"Yes, I know. My parents are starting to lighten up a little, since they see how dedicated I am to the music."

Paco paused a moment then reached into his breast pocket and pulled out a pair of sikus. Little ones. Chulis. He held them out to Lucy. "Here, take these. They're for you."

"Really? Are you sure?"

"Yes, I'm sure."

"Thank you so much!" Lucy accepted his delicate hollow reeds in both hands cupped, gazing into Paco's eyes in appreciation.

The pall bearers came out of the cathedral carrying the coffin. The sikuris played a funeral march and led the procession to the cemetery many blocks away.

The crowd, all in black, continued to grow. At the cemetery, still playing, the sikuris mounted the curved stone steps. They passed under a copula painted with heavenly scenes on its underside. Entering wrought-iron gates into the cemetery proper, they passed mounds of sand along the main thoroughfare lined with mausoleums.

At someone's signal, the sikuris halted their marching. In the silence a man started to talk in somber tones.

Suddenly, a woman screamed, "My daughter! My daughter!"

The crowd pulled the mother away from the coffin. Shrieking cries shook her whole being. People raised several plastic bottles of drinking water in the air above the crowd. They shook water on her. Someone pulled the black shawl off her head. Water poured over her exposed hair to wash away her excess of emotions. She calmed down somewhat. Then she drooped; went rigid. Someone tried to pry her jaws apart.

"Give her air! Give her air!" another person shouted.

Soon, she regained consciousness. Two people led her away.

With music and solemn speeches the crowd laid the dead señora to rest in a hole on a hill. Dirt mounded high. People laid the flowers all over the mound. Lucy offered prayers of Nam-myoho-renge-kyo for this woman who fell, hit her head and died.

At the gates of the cemetery, two receiving lines formed; men on the left, women on the right. Lucy inched ahead in line. She offered condolences to the family. At the end of the receiving line a woman handed Lucy a drink and a handful of coca leaves. Lucy joined the hundreds of mourners who sat on the grassy slope outside of the cemetery, thoughtfully chewing coca leaves, drinking beer, and whispering.

It started to drizzle. Lightening flashed on the horizon. And flashed again and again. Thunder boomed with some of the crackling bolts. Other flashes were silent.

Theories spread among the people. Lightening that hits the ground makes no sound. Or was it that lightening that doesn't hit the ground makes no sound? Lightening is attracted to nails. Don't wear hobnailed boots.

"My friend's uncle was struck by a lightening bolt while he was walking in the country and died," Lucy said.

Everyone was solemn at that one.

A cloudburst of heavy hail attacked. Frozen pellets, white as stars, shot from the sky and covered the ground in a blank canvas. Flash floods raced like watery lightening on the ground.

Boom! Crack! Lightening struck everywhere. The celestial nervous system was short circuiting.

"To the coliseum!" a voice shouted.

In a panic Lucy and the mourners ran. Towards shelter they all ran. Each person a black-clad spark of soul, pulled by the inexorable gravity of survival. Together, the seething mass of humanity ran. In their black mourning clothes they were like primordial darkness churning. The light of humanity in their hearts bound each to the other, as if to birth a new galaxy of life, in Warrior Town.

The only thing to fear is fear itself.
- Franklin Delanor Roosevelt

INTERLUDE, SHORT LETTER TO AUNT BERT

Dear Aunt Bert,
    You know how I was so nervous about going to Warrior Town? Well, I ended up making all these new friends and you know, I felt enveloped in a family. They invited me to come play again. I have a feeling we're going to grow really close.
    In some ways it felt more home than home. There's no place like home. Who thought that saying up? I never got that in the Wizard of Oz where Dorothy says that if she ever goes looking for her heart's desire she won't go further than her own backyard.
    Love, Lucy

CHAPTER TEN
METEOR CRATER

In her own "backyard" of the U.S, Lucy drove along interstate 40 in her company van, on her return trip to Los Angeles after attending an Ethnomusicology conference in Albuquerque, NM.

Near Flagstaff she came upon a roadside attraction.

"Meteor Crater, A Natural Landmark."

"How cool!" she thought, "I'll swing off the road for this!"

Exiting onto the recently paved road, she passed Meteor Crater RV Park. Winnebagos with Good Sam stickers huddled under shade trees at this AAA-recommended destination. Next door was a way-too-expensive gas station.

Autumn desert breeze wafted in the open window of Lucy's battered '85 Toyota Van. Wind ruffled blonde hairs on her sun-wrinkled forearm; tossed wisps of graying sandy hair into her hazel eyes. She smelled sage and sand damp from recent rain.

Ahead, the meteor crater mound rested on the horizon. Luminous half-moon rose above an adobe ruin silhouetted on the azure late afternoon sky.

"Looks like a postcard!" she thought, "'Wish I had a camera!"

As Lucy neared the crater, the paved road swerved to the left. Straight ahead a dirt washboard road ran through scrubby plain. Its sign warned, "Unmaintained Road" followed by a bunch of small print. She swung left, following the paved road through a gate, into a parking lot.

Lucy parked and walked up to the ticket window at the Meteor Crater Museum. A sign read, "$12 a person."

"I expected it to be $5, tops," she thought, "No way am I going to pay $12 to look at a Natural Landmark. It's not like they had to build it or anything. Hmmm, that dirt road I passed is intriguing. Perhaps it goes around a back way to the crater!"

With a toss of her uncombed head Lucy jumped into her van and headed to the dirt road.

"Washboard alright," she thought, "What does that fine print on the sign say? Don't take away hunks of meteorite. Something about no trespassing on the land around. Hunting is okay just about always. Very weird. How does one go about hunting without walking on the ground outside their car?"

Visualizing guys in pickups with rifles poking out of windows, Lucy jounced down the gravelly washboard. Barbed wire lined the road on both sides. The crater loomed over to her left. Wooden ruins scattered on its flank. The road continued straight.

"I don't see any way to get over to the crater and I'm almost past it now," she thought, "Bummer! There's barbed wire everywhere and all these signs that say 'No Trespassing.' Hey! What's that?"

On the horizon, beyond the sword grass and scattered meteor fragments, a cloud of red dust rose. The dust cloud moved from left to right, heading towards the road.

"It's coming from the crater!"

Lucy and the dust cloud reached the intersection at the same moment. Kicking up that dust cloud was a convoy of 4x4's. The lead driver was a white, serious, no-nonsense man in his 60's with a neatly trimmed mustache. He stared hard, assessing Lucy. Lucy stared back. She continued driving slowly ahead on the washboard road. She passed the intersection.

The man averted his gaze, dismissing Lucy as a lone 40-something overweight white woman of no consequence. He turned his Land Cruiser to the right onto the washboard road. He zoomed down it about five times faster than Lucy took it. The convoy followed in tight formation. Their dust cloud billowed high and long.

When Lucy no longer saw the cars for the dust, she figured that they couldn't see her, either.

She stopped. Turned the van around. Then moseyed down that side-road from whence they came.

"Shees, I feel nervous trespassing," Lucy thought, "But, I'm not really trespassing, because the 'No Trespassing' signs have a picture of a footprint with a red slash across it. I'm not walking. I'm driving. There's a difference!"

But, no matter how much she tried to convince herself that it was okay to drive down that dirt road, Lucy still felt nervous.

"I'll just stick to the tire tracks," she thought, "and go slow and hardly raise a dust cloud at all, in case that convoy of serious-looking white guys decides to stop and glance back."

Driving down the sandy road Lucy fondly recalled her mom and dad.

"Man, before the divorce, we went camping in all kinds of remote places! Like that time dad took the riverbed instead of the road. We never had a 4-wheel drive. He said, 'If I don't go under 40 miles an hour, I won't get stuck.' And we didn't. Well, not much. My ole van has good Michelins and high clearance."

CLUNK!

"Well, maybe not quite as high as I thought. Hmm, the temperature gauge isn't rising and there's no puddle of bleeding vital fluids trailing me so I guess I'm okay."

She rounded a bend.

"Cool! This road leads to those old wooden ruins on the slope of the crater!"

At the ruins fresh tire tracks curved and ended. The road ahead showed only sandy footprints.

"Heck, just because those 4x4s decided to park and walk it doesn't mean I can't drive it!"

Subconsciously Lucy was still worried that getting out of her car and walking equaled trespassing, so she continued driving as far as possible.

Pointy rocks big as jack rabbits covered the bumpy road that ran along a drop-off to the right into an abandoned open-pit mine. To the left climbed the eroded shoulder of the crater. She followed the road as it turned up the steeper sandy slope towards the rim of the crater.

The wheels bogged down.

"Oops."

She tried to back down.

No traction.

Stuck.

"Okay. Now I need to get out of the car. But I'll only walk as little as necessary and keep close to the van. The rim is so close. I would love to walk up and peer in. But, who knows what craziness the government is up to, what with that Patriot Act and all. I would be a target on the horizon. Some sharp shooter at the visitor's center could pick me off and chalk it up as a hunting accident."

Lucy picked up a gray weathered branch to scrape the sand and rocks away from the tires front and back.

"Too bad I don't have a shovel. Mom and dad always carried a little folding shovel for an emergency like this. No friendly passers-by to offer a push. Nope. Just me. Just me in the dimming day with a stuck van on semi-private land where hunters can roam-at-will shooting things."

As she dug, she thought about where she would spend the night.

"Hmmm, maybe I could sleep here in the van; these ruins are cool."

Fear churned in her stomach.

"Bad idea. Nope. Gotta get the van outta the sand and getta outta here!

Dig.

Try to drive.

Dig again.

Chock rocks under for traction.

Turn tires a different way.

Rock it rock it...

Nothing."

The only thing left to try was an old Turtle trick. When Lucy drove for the Brown Turtle Adventure Travel bus company, she learned that no matter how badly you got a 40-foot bus stuck in the sand, if you let the air out of the tires down to about 10 pounds, it would crawl out of anything. Then, you pumped the tires back up with your compressor kit adapted to the air brakes.

"Well, I don't have air brakes or a compressor kit or even a bicycle pump. I'll just let the air out a bit at a time, try to drive out, then remove more air if needed. I'll have to travel on these flat tires all the way back down the washboard, down the paved road to the way-too-expensive gas station by the RV park to pump them back up. Glad I have a tire gauge in the glove box!"

Lucy picked up a glittery meteor pebble off the ground and pressed it against the valve stem on first one drive tire, then the other.

Hssssssssss.

"Okay. Back in the driver seat, in gear."

Careful to not spin the tires and dig herself deep, she touched the accelerator gentle as a lover.

"Nothing.

Didn't budge.

Hop out. Let out more air. Check the pressure. 25 lbs. Good. Now the other side. Done."

Lucy climbed into the driver's seat.

"Hmm, the temperature gauge is rising. I'll keep an eye on it."

In gear, she tried again to drive out of the sand.

"Nope. Doesn't wanna leave yet. Hop back out. Deflate the front tires a bit. Drop the drive tires to 20 lbs. Hop back in. The temperature gauge is higher than I've ever seen it. But it's not into the red. Yet.

Okay. Gentle, gentle, baby, and ...

we ...

move!

I'm out of that spot! But, where do I go from here?"

Clunking the transmission into Park, Lucy got out to scope a plan.

"Hmmmm, too dangerous to back out with that drop-off right behind me. Better turn around somehow."

Back in the van, she got a running start and zoomed up the same hill she had got stuck on. But now the tires were softer. She had more traction. And she went faster, like she would have in the first place if she hadn't been afraid of raising a dust cloud. Momentum carried her higher up the hill. Then stopped. Turned the wheels. Rolled back. Slid between two scrubby bushes.

Turned.

Drove away.

Although she was unstuck and heading back towards the highway, disappointment tugged in Lucy's chest.

"I was so close to the crater! I could have just walked up and peeked in."

Hope surged.

"Maybe I could go back and just take a quick look."

Inner warning bells jangled. She continued driving away. Bitter experience had taught her never to ignore her intuition. Slowly she drove. No dust to reveal her to a distant observer.

Back down the side road marked with tracks of the convoy. Back down the washboard road.

Finally, plop plop, the tires rolled onto black-top.

"Hey! What's this? Are they shooting a film or something?

A dirt turn-out had filled up with cars, U Hauls, and assorted stuff. Lucy parked her dusty old van into the end of a row of neatly parked clean new cars. She slid out and walked around to see what was going on.

"I wonder what they're filming. Here are cables running to generators. There are white box-trucks open and full of crates of gear. But, it all looks odd. Everyone is a white man. No women or brown people. What are they fiddling with? There's a tripod with white sand bags anchoring it. But, where're the cameras? The lights? The catering people with the food table? Everyone is so serious and acts like they don't notice I'm here. Usually at a movie shoot they make eye contact and smile, at least!

Those gizmos on top of the tripods, how bizarre, they look like miniature solar panels, hardly bigger than the palm of that beefy man's hand. There's another group of folks across the wash, almost a mirror image of this one, with their tripod and solar panel-thing angled this direction.

Didn't I hear a buzz or hum as I got out of the van? It's stopped now," Lucy observed.

Mini "solar panels" angled up, as if triangulating on a point high in the sky.

Away from the other vehicles, was parked a large white American van. Its front hood was open. Two gigantic electric fans aimed at the grill. At the back of the van was a white four-legged canopy.

A tall broad-shouldered white man walked among the parked cars. Lucy caught his eye and politely asked, "Can I ask what's going on here?"

"This is a closed test for NASA... the Mars Rover," he said with military curtness.

"What's a 'closed test'?"

"A 'closed test' is closed to the public," his unblinking stare didn't waver from Lucy's eyes.

"Oh! Then I shouldn't be here."

"No," he said and turned away.

Authority radiated from him.

Lucy walked straight back to her van.

Driving away, her skin prickled with fear. It felt like that time when she was six years old and she had wandered away from her family in a crowded holiday campground. A man in a white car stopped next to little Lucy and motioned for her to come to him. She knew in her gut he was bad.

She tried to scream, but no sound came out. She ran. The running loosened her scream, "Maaaaaaaaaaaaaaaaaaaaaaaaaaaaaaaaaaa meeeeeeeeeeeeeeeeee!"

Even though her skin tingled with fear, Lucy was still intrigued with somehow seeing the meteor crater without paying $12.

"At the gas station I'll pump the pimply faced local for info. Like, 'Tell me about that dirt road I went up. How strict are they about folks wandering around up there? What would have happened if I had camped there? Do you think it's okay for me to go back and this time walk to the rim and peek in?'"

When she arrived at the gas station, she saw that the attendant was far from being a bored teen leaning on the counter. He was a middle-aged white man with a military haircut and posture clothed in a crisp uniform, overseeing an immaculate garage. Not an oil stain or grime anywhere.

Lucy felt it was best not to ask and not to tell anything.

But, her tires were still flat.

She swallowed, took a breath and said, "Is this the air for pumping up tires?"

A metal canister (not a scratch on its shiny green paint), with hose draped over it in meticulous loops, sat outside the garage door.

The military man lifted the nozzle as if he was retrieving a maiden's dropped handkerchief.

A loop of clean rubber slapped scrubbed concrete.

"Which tire do you want to inflate? This one?"

The long chrome attachment was his sword. He was a knight.

"All of them," Lucy said.

Feet planted unconsciously in a protective karate stance, Lucy gazed directly into the man's eyes.

He scanned the scene. Van with cracked windshield. Dents. Covered in red dust. Extremely low tires all around. Lady in dusty shoes. Red dust smudged white pants, shirt. Even her face was covered in dust.

He thought, "Cars that stay on the pavement, as they should, don't get dusty. Women, who know what's good for them, don't go poking around where they have no business. They do not get dusty."

He said, "You know how to work one of these things?" as he handed over the hose to Lucy, his arm outstretched as if she might have a contagious disease. Then he turned and marched back inside of the garage.

Compressed air shot geyser of dust from around valve stem. Heart pounding, Lucy filled the tires one by one. Carefully, she looped the hose back over the green tank.

She drove away.

Escaped.

Further down the highway Lucy came to Walnut Canyon Indian Ruins.

"Oh boy! I'll camp here and check out the ruins in the morning!"

She went down the road to the entrance gate only to find that it was closed for the day. But at least the sign said that it was only $5, not $12.

The sign also read, "No camping allowed."

Lucy thought, "There's gotta be somewhere to camp. How many times did Dad park in the middle of nowhere for the night when we were kids?"

Retracing her route she glimpsed a 4-wheeler disappearing off to the right.

"Where's he going?"

Lucy pulled up and peered. An opening in the fence. Dirt road. Headlights illuminated a sign, "Unmaintained Road."

"Well, it doesn't say 'Private,' so here I go!"

A little further along there was another sign, "Forest Camping 14 Day Limit".

"O joy! It's actually legal to camp here!!!!"

Smaller dirt roads snaked off into Juniper woods and Piñon pine. Lucy bounced down one of those side roads and found a meadow. The trees framed an expansive view of the valley she had just crossed. Lucy sighed.

How beautiful!

Humming to herself, she organized her stuff to make a comfy place to sleep on the carpeted floor of the van. All the food she stashed outside in order to keep bears out of her bed. Finally she laid her head on a goose-down pillow, tucked the sleeping bag under her chin, and gazed up at the star-strewn sky with the half-moon riding high.

"Look! A falling star!" Lucy thought, "No, it's going the wrong direction. It's going sideways. Now it's flashing red. It must be a plane. But look how fast it's going! I've never seen a plane go that fast! Well, maybe the Blue Angels went that fast in the air show in San Francisco when they buzzed the Financial District and set all the car alarms shrieking."

A long long time later she heard the plane's roar. It headed from the North to the ... meteor crater.

"Here's some more. Wow. Four of them in tight formation; truly like sideways falling stars blinking red. What could the Mars Rover possibly have to do with squadrons of supersonic planes like the Blue Angel? Blue Angels don't go to Mars."

Later, Lucy learned that the Blue Angels are Boeing F/A-18 Hornets that specialize in night attacks, each carrying up to 9,000 pounds of bombs.

Although Lucy felt safe in this woodland camping place - safe from lions, tigers, bears, and Bin Laden - her heart faltered at these falling stars that didn't fall as they should.

Those fake stars continued zooming silently over the NASA Closed Test in the darkness until dawn.

Space

INTERLUDE
VISIT TO AUNT BERT

"Aunt Bert," Lucy said as they visited together in California at Bert's handmade kitchen table, "those stars gave me the creeps. I thought going to Warrior Town was going to be scary. But it's scarier here."

"Well, people are people wherever you go," Bert said, "Just don't let the bad ones get you down."

They sipped black coffee out of chipped Beatrice Wood mugs and watched the sky turn orange then lilac out the back window.

PANPIPES
a poem by Lucy

Zampoñas.
Sikus.
Bamboo
sun-dried
color of vicuña
(llama's cousin
who would rather die
than be domesticated)

Shortest tube,
length
of my
index finger.
Longest,
of my shin.
Two graduated rows
of string-lashed
bamboo digits,
cut mid-knuckle,
clack together
like ancestors'
bones.

Cane
straight and hard
as an erection,
hollow
as a womb.
Lip
of the orifice,
sliced at just the right length
to form
resonating chamber
to birth
a tone
when wind
caresses
its edge and
vibrates
hollow core.

My palm tingles
against bamboo sheath,
that reverberates
with my breath.

Aiming my stream
of air
higher,
cane shrieks
an overtone
like condors' cry
coupling
midair.

Arca and Ira.
Two rows of pipes
for two people.
Seed and soil.
Inti sun,
killa moon.

Joined by invisible
breath
he and I
intertwine
sounds
into
melody.

Our chicha corn-beer
scented exhalations,
flecks of spittle,
impregnate cane corridors
that span
millennium.

CHAPTER ELEVEN
LUCY PLAYS WITH THE SYMPHONY

"...musical performance, while it lasts, brings into existence relationships that model in metaphoric form those which they would like to see in the wider society of their everyday lives."

- Christopher Small (C.S.)

SIKURIS	SYMPHONY
• Egalitarian participation • Dialog • Individuals forming community • Dependent origination • Everyone welcome to participate from every socio-economic sphere • No concept of "star" • No concept of "talent" - everyone is born with innate musical ability • Traditionally takes place outside, anywhere • Traditionally moves, as in a pilgrimage • Musical instruments handmade made by member of the community • Hollow reeds symbolize mother nature, the womb from which we all were born	• Embraces Western Industrial Society values • One-way communication • Individual as star, to the point of narcissism (soloist in a concerto) • Producers/consumers • Place where middle class people can feel safe together • Artificially controlled access to becoming a "star" • "Talented" few are empowered to produce music for the "untalented" majority • Takes place in a single-purpose modern building (usually built with no expense spared) on the forefront of design and building technology that is a prominent landmark[i]

LIMA

After Lucy's sojourn in the U.S., she returned to find that one of the artisan workshops in Bolivia hadn't come through on the Suburban Provisioners' order. So, she searched and found another group in Lima. Although she was stressed-out getting the order filled, she was excited when her cell phone rang and she heard Carlos of Jaqe Runa say, "We're in Lima to record with the symphony! The panpipes are rising in esteem in society! Come record with us!"

(Symphonies) and concert halls are expensive and can be afforded only, whether directly or indirectly, by the wealth generated by industrialization. C.S.

It was a weekend. She would do it. After all, it was a dream come true.

Lucy's vision of the panpipes bringing peace to the world included playing the panpipes in symphonies. Earthy mysticalness would influence Western society to be more in tune with nature.

...nature had to die and ourselves become split off from her before true science (and Western Industrialized Society with its symphonies) could be born. C.S.

Lucy believed that the Andean Cosmovision would inspire people when they heard the haunting sound of breath being the wind in the reeds. And the dialog aspect - not only dialog between humans and nature and the invisible spiritual realm, but dialog between human beings. The audience would be inspired to dialog, just as the musicians dialoged, each with half the instrument, listening and responding so that their notes blend with those of their partner to make a melody like a marriage. Duality. Two hands working together. That was why she felt the urge to play the sikus together in community, and felt good when she meshed well with the group - she was participating in the formation of her ideal egalitarian society.

Lucy got on a bus to go to the convent where the sikuris were staying. The traffic belched diesel smoke. Lane markings and traffic signals were ignored. Frantic rush to get from here to there carrying as many paying passengers as possible. Horns screamed urgent complaints. Drivers cussed at each other through open windows.

Lucy stumbled down bus steps as the bus assistant (muscled firm with voice to match) held the accordion door open and hurried her along yelling, "Baja! Baja! Baja! Vamanos!" The door rattled shut behind her. The bus surged forward and disappeared into the churning rapids of Lima traffic.

Pedestrians jostled past street vendors and spilled into the road.

Carried along like flotsam, Lucy turned into the convent driveway.

The convent, she imagined, would be a quiet colonial environment with an inner courtyard filled with abundant green plants and brown cowl hooded monks' footsteps echoing in the silence of the stone corridors that ran under high arches that led one's mind to contemplate heaven.

Instead, the convent driveway ran through a two-story shopping mall. Giant posters of skinny teens with tight tummies in jeans dominated the scene like Holy Relics.

The convent leased out part of their complex fronting the boulevard.

Up two flights of linoleumed stairs to an open door (a padlock dangling off its hasp), Lucy entered a room filled with bunk beds.

"Lucy!" her friends welcomed her.

Some were sleeping, others rehearsing.

"You'll be my partner," Carlos said. Carlos was middle aged, older than most of the sikuris in the group except for El Oso Perezoso - Lazy Bear. El Oso lumbered about as if just disturbed from hibernation. Many of the sikuris had nicknames. Carlos's nickname was Profe, since he was a professor of music. Carlos was slightly taller than Lucy. That was part of why she felt at home in the Andes. The people are short, like her. Carlos regularly shaved the few hairs off of his round bespectacled face. But he always left a wisp of hair under his chin; not off the tip like a goatee, but further back. Lucy was fascinated by this patch of long kinky hairs left to grow in an otherwise conventionally groomed face.

"Here's your instrument."

Carlos handed Lucy a giant siku, three rows deep, of thick-walled bamboo tubes tied together. In her two hands it spanned from shoulder to shoulder and down past her hips. Carlos held the partner siku.

"Hoooof," Lucy blew across the long tubes and the deep resonance vibrated out. The harmony of the natural overtones sent shivers of joy all over Lucy's skin.

"We're recording ten songs." Carlos informed her.

"Aack! Ten? No way! I'll focus on learning one," Lucy said.

"You can do it!" Carlos said. "Look, I'm just starting to rehearse, too. It will be fine. The session is at 3 PM tomorrow."

Lucy did her best to sight-read the sheet music on this new-fangled type of panpipe that was an invention of the composer.

She thought, "It's been over 20 years since I've been sight-reading regularly. Man, this is hard!"

Her 42-year-old brain cells sluggishly stirred at this unaccustomed task.

This was so different from how the sikuris usually learned new songs.

Traditionally the sikuris stood all in a circle, looking at each other, listening closely to the thread of the melody that one or more sikuris played. The melodic phrase was stated then repeated. The second section often mirrored the first or carried the same hook or melodic phrase, but transposed up or down to different tubes on the instrument. The group usually played the song over and over. With each repetition, the newer players joined in on more and more notes. An oral tradition. A tradition of transmission of learning life to life in personal interaction, in dialog. A musical dialog of sikuris in a circle, in the moment. Engaging their whole being, being part of the whole. Creating a society - a world - that they want to exist. A world where people are aware, awake, participants in. Sensing interconnection with each other, the Earth and the infinite.

However, in the convent not only were the sikuris not in a circle, they weren't even listening or looking at each other.

What was going on here? C.S.

Each sikuri was facing a different direction, blowing sounds oblivious of the people around him. Each stared at a piece of paper in front of him that had a portion of someone else's creation frozen in black dots. It was a portion not only because not all of the orchestration was noted - just the part for that particular size siku - but more importantly it was devoid of the spirit of the creative act of interactive musicking.

Musicking is a verb. The paper was like a ghost of a life. It was a whisper from the grave. The creative act of composition had happened and passed away. All that was left was this skeleton. Just a bone or two, disconnected not only from the whole frame, but even from the bones closest to it. Most importantly it was disconnected from the force that animates life.

"That's enough," Carlos said after about half an hour. "Let's go sightseeing."

Lucy had the sniffles and work to do. Carlos and the others kissed Lucy goodbye on the cheek. They would rehearse again in the morning at ten.

The next day, Lucy arrived at the convent.

"The guys from Puno went out to breakfast," a sinewy man with a broom told Lucy, "They left about half an hour ago."

She tried to practice patience as she walked up and down the stairs to while away the time. On a landing she gazed out a steel-barred window. To better see the view, she reached her hand between the rebar and wiped a layer of diesel soot off the glass. In the middle of the block, over a rooftop, a bit of a dome protruded above a tiny courtyard with big green leaves. That was the only remnant of the convent that bore resemblance to Lucy's fantasy. It was inaccessible.

Eventually the sikuris showed up. They all went into the bunk-bed room to rehearse.

Lucy practiced by herself. Her head ached. She tried to learn more than the two bars she had memorized so far. Cacophony of panpipes, each sounding a different tune all at the same time, filled the room.

Finally Carlos said, "Let's go!"

Panpipes in hands, bamboo clacking together, the sikuris and Lucy trooped out and got on a bus.

A clean cut young man followed the group on board. He stood in the aisle, faced the back of the bus and spoke from the diaphragm, to be heard above the rumble and honks of the churning traffic.

"Ladies and Gentlemen, please excuse this interruption in your day. I know that you care about your children and their education. But it is expensive to buy them the study materials they need - materials such as this booklet of the history of Peru from the Inka Empire to the current day. Normally, in stores, this book would cost twenty, twenty five, thirty soles. But, here today you can buy it for much much less. What is in this book? (He flipped through the pages, as he leaned against a seat back for support, demonstrating as he talked). Here is a summary of the history of the Inka Empire, from the Island of the Sun to Cuzco up to the time of the conquest. Complete. How your children will appreciate this knowledge that you bestow on them, having this valuable reference in your home. All good parents want their children to learn so that they can grow up to get good jobs and be successful. And for the special price of only five soles, you can buy this book of knowledge right now. Five soles. How often do you spend five soles on beer with your friends? Now you can invest in the education of your precious children for just five little soles. Not thirty. Not twenty. Not even ten. Just five tiny little soles. I'll pass through the bus so you each can have the opportunity to bring this valuable reference book home to your beloved families. Ma'am, how many would you like? Thank you. Thank you. Sir?"

The book vendor went the length of the bus, then skipped down the back stairs at the next stop. A shaggy haired teenager squeezed up past him and boarded with a charango, a zampoña hooked around his neck with a bent coat hanger, and a sack of hard candies poking out of his chuspa bag slung across his shoulders. He braced his hip against the shoulder of a hefty matron in an aisle seat and strummed and blew across the panpipes as the bus swayed and jerked down the road. His feet planted wide, one ahead and one behind his center of gravity, as he kept erect as a deckhand on a storm-tossed craft.

At the end of the song he announced in a loud voice, "Ladies and gentleman, I hope you enjoyed this little song that I play for you to brighten your journey. I am a father, with a little baby girl at home with my precious wife. I not only play for you, but I offer you sweets to give you energy for your day. These candies are only ten for one sol. This is how I make my living, to care for my wife and my beautiful baby girl. My baby is sick and we need to buy medicine. Just one sol for ten candies. I will pass through the bus. I humbly thank you for your collaboration," In a softer voice he said, "Thank you sir. Thank you. Ten for one sol. Thank you," as he offered the bag to each passenger in turn.

Lucy gave him a coin, like she did for all musicians, but refused the candy since she was watching her sugar intake. She knew what it was like to make one's living playing on the streets for donations from strangers. You give your all and you're lucky if you get applause, let alone lunch money.

Forty minutes later, after many more sales pitches for everything from ice cream to an herbal ointment that cures all that ails you from acne to prostitis, the sikuris started to worry that they had gotten on the wrong bus. It was taking too long to get to their destination.

"Great," Lucy thought, "We'll be late and miss the recording session."

Lucy walked up to the front of the lurching bus like a drunken sailor, hanging onto the bars.

She asked the driver, "Is it far to the National Museum?"

"Almost there! Almost there!" he shouted as he reached behind himself to shift the three-and-a-half foot long transmission gear shifter that rose up out of the floor well behind him.

"What a set up!" Lucy thought, "Who designs these things?"

But he shifted quickly and smoothly, by touch, behind him. Lucy, an ex-bus driver, admired his skill.

"There it is! Get off here!" the bus assistant commanded as the bus ground to a stop. The folding metal doors clanged open with their own momentum.

"Thanks! Bye!" Lucy and all the sikuris stumbled out of the bus and jaywalked across the six-lane road to the museum.

Carlos led the group confidently up to the employee's entrance.

"We are here to record with the symphony," he informed the uniformed woman behind the little window.

"The symphony is done playing and they've all left," she said.

"No, I'm not talking about the performance. We are scheduled to record with them now," Carlos said.

"Well, ask at the main entrance, then. Goodbye." The woman closed her little window with a thud.

Carlos led the way around to the main entrance and asked the ticket taker about how to get in to record with the symphony.

"Try the East entrance."

They walked around to the other side, to an open gate with a guard shack. In the shade of a tree just beyond the shack, a group of sikuris was rehearsing.

Lucy was relieved that they weren't late.

"Everyone pull out their ID to leave with the guard," Carlos commanded.

...human willingness to obey orders, however repugnant to conscience they may be. C.S.

"Uh oh," Lucy thought, "I didn't bring any ID with me. I'll just walk in with purpose and maybe they won't stop me."

As the group gathered around the guard, setting down their giant instruments with care and searching multitudinous pockets for their laminated ID cards, Lucy strode in like she was in charge and went directly to the sikuri group under the tree and started going around the circle shaking everyone's hands.

"Whew! No one challenged me! I'm in! I get to record with the symphony!"

She joined the circle and tried to rehearse. Even with her glasses she couldn't quite make out the notes on the sheet music on the stand shared by several musicians. So she searched out another player who was playing the same instrument (malta ira) who looked like he knew what he was doing. She watched what tubes he blew and when, and copied them as best she could.

"Lucy! Let me introduce you to the maestro!" Carlos called.

"Pleased to meet you," Lucy held out her hand.

"How beautiful!" the symphony conductor stroked her cheek.

Lucy felt like a cherished artwork with his tender touch and clear gaze.

The maestro hurried off to tune up the orchestra.

Soon, the sikuris followed. They walked down through an underground garage and entered a wide doorway to underground rooms. From one of those cement-walled rooms came a cacophony like a hundred seals mating.

It was the orchestra tuning up.

Lucy followed her friends as they grabbed black metal music stands from the back of the room and set up in a line behind the first violins.

Musicians in an orchestra are as interchangeable as pistons in a Ford. L.Y.

"Great!" Lucy lamented, "They've set up one of the two mics right over me. I better not make any mistakes. I'll just blow the notes I'm really sure about. Oh, and look. There's a video camera on a tripod. Aimed in my direction. O man, now it will be obvious I don't know the music. I guess I'll just pretend to play, moving the instrument around, on the songs I don't know. I can't just stand here like a dolt."

The composer scurried about with a scowl on his face, whispering last minute instructions to the maestro at his stand - baton at the ready.

Composers, like other artists, catch ideas and visions that are, as it were, still in solution in society and crystallize them in metaphorical form. C.S.

The maestro tapped his baton and lifted it. The room fell into attentive silence.

"We will run through the first piece from the top," he said, as if to a lover.

The orchestra was his instrument and every musician was a beloved part of this instrument. His words and tone of voice were as loving and gentle as if he had been stroking a Stradivarius. Lucy fell in love. She wondered if he was single. But then her life would be wrapped up in orchestral music if she were married to a maestro. No. The sikus were Lucy's true love. O well. Enjoy the moment, of being there, in the basement of the National Museum with the symphony, getting ready to record a performance of these new compositions. It was already a dream come true. Why add the fantasy of falling in love with the maestro?

Lucy stood attentive, waiting for the signal to play.

The timpani started with a low rumble like thunder in the distant hills. An oboe and other winds joined in.

"Wow," Lucy thought, "It sure sounds different with all the parts!"

It was time for the sikus to enter. The maestro nodded with a slight flop of his long wavy hair. The sikus entered all together. Fortunately this was the piece where Lucy had memorized the re-occurring two bar phrase, so she didn't have to fake as much of it.

But, the composer came striding over looking like flames were ready to shoot out of his ears.

Lucy wished she could hide under the chair.

"Don't make eye contact," she thought, "Just look at the music and put my heart into looking like I'm playing."

He passed Lucy.

"Whew!"

He marched along the row of sikuris until he came to extreme far end.

The composer yelled at the sikuris, "You are destroying my creation!"

They played a phrase over and over for him. He stomped back to his post by the video camera muttering in disgust, "Ugly! It's ugly!"

"From the top," the maestro directed.

Following his white baton, they played it again. The composer held his elbow in one hand and his chin in the other. His brow furled. Throwing down his hands, he stomped up to the maestro and whispered to him.

Rap rap rap. The maestro tapped his baton on the music stand. The orchestra stilled except for dwindling sounds as less attentive players continued on for a few more notes.

"The cellos will start at 57," the maestro directed, with the composer hovering nearby like a ticking bomb.

The cellos played a few bars while the composer shook his head.

He yelled, "Like the sikus. You are supposed to sound like the sikus with a sharing of the melody. Play it again!"

The cellos played the phrase over and over, but it always sounded the same. Defeated, the composer gave up that battle and retreated back to the video camera on the tripod. He adjusted the camera. The lens now centered directly on Lucy.

Drawing on her Kotekitai training, Lucy stood tall and summoned all of her life force to do her best and be an asset to the group.

"Recording," the sound engineer said

In the silence the maestro lifted his baton and the timpani started its distant rumble. The oboe entered. The strings swelled. The sikus entered. All together, it was a joyous dance of music of instruments from Europe and the ancient Andes. Lucy glanced sidelong at another player to see what tubes he played during the parts when that two bar phrase wasn't featured. Lucy moved her instrument around, copying the other player, and pretended to blow.

"Here comes that phrase!"

With confidence and gusto, Lucy contracted her abdominals and shot air into the tubes.

The piece drew towards the end. She focused on coming in on the last note with confidence. The maestro held his baton in the air. Everyone listened to the overtones disappear into sweet silence that was being preserved for posterity on the recorder. No one breathed.

Someone's cell phone beeped.

It was Lucy's.

The maestro dropped his hands. Musicians groaned.

Lucy slid her hand into her pocket and pushed the "off" button on her cell, slumping her shoulders in shame.

After the recording session, the sikuris and the composer left the room as the symphony started rehearsing other songs that didn't include sikus. They stood in a circle in another cement low-ceilinged room in the basement of the National Museum.

The composer thanked the sikuris for playing and said that these were easy pieces.

He hoped the sikuris would record again in December on new, more difficult pieces he was composing.

... deep malaise of western art - indeed of western society; ...the pursuit ... of the products (things) rather than the processes (experiences) of life... C.S.

Lucy inwardly groaned at the thought of even more difficult works. Her dream was to play the panpipes for peace and to one day jam with Yo Yo Ma. But, really, to learn those difficult parts would take up more time than Lucy wanted to dedicate to it. She preferred playing in festivals in tiny pueblos, in the traditional communal dialog style, rather than in a concert hall to an audience.

... musical performance of one-way communication. The performance is a spectacle for the audience to contemplate, and they have nothing to

contribute to its course. C.S.

Especially since it was some other composer's work. Now, if these were Lucy's compositions...

"Wow!" she thought, "That would be cool to have a symphony play your composition!"

But Lucy realized she was more a simple sort of person with simple melodies and harmonies in her head. The truth be told, the complexity of orchestral music often gave her a headache.

The middle classes reject traditional ways of musicking in their eagerness to align themselves with the international industrial culture. C.S.

Lucy had fulfilled her dream of playing with a symphony. That was enough.

The composer was winding up his speech to the sikuris and Lucy wanted to give him a token of her thanks for tolerating her. In her chuspa she found a DVD of the music video she had made. She was going to mail it to a TV station, but hadn't gotten around to it yet. She could mail them another copy. This one she would give to the composer. Too bad the jewel case was cracked. O well. It was kind of like Lucy herself; quality inside tacky packaging.

Lucy made eye contact with the composer and extended the DVD. He kept his attention open to her. She walked across the circle to him and in front of everyone made a tiny speech of how she appreciated being able to play on his composition and that this was a tiny gift of a work that she had done.

He accepted it graciously.

To the group he said, "Let's get together tomorrow at 3 PM for coffee and to plan for the future."

With handshakes all around, the composer left and the group trickled out of the basement, into the clammy cold night. One of the sikuris, while leaving the recording session, encountered a beggar on the street and swung wide around him. He looked sideways at another sikuri and pinched his nose with a conspiratorial smile. The sikuri was now one of the elevated select few, having recorded with the symphony. He had nothing in common with this beggar - not even shared humanity.

Lucy had a tickle in her throat, so she went home to rest. The other sikuris went out to party.

The next day at about 2:30 PM, Lucy arrived alone at the convent. The sikuris were out. Their room was locked. She tried calling their cell phones, but no one answered. She was so looking forward to having coffee with the composer. Finally one of the sikuris answered his cell.

"We're in Plaza de Armas," he said.

"Wait for me! I'll be right there!"

She hopped in a cab to the plaza. Where were they? The plaza was huge! She made another cell phone call.

"Hola?" a voice answered.

A car beeped. Lucy heard a tinny beep a fraction of a second later in the phone.

They're close.

"I'm in the plaza. Where are you?"

"We're in front of the cathedral."

"Okay. I'm walking over there right now. Bye!" Cell phone minutes were expensive in Peru.

Walking quickly towards the cathedral, Lucy scanned the steps. They seemed half a block long, with clusters of people gathered here and there.

"There they are! I can hardly wait to talk with the composer!"

Lucy walked up to her friends sitting on the steps. She shook each one's hands and pecked a few on the cheek.

"The composer just left a few minutes ago, but his colleague is here," Carlos told her.

"What? But it's just now 3:00!"

"There was a change in plans."

And they hadn't notified Lucy.

She thought, "They didn't call me because I didn't play very good. They're rejecting me from the group. Or maybe they were just too broke to pay for the cell phone call. Or maybe they were too hung-over to think anything at all."

She felt disappointed. Everyone rose and started walking. Lucy went along. At a restaurant they went in. Lucy wasn't hungry, but she was along for the ride. It turned out that the group only ordered big bottles of beer. Lucy passed. The tickle in her throat had turned into a slight fever.

The representative of the composer bought the first couple of rounds.

"The composer has a proposal for you," he addressed Carlos, as the leader of the sikuris.

"Yes?"

"He would like you all to record eight songs for a cassette tape that will accompany his method book. The songs aren't hard. Nothing like you just played. They're easy. Unfortunately there isn't any pay. Of course he will credit the group."

The representative bought one more round, hung around for a few minutes making chitchat, then made his formal exit.

Carlos put the proposal to the group.

"What do you all think? Pedro?"

One by one, he called on the sikuris around the table to express their opinion. He skipped over Lucy.

Had he asked Lucy her opinion she would have said, "He should pay you. This is a commercial project. Even if he doesn't have the money to pay you up front, perhaps you could work out an agreement where you get paid once the method books and cassettes start selling."

But no one asked Lucy.

The sikuris were young, hung over from a weekend of partying, rehearsing and recording in the big city. Their pockets were full with their payment. They had stars in their eyes.

"Let's do it!"

...the more western man seeks peace, security and the satisfaction of needs through the proliferation of material means, with the products of will and intellect divorced from values, the more does he find them receding from him; the more he tries to progress, the more he destroys that which he wishes to attain. C.S.

"Yes! And it will just be us! Us nine sikuris! We are the only ones who worked so hard to learn this music and to come all the way to Lima. We will be the only ones recording with the composer!"

"I'll buy the cane for us to make new instruments just for the recording," Carlos offered.

"They'll be our instruments!" el Oso said, "Our very own! They won't belong to the group, but to us!"

Everyone was elated.

Everyone, that is, except Lucy.

Lucy was sad to see the community spirit of this sacred instrument being destroyed by egotism and greed. She lost even more respect for the composer. If his style of music using this ancient instrument caused people to become exclusionary and arrogant, then she didn't want to associate with him. She had lost nothing by missing the meeting with him that afternoon. Carlos ordered Lucy a cup of herbal tea as the sikuris finished off the beer.

The sikuris all chipped in to settle the bill, magnanimously refusing to let Lucy pay.

They left the restaurant and started heading back to the convent. At the corner of a main boulevard, Lucy said, "I'm going to say goodbye here. My bus is the other direction."

The sikuris formed a circle on the wide sidewalk, the other pedestrians streaming around them. Lucy made a short speech more or less in the indigenous altiplano style.

"Thank you for inviting me to perform with you all. It was a great honor. Unfortunately there wasn't enough time for me to learn the music very well. But in the future, with more time to prepare, I can play better. It was a great honor. Thank you again. And I wish you all a tranquil journey to Puno."

Lucy went around the circle, looked each sikuri in the eye, shook his hand and kissed his cheek.

"Goodbye, Lucy."

El Oso blurted out, "You can fund the recording of our next CD."

Lucy pretended not to hear. Her head throbbed. Her sinuses were clogged. A deep rattling cough shook her. She walked away into the jostling crowd as the sky grew dark.

And there was still that Suburban Provisioners order to fill.

Lucy in Lima

AUNT BERT NOTE

Dear Aunt Bert,

You wouldn't believe it! We had to re-sew almost all the chuspas. One of the workshops was fine - the artisans completed their order on time and the work was beautiful. But, the other! Shees! Everyday I went to inspect the chuspas. I set aside the rejects - ones that had holes in them, that were stained, that their straps weren't sewed on very well. And soon I started to recognize the same rejects over and over. The artisans put them back in the good pile when I wasn't looking! The straps were the worst thing. They were sewn on so sloppily that they would pull off the first time someone put something in the bag.

"They're fine," the artisans said. "Tourists here buy them this way all the time."

"But it 'aint gonna fly in the States," I insisted. Finally I sat there myself with needle and thread sewing sewing sewing day after day. That kind of shamed the artisans into sewing alongside of me. Finally we got 1,000 bags that were clean, in good shape and had the straps sewed on strong. I pulled an all-nighter last night packing them into the shipping boxes. Today I did all the Customs export paperwork. The chuspa bags are at the airline cargo warehouse and ready to go out on the next plane.

Now I am ready to sleeeeeeeeeep.

Love, Lucy

CHAPTER TWELVE
LOS ANGELES

CLARA

In the home-office of Orqo Warmi (Mountain Woman), Clara spent a few hours redesigning the priority list that Lucy had hand-scrawled and tacked to the wall askew.

PRIORITY LIST
1. Process and ship new orders
2. SALES - Call contacts from Gift Show
3. SALES - Call all music stores in L.A.
4. SALES - Call museum stores
5. Organize files
6. Everything else

Clara thought, "What graphic should I use for 'SALES - Call contacts from Gift Show?' Hmmm...

This looks cute.

Or what about this?

But calling is more like communications. What clip art is in that folder?

Oh! I like this! I'll put this one for 'Call Contacts from Gift Show.'"

Clara went through this process to find a graphic for each item on the priority list. She experimented with fonts and formatting. Then she rummaged around to find the most appropriate paper to print it on.

She thought, "The white paper in the printer is too boring. Here's some yellow paper. Hmm... maybe. Oh! Here's some cardstock with a marbley finish! Perfect!"

Humming, Clara pulled the white paper from the printer, tapped it to line up the pages, and carefully slid it back into the open ream on the shelf.

She pulled out a single piece of the cardstock and loaded it into the printer.

Her cell phone rang,

"Hello honey. Uh huh. Sure, you can have a piece o' that pie. Now be sure and give a hug to your little sister and do what your auntie tells you. Okay. I love you too. Hugs!"

Resuming her humming, Clara sat at the computer and printed out the Priority List in four colors on premium cardstock, then carefully thumb-tacked it to the wall. Her only regret was that she didn't have a picture frame for it.

The phone on the desk rang.

"Hello, Orqo Warmi (Mountain Woman), how may I help you?" Clara sang with a smile. "Oh! How are you? What's the weather like where you're at? Really? You know, that reminds me of my cousin, you'd like her. Anyways, she said that Austin was hot, too. I just can't bear the heat. I feel like I'm melting into a puddle of Jell-O. How about you? You have air-conditioning in your store? Oh good for you! Your order from the Gift Show? Why yes, it went out yesterday. I have the tracking number for you right here, now just a minute... Uh huh, uh huh. You don't say? Well that's lovely. It's been nice chatting with you too. Now you take good care of yourself, you hear? Okay now. Bye bye hon'!"

Clara hung up the phone with a pleased smile and looked around the office.

Now what to do?

Making sales calls could come later, regardless of what the Priority List said.

"I know! I'll practice the QuickBooks program. I'll set up a new company. My girlfriend is starting her own record label. This could be helpful for her. Okay, new company, enter name, 'Elm Street Records,' design invoice. Oh good! I love graphics. Let's see, what logo would she like? I better call her..."

And so the days passed in the office of the North American Manager of Orqo Warmi (Mountain Woman).

LUCY

Lucy lurched through the front door lugging a scarred and dirty giant suitcase, a carry-on bag on wheels, a bulging shoulder bag and a huge pack on her back. Her clothes looked slept-in (which they were) and her hair was an uncombed mass bundled up with a hair tie.

"I got the Suburban Provisioners' order sent off," Lucy called out to Clara in the next room as she struggled to get the backpack off. Her luggage fell in a heap on the living room floor. "These are samples for the next show, plus stuff for some of the orders. But right now I have to go to the bathroom, bad." Lucy dashed through the office/dining room/bedroom.

Upon returning, Lucy plopped in a chair by Clara's desk, looked around the room and said, "Hey, the office looks great! Any new sales?"

"Thanks," beamed Clara, then adjusted her position to look as professional as possible and said, "No new sales, yet."

Lucy sighed again and said, "I'm tired."

"Why don't you rest, hon?" Clara said.

Lucy sat up straight, "I can't. There's too much to get done. I have to shoot photos of the new samples for the catalog, and Photoshop them ... and ... and ..." Lucy recounted her list of overwhelming tasks as she got up and started unpacking her bags in an adrenalin frenzy.

ORDERS

When Lucy was in Lima filling the chuspa order, she simultaneously prepared for the chullu order that the assistant to the buyer for Men's accessories at Suburban Provisioners told her they would be placing.

Lucy had double-checked her suppliers. They told her that the price had gone up because it was the coldest winter in 50 years. Alpaca and llamas were dying. Frantic, she found someone with a supply of chullus at the original price. She bought enough chullus to cover monthly orders of 1,000 units for five months.

But, silence was all she got from Suburban Provisioners. They never followed through on placing that order.

Since she was in the States, Lucy visited one of their stores. She saw chullus. They were identical to her samples the new Assistant to the Buyer said she was going to order. Same Andean designs. Same crotchet stitch. Same everything. Lucy peeked at the label.

Made in China.

And Suburban Provisioners never did reorder the chuspa bags.

Lucy took out another cash advance on her Visa to pay Clara's salary. Positive she would recoup the money, she pushed herself to work harder.

Back to the Gift Show she would go.

An offer came in the mail for a new credit card at 0% interest. She filled out the form, transferred the balance from a different card and pulled out another cash advance to pay for the booth fee

"It's just a matter of time before I'll be able to pay off my debts," Lucy thought, "$5,000 for a corner booth for the long weekend. Yikes! But the location will be great and the big clients will find me easier and this will all work out."

At the Gift Show on Saturday, a guy placed a verbal order for $9,000 worth of backpacks.

"I'll fax you the P.O.," he said, and left.

Lucy thought, "That's a help."

Monday, designers for Fortune Brand bought some samples to redesign for next Season's new line for Bloomingdales and Nordstrom's.

A week later, Lucy jetted back to Bolivia to work on their new designs.

ITEM 3003 LLIJLLAY BACKPACK

Backpack One Sheet

CHAPTER THIRTEEN
BOLIVIA

"Manuel, we've got work to do," Lucy said. "These big-time designers loved the beanies, gloves and scarves your mother and the other workshops knitted. They made some changes and want me to send them samples using their new ideas."

"Sure thing," he said.

The designers for Fortune Brand emailed pdf images that they created in Photoshop, showing what they had in mind. Manuel's mother whipped up the new samples. Lucy sent them by FedEx to the designers.

"The scarf is lovely," they said, "However, the buyers for Fortune Brands want to see it with fringe, three inches long, on both ends. Can you send us that new sample ASAP?"

Lucy went to Manuel's brother's handcraft store to deliver the message. She loved being with Manuel's family in their shop. It was like a cozy womb. The arched adobe ceiling towered overhead. The scent of alpaca, llama and sheep wool made her feel at home, somehow. Stacks of folded aguayos, llijllays, lined the walls, absorbing all sound. Each weaving was a work of art made by a woman who probably couldn't read or write and never was consulted in National elections, because she didn't have a birth certificate or an ID card. Electricity, running water and showers were luxuries that didn't exist where she lived, where her ancestors had lived. Where she had raised her children who left and went to the city to study and work.

Lucy marveled at the fine and even twist of the yarn, handspun with a drop spindle. The aguayos from the community of Llallagua were her favorites. On one, figures of condors flew across like an animated panel. Another had playful wiskachas. These native animals were endangered, just as were the women who wove the cloth. Mother to daughter for countless generations. But, the daughters didn't want to spin and weave. They wanted to be executive secretaries and wear high heels and hip huggers.

But, still, the calm and invisible love that emanated from these laboriously made textiles was almost tangible for Lucy. She felt loved and that she was in the right place. The place that the panpipes called her to.

All of this flashed through Lucy's mind as she strode up to Manuel's mother, doña Teresa, who was napping behind the counter.

"Hola," Lucy said.

Doña Teresa roused up. When she recognized Lucy, a Saint-like smile illuminated her face.

Lucy pulled a scarf and a folder out of her shoulder bag and asked, "How much would you charge to knit two more scarves just like this one you made, but add fringe, like in this photo?"

"Oh, I don't want to charge you, hijita. You're like family."

"Thank you. I feel the same way about you. But I have to pay you and have to know what the going rate is, to figure out what to charge the client."

"My son is better at that sort of thing," doña Teresa said. She looked ready to nod off again.

Lucy tapped her arm to keep her attention.

"Okay, I'll ask your son. When can you make these scarves? I need them right away."

"Let's see," doña Teresa concentrated. "What day is today? I have to cook for the Church, praise the Lord, on Friday."

"Today is Thursday."

"Oh, so I will go to market today and cook tomorrow. What time is it, hijita?"

"I don't know," Lucy said.

Doña Teresa dug under her layers of sweaters and pulled out an alpaca wool handknitted pouch. She untied the drawstring and drew out a cell phone.

"Can you read this? The numbers are so tiny," doña Teresa asked Lucy, handing her the phone.

Lucy couldn't read it either. She put her hand in her pocket and pulled out a pair of folding reading glasses she had bought at a 99 Cent store when she was in the States.

"It says 4:23."

"Oh, it's too late today to buy the produce. I'll go first thing in the morning," doña Teresa adjusted herself in her seat with great satisfaction at having made this decision.

"But the scarves," Lucy reminded her, "When can you knit the scarves?"

"Well, Saturday is our prayer meeting, and of course Sunday is Church..."

Lucy's chest clenched with worry. She tried to speak calmly, but her voice was getting a bit more urgent, "Please, doña Teresa, I need to send a scarf off on Monday and I need an exact duplicate to keep here as a model. It's really important."

"Do you have the yarn?" doña Teresa asked.

"It's the same yarn as last time. You know, that you spun and dyed. They loved it. It was so soft and the color was just perfect."

"Oh, that was some scraps I had stored from years ago."

"I thought you were going to make new yarn, just for these samples?"

"Oh, I was, but then I found this yarn in a bag tucked up in the rafters and decided to use it."

Lucy took a deep breath, then said, "Can you make more yarn just the same color and everything?"

Doña Teresa did not answer. She stared towards the street while smiling her Saint smile. She held her hands out, palms up. Her lips started moving. She bowed her head and prayed in Quechua, "Thank you, Lord Jesus, for bringing this gringa like a daughter to me. Keep her safe. Wrap her in your Holy Spirit, Halleluiah, Amen."

Lucy smiled as she thought, "I love her. She is so sincere. But when the order comes in I'll have to use the other workshops for the job. Work is work."

She gave a peck on the cheek to doña Teresa and rushed out of the store to find some yarn that was a close match.

Monday doña Teresa put the finishing touches on the scarves. Lucy shipped one to the designers for Fortune Brands.

Soon, the order came in for 10,000 hand-knitted scarves, beanies and gloves.

"Cool! Now I'll be able to recoup my losses and also spread indigenous culture through the handcrafts!" Lucy thought.

She just knew that the end-user would sense the Andean Cosmovision vibe emanating from the yarn handspun by an Inka woman.

Although Lucy was bummed that Suburban Provisioners bought copies of chullus from China and her garage was stacked high with those 5,000 chullus, Lucy just looked to the future. She was determined to recoup her losses, while spreading Andean material culture.

But, Lucy ran into problems. She didn't calculate her costs well. A major workshop backed out of their verbal agreement. She sought a new workshop. Labor costs rose. Raw materials needed to be found from a different vendor. None were available at the original price. Her costs doubled, tripled, quadrupled. She stopped calculating costs and just tried to fill the order, no matter what.

"So what if I go deeper in debt on this. Once I fill this order on time and with quality items, I'll have their trust. On future orders I'll recoup."

She ran all her credit cards up to their limits. Instead of new credit card offers coming in the mail, Clara informed her that the mail was full of offers to consolidate debts.

Finally the order was complete. Lucy shipped it off.

Fortune Brands loved it.

Lucy got to work on the Backpack Order.

Manuel's family worked on part of the order. Lucy enjoyed passing through their garden where a natural spring gurgled forth and Manuel's mom, doña Teresa, stirred the soup simmering on a wood-fired clay cookstove.

CHAPTER FOURTEEN
CLAY COOKSTOVE

Clay cookstove,
smudged black
with a million fires,
radiates warmth.

Flames flicker
under the clay pot
la olla
nestled in its nook.
Soup gurgles
in concave depths
like in a mother's embrace.

Manuel's mother stirs the soup
in la olla
on the clay cookstove.
The clay cookstove sits on a
hip-high
knoll
next to a spring.
The spring
drip drip dripping
onto the broad-leaf ferns
she has nurtured
since her children learned to crawl and run.

Her twin black braids,
the never-cut ends tied off with puffs of llama wool,
sway
against her voluminous skirts
as she stirs
the soup.

Soup made from water
she carried
on her head
in another clay pot.

A clay pot she made.
The clay
she dug

on the rising of the full moon.

The water
she carried
from the stream.

The stream
clear as laughter,
that caresses the multicolored pebbles.
Pebbles that hold the shapes
of the beings they once were.
Here a frog.
There a puma.
Over there a llama.
Each pebble remembers
and tells its story
to anyone
who listens.

The mother listened.
She conversed.
The sacred frog,
llama,
puma were her friends,
her guides,
her protectors.

At least she used to listen,
used to converse.

But not since
that traveling preacher
introduced her
to her Lord Jesus Christ.

He taught her
she was a sinner;
ancient ways were pagan,
evil,
of the Devil.

No longer
does she commune
with the sacred

frog,
llama,
puma.

Now she prays,
"Thank you for dying for my sins,
my sins,
my sins."

A worn stone-lined path
leads
from the clay cookstove
to a wooden door.
A door
whose
paint is chipping in long wrinkles
like the wrinkles
on the
woman's face.

Through that blue painted door,
in the cool darkness
on the warped wooden floor,
sunlight spills
into a soft beaming pool.

Against the side wall,
in this cool adobe room,
Juanita,
a teenage Inka girl,
slumps
over her homework.

Mickey Mouse
grins
from her notebook's
cardboard cover.
Juanita's hair is cut
short
and spiky
with gel.
Eye liner,
like Cleopatra's,
rims her lids.

A sigh escapes
from her strawberry scented
glossy lips.

She looks away from her notebook
and up
at
the TV
that is connected with jumper cables to a car battery.
Her jaw slacks
as she stares
at the flickering images
of a voiced-over
game show.

Hypnotized,
her eyes
widen.
She stares
at the contestant.
The contestant's face
is twisted
in worry and desire.

Through clenched teeth the contestant blurts her answer.
The host
(who looks like a Ken doll)
shouts
in a baritone voice,

"That's right! You win! You win the car! The trip for two to Hawaii! The
Chris Craft yacht and, but wait there's more! You... Have... WON ... 10
THOUSAND DOLLARS payable to you in 20 yearly checks, taxes the
responsibility of the contestant."

The contestant screams
and jumps up and down.

Juanita bows her head
and gazes at
the rough wooden floor
that is her job to sweep and mop.

Against the far wall
she sees
the rough hewn plank bench
that wobbles
on its legs.

Juanita looks
at
the bed.
The bed made with ropes
her grandfather twined
and crisscrossed on a square frame.
A straw-filled mattress on top.
The bed
she shares each night
with her snoring mom
and an occasional
flea.

Juanita walks out the door,
following the aroma
of the simmering meal.
Her stomach
feels
nauseous.

"Imanaylla, wawaycha?
(How are you,
my dear child?)"
her mother
asks.

"Fuck you!" Juanita yells
in English.
She bursts into tears
and runs
out
the street door,
down
the rutted lane,
to
the internet cafe
where her cousin works,
to chat

with her virtual lover
half
a world away.

Humming computers,
glowing green
with vision dimming rays,
radiate warmth.

Boys in uniform sweaters and neckties
sit in a rigid row
in front of
the radiating screens.
"¡Puta!" they cry
as they each wrestle
with a virtual enemy.

The soup is ready
in la olla
on the clay cookstove.
The mother eats alone,
leaning her hip
against the knoll
by the spring
drip drip dripping
on the broad-leaf ferns
she has nurtured
since her children learned to crawl
and run.

Culture Smash

MESSAGE TO AUNT BERT

Dear Aunt Bert,

Sometimes I get so sad. I mean, I came to the Andes to find this peaceful world of which the panpipes sing and what do I find? Indigenous people, the artisans I work with, are throwing away their culture. Thousands of years of wisdom being ignored and discarded.

You know what's replacing it? The same old stuff that is destroying the world.

I'll stop here. I don't want you to get depressed, too.

Don't worry. I'll be fine. And I'll continue on. Sometimes, though, I get so discouraged.

Love, Lucy

CHAPTER FIFTEEN
DOROTHY AND AUNT BERT

Bert's phone, on her bedside table, rang at three AM. She picked up the heavy black receiver of the one-and-only phone she had ever owned, a rotary that had never given her any problems.

"It's happened," Doro said, her voice tense.

"I'll be right over."

Bert clacked the receiver into its cradle. She wrapped herself in her threadbare terry-cloth robe. She slipped her bony feet into beach sandals. In the kitchen, she opened a secret compartment she had made in the table. Out of the compartment she extracted a key on a cotton string. Bert went out her back door into the ever-present city glow that blocked all but the brightest stars. A car alarm whooped through its series of sirens. Bert followed the dirt path that wound through her forest of sculptures to the nasturtium-covered archway. The archway Bert had made during the War when she and Dorothy shared Victory Gardens. Passing through the arch, Bert entered Doro's backyard. She walked over the mowed grass lawn past roses in border beds.

The key was oxidized. Bert wiggled it in the lock of Doro's backdoor. It didn't want to budge. Her sculptor's hands kept at the task. She worked at this key and lock with the same determination she used when she uprooted the stump from her Dutch Elm that had died from disease.

Finally it turned. The deadbolt clicked back.

"I'm here Doro," Bert said in a voice like she was coaxing a frightened kitten down from a tree.

"I'm in the bedroom," Doro said.

Bert opened the bedroom door and turned on the light. Doro was in a heap on the floor halfway between the bed and the bathroom, her walker unused in the corner.

"O Doro!" Bert knelt down next to her friend and embraced her cheek to cheek. Their tears mingled as they cried together there on the floor.

Doro cried in pain. Bert cried with long quiet sobs. She held Doro as if she could shield her with affection, protect her from pain, guard her from death itself.

They had discussed this possibility many times. Bert was older, but Doro was more delicate. What if she fell and broke something? They had both seen many of their acquaintances disappear into old folks homes from which they never returned.

Doro's cries wound down and their breaths harmonized, chests rising and falling in unison.

Bert nuzzled Doro's soft white hair and whispered in her ear, "Do you want me to call 911?"

"No. They'll just cause a ruckus with their sirens and all," Doro said, "Call Bobbie. He's in the phone. Oh, but I hate to wake him..."

Bert picked up the cell phone that Doro always safety-pinned to her nightgown at the urging of her grandkids. The grandkids had all chipped in and bought her the phone and paid for her monthly service.

"Which button do I push?" Bert asked.

"Here, give it to me," Doro summoned all her energy and pushed the buttons, then her arms fell limp as she fainted.

Bert took the phone and held it to her ear. Someone answered.

"Bobbie, this is Bert. Your Grandma Dorothy fell. I think she broke her hip."

Ten minutes later, Robert pulled up in his SUV. He had the build of a linebacker - which he had been in college. He carried his grandmother to the car. Bert helped arrange her on sleeping bags in the back of the SUV. Then Bert climbed into the front seat.

At the hospital a doctor treated Dorothy's broken hip.

"She'll need to stay here for two or three days, then go to a skilled nursing facility," the doctor told Bobbie and Bert.

"See you soon, Doro," Bert said, embracing her friend propped up on pillows in her hospital bed.

"Yes," Doro said, groggy with pain killers.

It was now late in the day. Bobbie gave Bert a ride home as the sun splashed purple and magenta across the Pacific.

Sitting alone on the edge of her bed with the dip in it from over seventy years of use, Bert sighed, "It's been a long day."

On the nightstand she noticed a card that Lucy had enclosed with her letter. It said, "Nam-myoho-renge-kyo, SGI-Bolivia."

Bert, an athiest, picked it up with a smile. Lucy had been giving her cards like this off and on for years. One from San Francisco, another from Los Angeles, one from Guatemala. Those Buddhists were everywhere.

How did Lucy say to do it? Sit up straight, look a point on the blank wall and repeat the mantra.

"Nam-myoho-renge-kyo nam-myoho-renge-kyo nam-myoho-renge-kyo..." Bert repeated over and over until she felt something change. Her forehead relaxed and the worry lines eased. Her cheeks lifted in a smile. She sighed a deep breath. In her chest she felt a huge expanse as if the entire universe and everyone in it from the past, present and into the future was right there. Or had she grown big? It didn't matter. Bert felt a happiness and confidence that was beyond words. She set the card back on the nightstand. She lay down and pulled the quilt up to her chin, reached over and tugged the chain on the Depression Glass lamp she had received in 1933 from the artist in exchange for carpentry work, closed her eyes and went into a long dream.

In the hospital, Doro fell asleep. The pain killers were working. She hardly noticed at all the moans and yells of the woman in the next bed who was in the late stages of Dementia.

Doro dreamt.

In the dream Bert held a white ticket in one hand and extended her other hand to Dorothy.

"Doro! You know I've always wanted to travel! Now I am! Come with me!"

Bert looked great. So happy - and young! Her braid was thick and brown. Behind Bert was a bus. A huge bus. A bus as long as a freight train whose caboose was invisible beyond the horizon. And what a bus! Covered in jewels. It was a mosaic of everything precious or even halfway so. The glass in the windows was transparent sheets of quartz. The bumpers and window moldings were solid silver. Hammered gold were the panels. Inset were diamonds of all sizes and shapes, rubies, emeralds. Lapis lazuli bordered the diamonds to spell out letters on the side of the bus, "Nam Myoho Renge Kyo Express."

"Come on!" Bert said.

Bert's face was happier than Doro had ever seen. There was a glow to her, an aura of white that shimmered with all the colors of the rainbow. Holding Bert's hand, Doro boarded the bus. The bus was filled with people. The people sat on seats that were like thrones - or more like carved carousal seats. Some seats were shaped like roaring lions. Other seats were giant Lotus flowers. All the passengers were overjoyed to see Bert and Doro and waved to them with an exuberance that felt like the bus would levitate.

"There's the boy who mows my lawn!" Doro thought, "And there's Bobbie's ex-girlfriend, Nancy!"

And there was an Arab in a turban. A veiled Muslim woman. A gay man with nipple rings and leather chaps. A soccer mom. A Zimbabwe man with his mbira in hand. A judge in her official robe. A university rector. A six-year old karate champ in his tiny ghee. Even Tina Turner was on this bus.

They were all saying something - something in unison. It was a buzz, a roar, a force that stirred the cosmos.

The driver was a funny looking Japanese man with a shaved head and a white robe. He sat with his hands on the steering wheel and turned to Doro with the happiest possible expression on his odd face. His intestines rumbled. He and everyone on the bus chuckled in amusement.

"I have digestive problems," he explained with a laugh, then resumed singing that great song of life.

Doro turned to Bert with a questioning look on her face.

Bert held out the ticket to her. It said, "www.sgi.org, Nam Myoho Renge Kyo"

"Remember that day when we practiced saying Lucy's chant in my kitchen? It's the ticket! Let's travel!" Bert chanted along with all the other passengers, "Nam-myoho-renge-kyo nam-myoho-renge-kyo nam-myoho-renge-kyo..."

Doro awoke to sunlight streaming in her hospital window. She felt more alive and energized than she had in years, even though she had a broken hip. She picked up the bedside phone and called Bert's house. The phone rang. And rang. And rang.

Then she called her grandson.

"Bobbie, I think something happened to Bert. Will you please go to her house and check on her? The key is under the flowerpot of magenta begonias on the back stair."

Bobbie went and knocked on Bert's door. When there was no answer he lifted the flowerpot. In the damp spot underneath, a sow-bug curled into a ball. A few hair-like roots clung to the stair and even around the key. As he picked up the key, some roots tore off and floated to the ground. He unlocked Doro's backdoor and went in.

"Bert?"

No answer.

He opened her bedroom door. He saw her asleep in bed. She was so beautiful! Her face was relaxed and seemed somehow to look younger. A slight smile lingered on her lips.

"Bert?" he said softly, then repeated more loudly. Gently he shook her shoulder to waken her. Her arm fell from under the quilt. Her broad hand dangled alongside the bed. He took her hand. It was cold and limp.

He lifted her hand and placed it over her heart, and gave it a loving pat.

He pulled out his cell phone and called Dorothy's hospital room.

"Grandma Dorothy, I don't know how to tell you this..."

"She's gone. I thought so," Doro said with a firm voice. She had more life force in the tone of her voice than she had even before she fell. "Bobbie, now Bert keeps her important papers in a secret drawer in her kitchen table. You take off the table cloth and rotate the table top and you'll find the papers. She has a pre-paid funeral plan. Call me back and read the pertinent information to me. I'll make the calls from here. You stay there with her until someone comes to pick her up. Is that alright?"

Bobbie followed his grandmother's instructions. From her hospital bed with the telephone on the nightstand, and later from Whispering Oaks skilled nursing facility, Doro oversaw the settling of affairs of her dear friend Bertha Matilda Hawkins.

"Grandma Dorothy, I don't know how you do it..." Robert said during one of a daily visits.

"Now Bobbie," Doro said from her regal position in the throne-like bed, "I may not be able to walk, but I can still think and I can talk. So,

Bobbie... Wait a minute. 'Bobbie' is a little boy's name and you've been all grown up for some time now. I should call you by a more adult name."

"You can call me 'Bobbie' if you like," he said.

"How do you introduce yourself, nowadays, to people from whom you want the deepest respect?"

"Robert."

"Then 'Robert' it is. Now, Robert, what I want to talk about is that retrospective of my photographs you've been pestering me about. I'm ready. Let's do it. Bring me my boxes of prints and we'll go through them right here in this warehouse of old people. I'll show you which ones to exhibit. And please bring me my phone directory. I have a lot of calls to make. On another topic, I know you haven't been keeping in touch with your ex-girlfriend, Nancy. But, will you please call and tell her that I would like for her to visit me? I am ready to take her up on her many offers to chant Nam-myoho-renge-kyo."

Nam Myoho Renge Kyo Express

CHAPTER SIXTEEN
RED OCTOBER

October 2003, La Paz, Bolivia

THE DECISION

Lucy cleaned her apartment and put everything in order in case she never returned.

While sweeping the floor, she thought about her phone call an hour before with one of the artisans, Sergio.

"I finished making the backpacks, but it's too dangerous to deliver them. Two army tanks came down the street shooting at everyone. I just got back from the cemetery. There were thousands of people at the funeral. Everyone dressed in black, walking walking, carrying the caskets to the cemetery. We buried twenty eight people. Twenty eight! A baby that was in his mother's arms when the military shot her in the back. A grandmother who was sitting in her living room and a military hand grenade came through the window. One of the dead was my best friend. He was an artisan, a folklorista. He just stepped out of his front door for a second and BOOM! The police shot him dead."

His sob crackled over the phone lines, "This government is unbearable!"

Unbearable.

Lucy had to do something. But what? Of course her first thought was to try and end the war by playing her panpipes.

But this wasn't a handful of farmers on a dirt road. This was U.S.-supported massacre of the people in the streets.

Army tanks.

Hand grenades.

Automatic weapons.

Lucy glanced out the window. A pair of sparrows, unaware there was a massacre going on beyond the ridge, carried a bent leaf of grass to a hole in the brick wall outside. Their song was crystalline in the silent city.

Dissonant buzz sounded high above. A reconnaissance plane crossed the silent sky. The only plane in days. All commercial flights were cancelled. The streets below were empty. No busses. No taxis. No smog.

A girl's laughter echoed in the eerie quiet of the city under siege. Children ran out into the empty streets to play. Doppler sound of skate board wheels followed gravity down the asphalt. Asphalt that usually knew only double-axle trucks pressing worn tread and tooting Toyota vans, overweight with passengers, careening around each other like the plastic flotsam in the river that carved this valley. The walls of the valley echoed distant explosions.

The asphalt road outside Lucy's window was an ad hoc playground of children who didn't understand what the grown-ups were fighting about.

Mother's urgent voices called the children inside. Metal doors clattered down over storefronts. A march passed by. The street was lined with flags. Every family flew a flag from their home; Bolivian flags, indigenous Wiphala flags. Each topped with a black bow. Black plastic shopping bags tied on in mourning. Mourning of the killing that went on and on and seemed that it would have no end.

Where was this peaceful world of which the panpipes sing? Where was Lucy's soulmate? Where was any like-minded person with whom Lucy could feel at home?

If it was anyplace, it was there in the Andes, where panpipes for thousands of years endure. Lucy knew she had to continue her quest to find or create this peaceful world right where she was. While other foreigners fled the country, Lucy stayed.

Although she stayed, her courage battled with her fear. Lucy was too afraid to go out by herself and play her panpipes and attempt to stop this war. It was too big. She was just one person.

"Maybe other musicians will join me!" she thought.

She got out her phone book and started calling.

Nancy, no answer.

Jorge, no answer.

Jose Luis, no answer.

Finally, Charo answered.

"Let's play music for peace!" Lucy said.

"Jose Luis tried that during Black February and they tear-gassed him. I'm staying in my apartment. You should, too. It's dangerous," Charo said.

"I've got to do something! I'm not going to hide in my apartment and wait for the world to end," Lucy said.

"Well, some folks have gone to the Hunger Strike at Our Lady of the Miracles Church," Charo said.

The Hunger Strike.

When Lucy was a little girl her mother taught her about Civil Disobedience. Gandhi and his hunger strikes made a difference in India. When nothing else worked, a hunger strike was effective. And even if it wasn't effective and hunger strikers starved to death, they died with a clear conscience that they had done absolutely everything possible to speak out for justice.

That moment had arrived for Lucy. There was nothing else she could think to do to stop the massacre. If she fled the country she would feel like a failure. The time had come to offer her life in the cause of peace.

Like Gandhi, Lucy would fast until the killing stopped, or she starved to death.

Now that her decision was made, all her fear and uncertainty fled. Courage swelled as Lucy swept the floor, perhaps for the last time.

Yet, she also looked for a way to procrastinate just a bit. Her gaze fell on the dusty items that lined her window sill.

"I'll wash my rocks and bones," she decided.

As she washed soil out of sheep knuckles she thought about that dream she had with the Puma.

PUMA DREAM

Puma. A sacred animal here in the Andes. He entered the room I was in, confronting me with his sharp teeth and sleek strong body. The only defense I had was the book in my hand, a traveler's guide to Bolivia. I held it out like a shield. He bit into it, taking it out of my hands. He opened his mouth to let it drop. It clung to his upper fangs. After a few moments it dropped to the ground. I picked it back up, staring at two large punctures.

He started pacing again. I felt afraid. There was a bed next to me. I scrambled up into it. It raised like an elevator and I was high, away from the Puma. He didn't pursue. He exited from a door on the opposite side. Awhile later, I followed his path. Through the door was a long room that had a roof but no walls. In the rafters were streamers. The streamers were of various materials connected together. First I saw pastel colored serpentina like to bless people on their birthdays or on the Tuesday of Ch'alla. These streamers were connected to a piece of used fabric. The old fabric was connected to dry bunch grass, which was connected to..... the Puma!

But he was deflated. Desiccated.

In my hand appeared a letter. It was from the Puma. I unfolded the letter.

"Everything is connected. Everything is one," he wrote, "like dancers holding hands in a circle, we are one."

The rocks and bones of her collection, Lucy had found one by one in cobble stone streets and along footpaths in hills far from town.

As she washed them, she said goodbye to the white splintered sheep shin, mandibles, hip sockets shiny and round, igneous rocks, and a hunk of quartz that glistened and had a knob like it was the missing end of a stone femur.

She arranged the moist clean bones and rocks on the window ledge. The rocks sat a few inches apart. On top of the rocks, connecting them, she lay the bones.

Everything is connected. We are one.

JOURNEY

A last meal she cooked, using the last propane in the tank and the last food in the house; pasta and margarine. Stomach full, hair shampooed, body clean - Lucy gathered up the essentials that would accompany her to the Hunger Strike and possibly for the rest of her life: miniature gohonzon strung around her neck, her musical instruments – kena, charango and of course panpipes, two-liter bottle of boiled water, sack of coca leaves, and handwoven llama-wool poncho to keep her warm in the Altiplano nights.

Those nights, Lucy envisioned, she would sit on a pew, wrapped in her poncho, chewing coca leaves, playing her instruments (when a mass wasn't being said), sipping her water and chanting Nam-myoho-renge-kyo softly until the killing stopped, or she died.

Once she decided to give her life to stop the killing, there was no longer anything to be afraid of.

Like a prisoner who suddenly realized she had been her own jailer, Lucy opened the apartment door and walked out. She closed the door upon her past and turned the key. The deadbolt clunked home. She had set herself loose, free.

She walked outside onto the empty silent street. A light filled her. A light of justice; like the light at the blockade when she entered Bolivia. But this light was deeper. Deep like roots - roots of strength and perseverance.

No longer was she one of those furtive people dashing out with a plastic bag in hand to buy bread sold out of cardboard boxes on street corners with a line a block long. At the sound of an approaching march, everyone would scurry to hide inside buildings. Once the march passed, a brave or desperate shopkeeper would slide his metal roll-door up a meter for potential customers to duck inside and buy food. At the sound of another approaching march, the door would slam down shut. Heavy Yale padlocks clicked inside.

Lucy strode down the avenue as if she were a one-woman victory parade. A man darting-by glanced over at her with shock - a gringa walking down the street alone, in a hand woven poncho, her head held high and a light in her hazel eyes. Lucy smiled at his puzzled face and strode along. Her gaze caressed the hollow brick buildings scattered over the mountain side. In her heart she imagined embracing all the people huddled inside those buildings with maternal love. This might be her last view of the city.

All was empty and still. No pedestrians jostled elbows or jay-walked amid lurching traffic blaring horns and spewing black clouds. Instead, the air was a clean cool shock to Lucy's nostrils.

After walking a few miles through empty streets, she arrived downtown. Shouts echoed off the buildings of a march on the main boulevard, the Prado. At first she thought to take a side street, but then she thought how silly that was. If she was going to confront death, why take a side street?

Lucy decided, "I'll walk right up to the marchers and see what happens."

The chants of the marchers grew louder as Lucy drew near, the sole spectator.

A parade of women in velvet pollera skirts, poofed out with layers of lacy petticoats, strolled by in formation. They bounced their fists in the air in time with the chant led by a man with a bullhorn. Their broad feet were shod in molded plastic shoes. Layers of sweaters warmed the women, under their embroidered and macramé-fringed shawls. Small bowler hats rimmed in ribbon balanced on the crown of their heads.

Lucy walked up to the marchers. Their eyes met. They smiled.

One of the rows had an empty spot.

"May I join you?" Lucy asked.

"Welcome!" three women said, smiling. They motioned Lucy into their formation.

She slipped into place and strolled along chanting with the women:

"Fuerza fuerza fuerza!

Fuerza compañero!

Que la lucha dura

Pero venceremos!"

A new chant started. Hearing it, the women giggled behind their hands. Laugh lines crinkled around eyes. Lucy listened closer to see what it was that they were giggling about. The most she caught was:

"Goni!

Ladron!

Baja tu pantalón!

la de da de da de da de da

con Washington!"

Goni!

Thief!

Drop your pants!

la de da de da de da de da

with Washington!

Lucy could fill in the blanks. She smiled, too.

At Plaza del Estudiante, the march took a u-turn to head back up the other side of the Prado.

"I've got to go now. I'm off to the Hunger Strike," Lucy said.

"Que le vaya bien," a woman said with a smile of camaraderie.

ARRIVAL

Lucy tromped down the road to the church. She mounted the steps to the sanctuary.

Someone stopped her, "Are you here for the hunger strike?" Without waiting for an answer he pointed to the door of another building and said, "They're in there."

Lucy walked in. There was a little table staffed by two women.

"A registration desk to be a hunger striker?" Lucy thought, "What will bureaucracy think of next?"

"I'm here for the hunger strike," Lucy said, her eyes alight with higher purpose.

"All full up! Go away! There's no more room!" one of the women said.

All full? How could that be?

Lucy just stood there, immoveable as a statue. Once her mind was made up, nothing could sway it.

Another woman at the table said, "Thank you for volunteering to fast."

Lucy smiled and continued to stand there.

A man strode in and said, "I just got word. There's room for more hunger strikers at the Monticulo."

Towards the Monticulo she walked up a steep and empty street.

Empty except for the armed military police standing guard outside of the Department of Defense.

Empty except for a lone car coming down the hill. A huge white flag of truce, big as a king-size sheet, flapped above its roof and fluttered across the windshield. The driver hunched down behind the steering wheel. He peered out just enough to see over the dash. Hand-lettered sign in his car window read large, "PRENSA."

Prensa. Press.

"Don't shoot me, I'm just a journalist!" the flag and sign seemed to shout.

The car passed and Lucy kept walking. Huffing and puffing she climbed the hill. Cresting the top of the road she paused to catch her breath. Stretched across a side street was a banner made from a sheet. Red and black letters hand-painted, "Monticulo-Group Hunger Strike."

Lucy had arrived.

She knocked on the door of the church. A woman opened it. Lucy entered a tiny hallway. Another woman sat behind a little table in the corridor.

"We're all full," the woman at the table said, looked down at her paperwork and dismissed Lucy from her mind.

Standing firm Lucy remained.

When it became apparent that Lucy wouldn't go away, the women conferred in low voices and shuffled papers.

After a couple of minutes one said, "Another group is forming in a church in Miraflores. You can wait here. Human Rights will come by and pick up our overflow. Sign in."

With a sigh and a smile, Lucy gave her name, address, nationality and passport number. Red tape completed, she passed through the inner door.

HUNGER STRIKE

The door led into a small room, like a Sunday school classroom from Lucy's childhood. But this room was arranged differently than any she had ever seen. In the corner was a rustic wooden table with a couple of thermoses and mismatched mugs and herbal teas. Mattresses, foam pads and couch cushions lay in rows on the floor. On each mattress reclined a Hunger Striker. They all looked at Lucy. She smiled and introduced herself to the group. Out of her chuspa shoulder bag she pulled her panpipes. Kara Llanta she played, each note a soulful prayer. The Hunger Strikers, with a burst of energy, applauded.

"I've got a charango, kena, zampoñas," Lucy held out the instruments, "Who wants to play?"

A scrawny young guy reached for his guitar that leaned against the wall. An old guy with deep laugh lines politely asked to play Lucy's charango. A bearded man took the kena and warmed it up in his hands. The ad hoc ensemble gathered on a bench and a wobbly chair and played a wayño. The other hunger strikers clapped and sang along from their mattresses to the Bolivian folk tunes.

After a few songs, a woman from the table in the hall came into the room with a sheet of paper in her hands. She said, "The following people will be going to the newly formed piquete in Miraflores: Lucy ..."

"Can't I stay here with the musicians?" Lucy asked.

"No. You're going to Miraflores," the woman said.

The hunger strikers protested, "You can't break up the band! Lucy stays here with us! "

"But her name's on the list. She has to go."

"This is a democracy! We vote for her to stay! Luc-y! Luc-y! Luc-y!" they all chanted in unison.

People fasting in protest of authoritarianism weren't about to be cowed by a person holding a piece of paper.

The woman, flustered by the rising protest, capitulated.

"Okay, Lucy can stay."

"Yay!!!!!!!!!"

Two foam cushions, flattened with years of use and covered with faded fabric of Disney-like characters were offered to Lucy, along with a blanket. She laid her poncho on the cushions, set herself down and got comfortable. After all, this may be the last place she would be in this life.

Blowing into her panpipes, she played the refrain to Viva Cochabamba. The guitarist, resting on the mattress next to hers, strummed softly along.

Their last notes whispered into a sigh.

The skinny guy leaned his guitar back against the wall and relaxed into his bed.

Everyone lulled into nap mode. Amidst grunts and wheezes of tired and hungry people, Lucy drifted off to sleep.

The next day, she got to know the other Hunger Strikers. The skinny guy with the guitar was named Hochi. Hochi was quiet; Saint-like. He'd been in the Hunger Strike longer that anyone in the room. Two weeks.
On her right was Dora. Dora was an overweight salt and pepper-haired woman who worked at a radio station. A black wire ran from her ear to a transistor radio in her hand.

Dora said, "I came to the Hunger Strike after the government dynamited our transmitter in Oruro. Radio Juan Pablo II has an open door policy. Anyone can come in and talk live on air. Campesinos were talking about their experiences, the atrocities of the government massacre, on the radio; so the government blew it up," Dora said.

Lucy asked how Dora knew the government blew it up and not some terrorists.

"When a terrorist group blows something up, it's to get people's attention so they'll listen to what they have to say. They do it to be heard. Immediately they issue a manifesto; a list of demands. When it's State terrorism, the government doesn't say anything. No manifesto gets issued. They just blow something up and figure that will scare you and everybody else into being passive."

Dora paused to listen more intently to the transistor radio.

"U.S. Embassy Evacuates All Their People!" she shouted the news update for the edification of the Hunger Strikers.

"I'm not leaving," Lucy said, her voice choking with emotion, "I'm here with you. Forever."

On the next mattress down sat Ruth, a newscaster for the government-owned TV station. Her suit was rumpled from days of sleeping in it. Lucy brought her a cup of herb tea from the tea table and sat to visit.

"I was live on air," Ruth said, "reading a list of the wounded at Clinica Poder de Jesùs and I just couldn't take it anymore. I set the list down and said what was in my heart. 'This is far too many wounded for one tiny clinic to handle. You police and military are the ones causing this chaos. Stop the violence.'" Ruth sipped her tea. "Then I walked off the set and into the hunger strike." She set down her teacup, too agitated to drink. "That was four days ago. I don't care that I lost my job. Who would want to work for such an evil government? Pucha! Goni has killed more civilians than did all the military dictators; combined! Later that day most of my co-workers left too. The station went off the air."

Radio Dora shouted a news update, "CNN Reports Violent Protests in La Paz, Bolivia, But Military and Police are Calming the Situation. Calming!"

The Hunger Strikers snickered in disgust at this blatant lie.

Gabriel, a wiry mestizo Sociologist, reclined on a mattress across the room. Huge wad of coca leaves bulged one cheek. Palestinian scarf wrapped his sinewy neck. Even fasting, he had hyper energy. This was his fifth Hunger Strike in the last twenty years or so. He had protested military dictators installed by the U.S. and peace activists being "disappeared."

Gabriel liked to organize. At one point he gathered everyone into a circle and held a meeting.

"We'll issue a list of demands. Let's come to consensus on the wording..." Gabriel said, pen in hand.

Obligatory meetings irritated Lucy. Wasn't it enough that she was fasting until the massacre stopped or she died?

The next day the Human Rights woman from the hall ushered in a two-man documentary crew to interview the hunger strikers.

They went around to each mattress and filmed an interview with each person. When they got to Lucy they pointed the camcorder at her and asked, "Are those your zampoñas? Can you play us something?"

Lucy played a song. When it got to the singing part, she sang acapella in Spanish and Quechua -

"Tenemos la riqueza del espiritu
Somos la Pachamama
Somos la Virgen
Somos la divinidad
Somos la eternidad
Con nuestra musica y cultura podemos cambiar el mundo

Nubes de muerte
Nubes de inundacion
Nubes de guerra
Nubes de miedo

En La Paz cambia el clima con el sol
Noqanchis Inti kanchis

Llamamos el sol de felicidad
Dentro de nuestro corazon

Cantando nam-myoho-renge-kyo nam-myoho-renge-kyo nam-myoho-renge-kyo cantando nam-myoho-renge-kyo"

"I've heard that song once before," the guy with a camera in front of his face said, "It was on the radio, live."

"I wrote it a few months ago during Black February," Lucy said.

"Tell us about it."

"Well, I was going by Plaza Murillo in a minivan full of passengers, on my way to visit some artisans. Out the window I saw a march coming down the street. Now I've seen countless marches here. The police usually are leaning on their riot shields and look bored. But this time the plaza was filled with soldiers. They were all in formation, in a stance with one leg in front of the other and each had his rifle raised and was looking through the sight and his finger on the trigger. All the soldiers aimed at the approaching marchers."

Historians later would analyze Black February[ii] from a broader perspective than was possible for Lucy. Those two days of civil war in Plaza Murillo had their roots in the United States. One day in rural New Hampshire, in a resort-like building called Bretton Woods, the role of the International Monetary Fund (IMF) was transformed, which allowed it to grow more powerful than many governments. The IMF was controlled primarily by the United States and was charged with the task of imposing economic adjustments on the poorest of countries. Many people observed that starting about twenty years before Black February, the IMF and the World Bank had more influence on the running of Bolivia than the elected government. These financial institutions loaned Bolivia 350 million dollars on the condition that Bolivia adopt specific economic policies, such as selling the rights to natural resources (oil, water) to U.S.-based transnational corporations and devaluing Bolivian currency.

At the beginning of 2003, although Bolivia had completely repaid the 350 million dollars, the compound interest kept mounting. The IMF and World Bank put pressure on the government to put the squeeze on the people to pony up more money. So, the government announced a raise in taxes. The people took to the streets in protest. Also marching in protest was the Special Security Force of the Police Department. Their wage increase demands were refused (15 cents an hour was their average wage) and their January wages were not paid to them at all. The tax increase was the straw that broke the camel's back. They, too, took to the streets. They accompanied the marchers that Lucy saw approaching Plaza Murillo. Thirty four people died in the two-day shoot-out between the police and the military in a plaza that is usually known for its photo opportunities of feeding corn to pigeons next to graceful statues and flowering trees.

Lucy continued, "When I returned from visiting the artisans, there wasn't any transportation so I walked. Police tape closed off the entire area around Plaza Murillo. I heard shots. Down the street, some high school boys smashed a store window and started looting. Next to me, a grandmother hunched over with her stick, told me she was shocked to see youth looting. In her life she had seen many uprisings, but never had she seen high school boys breaking store windows and stealing things.

I told her that I had seen it. In the United States. In Los Angeles.

When I got home I thought about what I had witnessed. The boys looting weren't dressed in clothes of the countryside. They looked like boys I sit next to in any urban internet cafe. While I'm checking my email they're playing computer games like Grand Theft Auto. They practice stealing cars and looting stores everyday. Instead of learning how their ancestors lived in equilibrium for thousands of years, they are learning the value, 'Tener es mejor que ser. To have is more important than to be.'

I read that synopsis of Western thought in a book by Father Gregorio Iriarte. The book is, 'Globalismo, Post-Modernidad, Neo-Liberalismo'. Also I thought about writings of Daisaku Ikeda where he stresses that education is what makes us human. As an example he mentioned some children in Europe who were raised by wolves. As I remember it, people found the children and took them in and tried to teach them to talk and live like humans. The youngest siblings learned to talk and walk on two legs and eat with a fork. But the oldest sister never learned more than about fifteen words and behaved like a wolf for the rest of her life.

So, if education is what makes us human, and if TV, radio, the press and internet is our global classroom, then I decided to write a song and send it out to educate people to value the wisdom in the Andean Cosmovision and how that wisdom is in harmony with the Buddhism of Nichiren Daishonin.

A couple of days later when the shooting stopped and the tear gas cleared, I went to a radio station with a guitarist friend and we performed the song live on air to give hope to the people."

"I felt hopeful when I heard it," the film-maker holding a microphone said, "Where are you from?"

"I'm from the United States and I hate what my government is doing. They are causing so much suffering in the world. They are supporting the government murdering people in the streets."

"Why are you in the hunger strike?" he asked.

"I'm here as a last resort. This killing has to stop. I'm fasting until it stops, or until I die."

They got a solemn respectful look on their faces, nodded and quietly said, "Thank you."

After the documentary guys left, the Human Rights lady came in and opened hand-carved wooden shutters in the meter thick adobe wall. Round wrought iron bars caged the window on the outside. Outside were smiling people in red shirts and sweaters. All the hunger strikers gathered close to the window.

The people chanted, "¡Huelgista! ¡Amigo! ¡El pueblo está contigo!" (Hunger striker, friend, the people are with you)

The faces of the people outside were illuminated with joy, with ecstasy - ecstasy that people had the power. Democracy would triumph over tyranny. A new age was dawning.

Gazing through the bars at the visitors, tears of joy, of solidarity, sprang to Lucy's eyes.

This was something of the happiness that Lucy sensed in the sound of the panpipes.

The hunger strikers applauded their visitors. They felt renewed. The visitors left on foot, to encourage other groups of hunger strikers in the silent city. A military plane buzzed the sky, heading towards the massacre in El Alto.

Radio Dora shouted, "U.S. Ambassador David Greenlee Supports Goni 'Maintaining Order'!"

On Lucy's third day in the Hunger Strike, a nurse came to visit. One by one she checked everyone's health. Lucy was lethargic, but her vital signs were strong.

When the nurse took Hochi's blood pressure and pulse, she looked worried.

"You should break your fast, Hochi, to protect your health. Your life," the nurse said.

Hochi looked more saintly than ever.

In a soft voice he said, "The massacre is still happening. I will keep fasting until the end."

The nurse shook her head in sadness, sympathy and deepest respect as she left the room.

Lucy wanted to say something to Hochi. How could she honor his courage? She felt timid. What to say? She blurted the first thing that came to mind.

"Hochi, I've never heard that name before. Where's it from?"

"It's Vietnamese."

"Are you Vietnamese?"

"No. I'm 100% Bolivian."

"Then how did you get your name?"

"When I was born, my dad was the youth leader of the Bolivian Communist Party. My folks named me in honor of the Vietnamese Revolutionary Ho Chi Minh. It means, 'he who illuminates'."

"How interesting! What does your dad do nowadays?"

Hochi looked down at his mattress and said, "My dad died when I was nine. I'll never forget that day. It was September 5, 1982. He died in a car accident."

"I'm sorry," Lucy said.

He paused, as if to rest. Lucy had all the time in the world, so she waited silently to see if more words were coming. Hochi closed his eyes for a couple of minutes.

"He was with two other passengers and the driver. They all knew each other and were on their way to a meeting. My dad was running for office at the time - in Huanuni - the mining town where we lived." Hochi sighed, shifted on the mattress and paused to regenerate strength.

"He had just gotten back from Chile not that long before, where he lived with Pablo Neruda for months - studying the books in his library. Well, the car went off the road and no one else was seriously hurt. But my dad died." Hochi paused and swallowed.

Lucy listened with the utmost sympathy, waiting for the next words.

"After he died, men from the U.S. Embassy came to our house. They wore suits and ties. Their hair was cut so short I could see the wrinkles of their scalps. As I stared at the reflections on their patent leather shoes, I heard them offer to my mom to pay for her and me and my four little brothers and sisters to move to the United States. They would pay for our college education and everything. My mom told them that she didn't want anything to do with the United States. They went away."

Hochi looked at Lucy. Tears spilled down her cheeks.

"Why are you crying? You didn't do it."

He continued, "A few days later the driver of the car came to our house. He was trembling and stuttering. He only said a few words. He said, 'I'm sorry. I didn't want to do it,' then he left." Hochi paused, then said, "I miss my dad. There's so many things I want to ask him! About ... life."

Hochi looked into Lucy's eyes. Together they silently grieved.

Radio Dora shouted, "There's Over 500 Hunger Strikers! Even in Argentina They're Striking With Us!"

Murmurs of approval. The Hunger Strikers rested on their mattresses, conserving their dwindling strength.

A woman from the table in the hall came in waving Xeroxed papers in the air.

"Here's copies of an official letter from U.S. Congress to Goni!" she said as she handed one to every Hunger Striker.

Lucy wanted to go to sleep, but she read the letter, which said:

**Congress of the United States
House of Representatives
Washington, DC 20515·0307**

October 16, 2003
President Gonzalo Sanchez de Lozada
Presidential Palace
La Paz, Bolivia

Dear President Sanchez de Lozada:

I wish to express my serious concern for the safety of demonstrators based on the human rights violations that have taken place during the mass protests currently occurring in Bolivia. In four weeks of demonstrations, roadblocks and strikes an estimated fifty people have reportedly been killed, several hundred injured and an undisclosed number arrested. The majority of the victims in El Alto and La Paz appear to have sustained gunshot wounds.

According to reports by Amnesty International and Human Rights Watch, most deaths occurred when armed forces were sent to the El Alto area with the authorization to use force to secure safe passage for convoys of gasoline tankers headed for La Paz. Troops fired tear gas at protestors and opened fire with live ammunition and rubber bullets. Machine guns were also reportedly used. As a result, scores of demonstrators were injured from gunshot wounds, among them women and children. Most protesters appear to have been armed only with sticks, stones and slingshots, although some may have used sticks of dynamite.

Representatives of the Catholic Church, human rights groups, and civil society in Bolivia and around the world have criticized the use of live ammunition by the armed forces.

While recognizing the duty of Bolivian authorities to uphold law and order, the deaths suggest that armed forces failed to exercise proper consideration for human rights. International standards dictate that lethal force can only lawfully be used when strictly unavoidable to protect life.

I would respectfully urge you to ensure that local authorities respect the human rights of the demonstrators and to ensure compliance with UN International standards including the 1979 UN Code of Conduct for Law Enforcement Officials and the 1990 UN Basic Principles on the use of Force and Firearms by Law Enforcement Officials.

I hope that the authorities will work towards a peaceful solution to the conflict. I will be monitoring this situation closely and would appreciate receiving new information on this matter as it becomes available.

Sincerely,

Raúl M. Grijalva

Lucy set the letter down. Her arm was fatigued from holding it. The room was quiet. The Hunger Strikers rested.

Hochi struggled to get up. Lucy overcame her own lethargy and got up to assist him. She helped him stand, then supported him with her arm hooked through his as they walked together towards the bathroom.

Later that night, Lucy awoke. Soft snores around the room rippled the quiet.

Hochi shivered visibly under his blanket. Lucy crawled onto his mattress and spread her blanket and poncho over him. She spooned with Hochi to warm him.

They slept.

Lucy dreamed.

In her dream there was a giant book. The book opened up. The pictures came to life. There was William Randolph Hearst talking on the phone with his press artist on assignment in Cuba.

"But, boss," the artist said, "There's hardly any shooting. There's nothing to draw."

"You do the drawing. I'll make the war," Hearst said.

The page turned.

A Nazi concentration camp was full of screaming dying people. A face appeared. Franklin Delanor Roosevelt. He was on the phone, listening to William Randolph Hearst.

"You do what I say and I'll make you president. Don't mention Hitler.'

The page turned.

A Bolivian man in a shirt and tie was on the phone.

He was trembling.

A voice said, "You will give the order for the military to accompany the gas tanker trucks through the blockade. Shoot to kill."

Behind the man there was a painting on the wall. Wild brushstrokes of a man in a suit cradling his sleeping six-year-old son in his arms. He looked at an off-canvas threat.

The page turned.

There was Gandhi. He stood there so serenely, gazing at the world through his spectacles. Gandhi morphed into Hochi with loin cloth and staff.

Hochi/Gandhi said, "All you need is love."

Lucy woke up. It was morning. A sunbeam illuminated Hochi's face. A little smile curved his lips. He looked angelic.

Lucy sensed something was different.

She stroked Hochi's shoulder. It was so cold. She nudged his arm. It flopped down from his side, completely limp. Her hand she placed under his nostrils. Nothing. His neck she felt for a pulse. Nothing.

"Hochi died!"

Lucy's cry woke up the other hunger strikers. The Human Rights worker from the hall bustled in, assessed the situation and bustled out again.

Gabriel called a meeting.

"Let's all gather in a circle."

The Hunger Strikers sat or reclined on the floor. Hochi on his mattress was part of the circle. Lucy sat next to him, her hand resting on his calf. People said eulogies for Hochi.

Soon, two guys with a sheet came in and lifted Hochi away. Tears blurred Lucy's vision. Her throat clenched.

"We can't chicken out just because Hochi died," Gabriel said. "No one is allowed to leave the Hunger Strike. The public will think we are sneaking food if we go outside. Let's go around the circle and each person recommit to the Hunger Strike."

This was just too much for Lucy.

"It wasn't no meeting that brought me here, Gabriel, and I don't need no damn meeting to stay!" Lucy said.

The other hunger strikers started chanting, "No more meetings, Dammit! No more meetings, Dammit! No more meetings, Dammit!".

Gabriel shriveled in embarrassment and decided it was time to step out of the room and go to the bathroom.

Dora shouted out a headline she heard on her transistor radio that was plugged into her ear, "Hunger Striker Dies."

Everyone got quiet. Hochi. Dear Hochi. Which one would be the next to die? How long would the massacre continue? Like a dozen Gandhis they continued fasting for peace.

Later, Dora shouted another headline. "Goni Flees Country, Escorted by U.S. officials to American Airlines to Miami."

Fled the country? Lucy didn't expect that. She just wanted the killing to stop.

Now what?

The Human Rights lady from the hall brought in a TV. The Hunger Strikers watched Congress convene late into the night and vote Goni out of office. Vice President Carlos Mesa was sworn in as President in a solemn ceremony. His inauguration speech rang true and sincere.

What joy shone on the faces of the Hunger Strikers! Lucy's eyes moistened with emotion.

"He understands!" she thought, "He understands the suffering of the people!"

Congressmen and women applauded Carlos Mesa. The Hunger Strikers and all of Bolivia jumped up with joy, shouts, tears, hugs, more hugs and laughter. It was like the best New Year's ever.

Dora with her radio and earphone called out, "Hunger Strike Called Off!" She yanked the earplug from her ear and gazed at each person in turn with a look of awe on her face. She said, "We won!"

The newscaster grabbed Lucy by her upper arms, looked her in the eyes with a look of extreme joy - the joy of someone who had put her life on the line for what she believed, for the truth, and had triumphed. Her voice cracked with the physical weakness from days of fasting but was loud with spiritual strength, "We did it! We did it! The people have stood up for justice and we won!"

Gabriel went to the tea table and ate all the honey in big dripping spoonfuls.

The priest of the church came into the Hunger Strike room and interrupted the celebration.

"Now that the crisis is over, you Hunger Strikers have to go," the priest said. "Be sure to clean up the mess you made."

After sweeping and mopping and folding blankets, at midnight, weak with hunger but elated, the Hunger Strikers trickled out into the streets and joined the ecstatic multitudes.

CELEBRATION

Outside, laughter and cheers of pure-hearted celebration and camaraderie blossomed and flew like petals of sound that fluttered off of the mineral walls of the mountain womb that cradles La Paz.

Euphoria filled everyone.

On a blockaded mountain road, the blockaders laboriously moved aside the debris of a dynamited overpass to let transport pass. Men and women pulled and shoved the twisted metal and hunks of concrete to the side of the road. It looked as if a major earthquake had happened.

In the empty street near the stadium, an orange bonfire of celebration warmed hundreds of women and families, wrapped in blankets. They were lined up on the sidewalk in the frosty night with empty propane tanks (the yellow chipped-paint in the darkness looked like they were sprinkled with confetti) waiting for the arrival of the first truck in a month to arrive and exchange their empty tanks for full. Once again they would be able to boil water and cook.

In the cold midnight, people left their houses and went out into the now safe streets. Lucy walked past a store just as it rattled up its metal door and light spilled out onto the sidewalk. People gathered in that light, laughing and smiling. Brown bottles of beer passed from hand to hand and the shop keeper clanked coins into his wooden money box that had sat unused during the massacre.

On another street Cholitas danced with each other, holding hands and spinning their velvet pollera skirts and layered eyelet petticoats high in joy.

Lucy smiled and wanted to join the dance, but it was all the energy she had to keep walking up hill.

On one corner a gas station, that had run out of gas two weeks earlier, was crowded with vehicles waiting for the arrival of a tanker that was sure to come with the new day. Leaning against a battered stake-bed truck with a For Hire sign in the window was a grey-haired man. His work-hardened hands thrust into his pockets. His face was creased with a lifetime of worries and joys. Standing next to him was a necktied taxi driver whose car was in line.

"It was the hunger strikers that did it," the grey-haired man said. "The blockaders with their rocks and sticks and the miners with their dynamite could have continued forever and Goni would have just sent more soldiers and police and kept massacring people. But the hunger strike. Hundreds of people fasting. All kinds of people. Not a union or an association with a leader. But hundreds of individual folks. More every day. That's what made him run. He couldn't bear the international opinion of the hunger strikers starving to death."

The taxi driver said, "That's right."

Lucy smiled with a job well-done.

When she arrived at her building, she turned her key in the lock and re-entered the apartment where everything was in order, just as she had left it.

BACKPACK ORDER

The next morning, Manuel accompanied Lucy to collect the Backpacks. They took a bus for as far as it went, then walked the rest on foot. The buses weren't entering the artisan's neighborhood because the dirt roads were still littered with blockade debris. Walking in, they stepped over broken glass and rocks scattered across the road. Goni hung in bloody effigy from telephone poles. Tires smoldered in smoky heaps. Acrid smoke stung Lucy's eyes and throat. Above the houses black flags of mourning flapped in a gentle breeze.

At Sergio's house, Lucy and Manuel gathered up the backpacks and found a neighbor with an old truck to transport them to her apartment. They carried the backpacks upstairs and into Lucy's bedroom. Then they went to an internet café to check their email.

A letter from Fortune Brands was in Lucy's inbox.

"Maybe it's a new order!" she thought.

The email read, "The prices for the new samples you sent are too high. Can you come down in price? We can have them made for half the price in China. Or India. Or even Brazil."

Lucy felt sick to her stomach. Those were realistic prices she had quoted them. There was no way she could come down.

The next email she opened up. It was from the Backpack Client. Although they had been corresponding for a few months about the order, somehow he had never actually faxed her a P.O.. Now he wrote that he was canceling the big backpack order. He bought them cheaper from China.

In addition to feeling sick to her stomach, now her chest clutched in panic.

Nine thousand dollars worth of backpacks sat in Lucy's room; boxes stacked to the ceiling. She had paid the artisans. She had gone on a hunger strike. She had done everything she could to fill the order.

Now she faced bankruptcy.

She turned to Manuel for sympathy and support.

"Don't worry," Manuel said. "I owe thousands of dollars to all kinds of people. Life is to enjoy. You play sikus, drink, laugh with friends. You die. You get reborn. You do it all again. Don't worry."

He gave her a brotherly peck on the cheek and left, without paying for his internet time.

Learning about this life-philosophy of Manuel's, Lucy realized she hadn't lost a thing when they ended up "just friends".

But, how was she going to get out of this crisis? Even if she declared bankruptcy, how would she be able to stay in the Andes and continue her quest to find or create the peaceful world of which the sikus sing?

"Nothing is impossible," Lucy thought, "There has to be a way to change this poison into medicine; to not only get out of this crisis, but to have a much better situation than ever before."

The only thing Lucy knew to do was chant. Back to the apartment she went. She would use the strategy of the Lotus Sutra. Solidify her embankment of faith. Bail the seawater of doubt out of her ship of faith.

Alone in her room, surrounded by backpacks, Lucy chanted to her gohonzon. She chanted with the determination to change the direction of the tide, to re-steer the heavens.

"Nam-myoho-renge-kyo," she chanted and chanted.

Bit by bit she felt her chest relax, the panic fade.

Slowly, again, she saw the bright sun of hope within.

Hope.

Confidence.

Confidence that all of this was really exactly what she needed to grow stronger, strong enough to create the world of which the panpipes sing.

Like a Phoenix she rose.

Her feet led her to the post office. Why, she did not know.

Lucy checked her mail at General Delivery. There was an official-looking letter covered in dust. (Lucy didn't check her mail in Bolivia very often. Most mail went to her home-office in Los Angeles where Clara took care of it).

She blew the dust off. She walked to the plaza, sat on a bench under a flowering tree and opened the envelope.

It was from a lawyer.

"Before all else, please accept my deepest condolences on the death of Bertha Matilda Hawkins..."

"Aunt Bert!," Lucy said aloud, "No!"

Her favorite person in the world.

Gone.

Dead.

Lucy's throat felt like a lemon got stuck halfway down. Her eyes got hot. Grief spilled out in racking silent sobs. She covered her face with her hands. Sadness washed through her and spilled out onto the earth.

"Aunt Bert," she mourned, "You understood me when no one else did."

Tears flowed like pulsing river rapids. Bert, who taught her how to fix a car, how to use hand tools, how to not give no mind to what anybody thought about you. How to live true to yourself.

Each memory a throb, like a cloudburst swelling a river that surged over boulders, washing away flotsam. She cried till all was purged.

Clean.

Gone.

The flood had run its course.

"I still understand you," Lucy heard in that intuitive place that science will never be able to map.

"I know. Thank you."

Looking up, Lucy saw a vendor with a cart. The vendor squeezed oranges into a glass. Lucy wiped her eyes with the back of her hands and rubbed her face. She stood up and walked to that vendor. That glass of fresh juice Lucy bought. Down she drank. Tart sweetness cooled her throat.

She sat on the bench and read more of the letter.

"...You are sole beneficiary of the property of Bertha Matilda Hawkins; specifically, her house at 133 Driftwood Lane, Santa Monica, California and its contents..."

"O my god!," Lucy thought, "Your house! Aunt Bert! I had no idea..."

And Lucy's tears rivered all over again. This time mixed with deep appreciation.

When people asked on which side of the family was this aunt, Lucy always responded, "It's kind of complicated."

Sometimes the family we choose is as precious to us as the family whose blood we share.

The lawyer was a friend of Bert's. She had pro-bono set up this Living Trust. The lawyer would help Lucy sell the house and invest the money. The market was peaking. That funky house handmade during the Great Depression by a poverty-stricken woman a block from the ocean would soon sell for piles of cash to a movie mogul.

Lucy would pay off her debts. Interest from investments would cover her modest living expenses.

TODOS SANTOS
November 2, 2003

Todos Santos, All Saints' Day, when the spirits walk the earth. Everyone went to visit deceased loved ones in the graveyard. Lucy dressed up in a traditional velvet pollera skirt and went to visit Hochi.

Crowds filled the cemetery. Ferris wheel turned. Vendors sold soup and flowers and beer. Roving musicians played at one tomb and then another. Brass bands, guitarists, accordion players and of course, sikuris. Around Hochi's grave gathered the hunger strikers, Lucy and Hochi's family. A panpipe group wandered up.

"That's the gringa sikuri I saw on TV in the Hunger Strike!" one sikuri said to his partner in Aymara.

He walked up to Lucy and held out a siku. She accepted it with an appreciative smile.

"What was that tune we heard you play on TV?" he said, handing her his siku of seven tubes so she could demonstrate the whole tune.

Lucy softly played once through her composition, "Nam-Myoho-Renge-Kyo", and handed the seven tube siku back to her new friend.

All the sikuris softly played the melody over and over, quickly memorizing the tune.

When everyone got it, the guia raised his maso high, swung it down, up again and down. Music emerged triumphant. Someone blew a long celebratory note on a conch shell.

The Hunger strikers and sikuris formed two concentric circles around Hochi's grave. The sikuris danced, playing, in one direction. The Hunger strikers danced in the other. They danced a dance of joy, of victory, celebrating the life of this man dedicated to justice.

Lucy sensed Hochi's spirit rise from the grave. Space she made next to her so he could join the circle. Manuel and Ayllu strolled over from different directions and joined the dance. Sergio the artisan saw Lucy and came over to dance. Together they all danced. Spontaneously Lucy's new friend smiled at her, hooked elbows with her and they spun in circles in the warm sunlight. Her face turned up to the sky, laughing. Her skirt flared out as she twirled. Their feet patted cool freshly turned earth.

A man in a suit and tie took someone's outstretched hand and joined the circle.

"Hey!" Lucy thought, "That's the guy I saw in my dream! The Bolivian guy getting that phone call that freaked him out!"

He was the Minister of Hydrocarbons and he danced with a happiness he hadn't experienced since he was a wonder-struck child watching the magic of dust motes dancing in a sunbeam.

Other sikuri groups joined in the celebration. The concentric circles of music and dance expanded to the neighboring graves. Those families started dancing. Everyone at the cemetery started playing and dancing in more and more concentric circles like ripples on a human pond, dancing with a joy they had never experienced before.

The sound of them all singing Nam Myoho Renge Kyo echoed up to the glacier-topped peaks and beyond.

Healing joy spread across that blue orb hurtling through space. The universe resounded with the vibration of Nam Myoho Renge Kyo.

The End

Rather than fleeting satisfactions, one's ultimate goal should be to attain "the Buddha land," or enlightenment - that state of boundless joy in which one realizes the eternal truth within one's life.

- The Writings of Nichiren Daishonin I
(Background on "Aspirations for the Buddha Land)

APPENDIX A
PHOTOGRAPH AND ILLUSTRATION CREDIT
All art used by permission

Chapter 3 Aunt Bert
Aunt Bert (digital) Woodblock print by Lynette Yetter
Based on Matthias Sebulk's Public Domain (Wikipedia) photograph
"95-year-old Woman"

Chapter 4 Oruro
Coca Vendor, oil on canvas by Lynette Yetter

Chapter 6 Don Jaime
Adobe house by Lynette Yetter

Chapter 7 Candelaria
Self Portrait, oil pastel by Lynette Yetter

Chapter 8 Conima
Lake Titicaca, digital art by Lynette Yetter based on a photo by
Claudia Risch

Chapter 10 Meteor Crater
Space Collage by Lynette Yetter with photos by NASA

Chapter 12 Los Angeles
Orqo Warmi (Mountain Woman) Backpack One Sheet by Lynette
Yetter. (Collage element, photo of the painting: Virgen del Cerro. In La Casa
de La Moneda museum in Potosi, Bolivia)

Chapter 14 Dorothy and Aunt Bert
NMRK Express by Lynette Yetter (Digital collage using found
        images with permission)
        Found images -
Hammered Gold: Joshua Treviño, flickr.com/photos/trevino
Crystal: NASA
Wurtzite: Alan Guisewite
Raw Ruby: Wikipedia
Lapis Lazuli block: Wikipedia
Galaxy: NASA
Grill: Curtis Hart, MuscleCarRanch.com
Lapis Lazuli raw: copyrighted image item lapl117 used with
permission from catalogue http://www.mineralminers.com
Tire Tread: Wikipedia

Aguayo	Aymara. See Llijllay.
Alba	Spanish. Sunrise Mass.
Altiplano	Spanish. High plain. Name of the region in the Andes in which most of this story takes place.
Amiga	Spanish. Female friend.
Anata Andino	Aymara (anata). Game, play. Spanish (andino). Andean. Name of a festival in Oruro, Bolivia
Apu(s)	Quechua and Aymara. Deity. Often associated with distinctive landforms.
Arka	Aymara. Follow. Name of the row of seven tubes of the siku.
Awkinaka	Aymara. Old men.
Bayeta de la tierra	Spanish. Homespun wool fabric.
Bloqueros	Spanish. Blockaders.
Boliviano	Spanish. Literally "Bolivian." The name of the monetary unit used in Bolivia. One Boliviano is a silver colored coin that was worth approximately fifteen cents in U.S. dollars at the time this story took place.
Bombo	Aymara and Quechua. Large (approx one meter tall and half a meter wide) cylindrical drum with a drum head on each end. Often made with goat hide on the top and alpaca hide on the bottom. The fur may or may not have been removed from the hide. Played by striking with a single mallet.
Buddha	English. "Awakened One." One who perceives the true nature of all life and leads others to attain the same enlightenment. This Buddha nature exists in all beings and is characterized by the qualities of wisdom, courage, compassion, and life force.
Bueno(a)s dias /tardes /noches	Spanish. Good day/afternoon/evening.
Bungee	English. Elastic rope.

Byakuren	Japanese. Literally, "White Lotus." Name of a young women's service group in the Soka Gakkai International.
Caida de bombos	Spanish. Literally, falling drums. The name of a drum sequence played by sikuris.
Campesino(s)	Spanish. Rural farmers.
Campo	Spanish. Rural, countryside.
Candelaria	Spanish. Name of a holy Virgin and her festival. Literally "candlestick", for the distinctive candle she carries in her right hand. The infant Jesus is in her left hand. She is a syncretism of the Pachamama with Catholicism.
Carnaval	Spanish. Carnival. Syncretism of Catholic and indigenous spirituality expressed through public musical and dance performance.
Ch'alla	Aymara and Quechua. To bless. Usually involves drizzling alcohol on the ground.
Chao	Spanish. Bye.
Chajra	Spanish (chacra). Quechua pronunciation. Field. Garden plot. Plot of land farmed by a family or community.
Charango	Quechua. Fretted musical instrument with ten strings. Originally made from Armadillo shells. Later hand-carved from a solid block of wood to resemble the form of an Armadillo body.
Charanguista	Spanish. Person who plays the charango.
Chicha	Quechua. Homemade corn beer.
Cholita(s)	Spanish. Indigenous women in traditional dress.
Chullu	Quechua. Knitted pointy beanie.
Ch'uñu	Quechua and Aymara. Traditional freeze dried potato.
Clinica Jesus de Poder	Spanish. Health Clinic named "Jesus Power."
Cochabamba	Spanish version of Quechua word. City in Bolivia. The Quechua is Qocha pampa. Lake Plain.
Compañera(o)	Spanish. Comrade.
Conima	Aymara. Name of a town on the North shore of Lake Titicaca.
Contigo	Spanish. With you.

Desaguadero	Spanish. Drainage. Name of a city on the river that flows out of Lake Titicaca.
Doña	Spanish. Missus.
Double-wide	English. U.S. slang for a mobile home. Sometimes used in a derogatory way in reference to the living conditions of working-class people with little education.
El Prado	Spanish. Broad urban walkway with park-like plantings.
Esta	Spanish. This.
Faja	Spanish. Brightly colored woven cummerbund tied around the waist. Used to support the lower back when lifting heavy weights. Also worn as an adornment, especially in autochthonous Andean musicking.
Folklorista	Spanish. Person who studies and practices folklore traditions.
Fuerza	Spanish. Force, as in summoning up all of your inner fortitude to continue to battle obstacles.
Gohonzon	Japanese. The object of devotion in Nichiren Buddhism. It is a sacred scroll that embodies the Law of Nam-myoho-renge-kyo, expressing the life-state of Buddhahood, which all people inherently possess. Go means "worthy of honor" and honzon means "object of fundamental respect."
Gringa	Spanish. Woman from the United States.
Gringa facil	Spanish. Woman from the United States of easy virtue, i.e., easy to have sex with.
Guia	Spanish. Guide. Specifically, the conductor musician in a group of sikuris.
Hasta luegito	Spanish. See you a little later.
Huelga de hambre	Spanish. Hunger strike.
Huelgista	Spanish. Striker. Specifically a hunger striker.

Human Revolution	English. The "human revolution" is a term used by Josei Toda, second president of the Soka Gakkai, to describe the process by which an individual gradually expands his life, conquers his negative and destructive tendencies, and ultimately makes the state of Buddhahood his dominant life condition. Rather than changing society directly, through improving or reforming social or political systems, the object of change lies deep within the life of each individual. SGI President Daisaku Ikeda wrote these words in the foreword to his novel The Human Revolution: "A great revolution of character in just a single man will help achieve a change in the destiny of a nation and, further, will cause a change in the destiny of all humankind."
Ilave	Aymara. Rich farmlands. Name of a city near the shore of Lake Titicaca.
Ilaveño	Spanish. Person from the city of Ilave.
Illimani	Aymara. Literally "ray of light". Name of the sacred glacier-capped volcano that guards the city of La Paz, Bolivia.
Imanaylla kasanki	Quechua. How are you?
Indio	Spanish. Derogatory word for indigenous person. Connotates "sub-human" or "animal".
Inka	Quechua. Inca. The "k" is used instead of the "c" to express pride of culture.
Inti	Quechua / Aymara. Name of the Sun god. The sun.
Ira	Aymara. Teach or lead. Name of the row of six tubes of the siku.
Janaq Pacha	Quechua. Sky. Sacred realm above the Earth. Deity.
Jaqe Runa	Aymara (Jaqe) and Quechua (Runa). Person.
Jilata	Aymara. Brother.
Juan de Baile	Spanish. Name of mountain in Bolivia. Literally John of the Dance.

Kallawalla	Quechua. Name of a wiseman/healer from the Charazani region on Lake Titicaca.
Kara Llanta	Quechua. Name of drought-resistant bunch grass native to the Andean high plain.
Karma	Sanskrit. Literally "action." The life-tendency or destiny that each individual creates through thoughts, words and deeds that exert an often unseen influence over one's life and environment.
Kenista	Spanish. One who plays the kena (end-notch flute of the Andes).
Killa	Quechua. Moon (deity).
Kosen rufu	Japanese. Literally means "to widely declare and spread (the Lotus Sutra)"; to secure lasting peace and happiness for all human kind through the propagation of Nichiren Buddhism. More broadly, kosen-rufu refers to the process of establishing the humanistic ideals of Nichiren Buddhism in society.
Kotekitai	Japanese. Literally "Drum and Fife Band". Name of young women's marching band in the Soka Gakkai International.
Kusillo	Aymara. Literally monkey. Also name of a dance character. See Candelaria chapter for details.
Ladron	Spanish. Thief.
Law	English. Nichiren Buddhist term. See "Mystic Law".
Llijllay	Quechua. Handspun, hand-dyed, handwoven wool fabric used to carry nursing baby on back and other uses.
Loqhe Palla Kuya	Aymara. Name of an autochthonous music and dance that uses only one half of the siku. The musicians wear large paper hats and long crescent-shaped paper tails, with which they whack people.
Magica Blanca	Spanish. White Magic. Brand name of a laundry detergent.
Maricon	Spanish. Derogatory word for homosexual.
Martes	Spanish. Tuesday.
Maso	Spanish. Soft-headed mallet for playing a drum.

Mbira	Shona. Thumb piano. Traditional trance musical instrument of Zimbabwe.
Mestizo	Spanish. A person with ancestry of both indigenous and European peoples. Also used to refer to an indigenous person who has adopted Western ways and abandoned their traditions.
Mikisito	Spanish. Little Miki. Affectionate term for Saint Michael.
Mineria	Spanish. Mining.
Ministerio	Spanish. Department of national government.
Miraflores	Spanish. Flower view. A residential neighborhood in La Paz, Bolivia.
Mistura	Spanish. Confetti.
Monticulo	Spanish. Small mountain, viewpoint.
Moqor Puriña	Aymara. To reach the maximum, all that one can bear.
Morenada	Spanish. Name of folk dance that references the African slaves that the Spanish brought to the Andes.
Musicking	English. Verb. Definition proposed by musicologist Christopher Small: To music is to take part, in any capacity, in a musical performance, whether by performing, by listening, by rehearsing or practicing, by providing material for performance (what is called composing), or by dancing.
Muzak	English. Brand name that has come to mean recordings of generic renditions of instrumental music that subliminally tranquilize people.
Mystic Law	English. Nichiren Buddhist term. Japanese myoho. The ultimate law, principle, or truth of life and the universe in Nichiren's teachings; the Law of Nam-myoho-renge-kyo. This term derives from Kumarajiva's Chinese translation of the Sanskrit word saddharma, from the title of the Sad-dharma-pundarika-sutra, or the Lotus Sutra.

Nam-myoho-renge-kyo	Sanskrit and Japanese. The fundamental law of the universe expounded in Nichiren Buddhism, it expresses the true aspect of life. Chanting it allows people to directly tap their enlightened nature and is the primary practice of SGI members. Although the deepest meaning of Nam-myoho-renge-kyo is revealed only through its practice, the literal meaning is: Nam (devotion), the action of practicing Buddhism; myoho (Mystic Law), the essential law of the universe and its phenomenal manifestations; renge (lotus), the simultaneity of cause and effect; kyo (Buddha's teaching), all phenomena.
Nichiren Daishonin	(1222-82) The founder of the Buddhism upon which the SGI basis its activities. Based on his enlightenment, he inscribed the true object of devotion, the Gohonzon, for observing one's mind and established the invocation of Nam-myoho-renge-kyo as the universal practice for attaining enlightenment. The name Nichiren means "sun lotus," and Daishonin is an honorific title that means "great sage."
Nuevo(a)	Spanish. New.
Ojotas	Spanish. Sandals made out of recycled tires or other materials.
Oqa	Quechua. Botanical (Oxalis tuberosa Molina). Edible tuber native to Andes.
Orqo	Quechua. Mountain.
Oruro	Spanish. Name of a city in Bolivia. Derived from the name of the inhabitants at the time of the Spanish conquest - the Uru peoples.
Oso	Spanish. Bear.
Pachamama	Aymara and Quechua. Principle deity. Often translated as "Mother Nature." Embraces the entire space/time continuum.
Palla Palla	Aymara. Literally "chosen" as in the military draft. Name of a dance in Conima, Peru that mocks the military draft.

Papito	Spanish. Literally "little father." Used with affection when talking to little boys.
Parque	Spanish. Park.
Percodan	English. Brand name of an addictive pain-killing drug widely used in the U.S.
Perezoso	Spanish. Lazy.
Piel de lobo	Spanish. Wolf skin. Name of satin-like acrylic fabric.
Pino	Spanish. Pine.
Pio	Spanish. Pope.
Piquete	Spanish. Squad.
Pixcha	Aymara and Quechua. To chew the sacred coca leaf.
Plaza Avaroa	Spanish. Plaza in the Sopocachi neighborhood of the city of La Paz, Bolivia.
Plaza de Armas	Spanish. Weapons' Square.
Plaza del Estudiante	Spanish. Student Plaza. A principal plaza near the University Mayor de San Andres (UMSA) in the city of La Paz, Bolivia.
Pollera	Spanish. Voluminous skirt worn by Quechua and Aymara women. Gathered at waist and tied at the side.
Prefectura	Spanish. Government office.
Prensa	Spanish. Press, as in journalism.
Pucha	Spanish. Exclamation. Some say it evolved from a softer way to say the cuss word, "puta". Also means "daughter" in Aymara, but Aymara informants insist the two uses are unrelated.
Puta	Spanish. Misogynist exclamation. Bitch.
Qanri	Quechua. And you?
Qhepi	Aymara, Quechua. A bundle carried on one's back. Traditionally the square cloth was hand woven by the user or a member of the user's family. Recently factory produced synthetic fabrics made by the hundreds of meters, incorporating traditional iconic designs such as Inti, the Sun god, or the endangered Andean mammal - the wiskacha, are used to carry the bundles. The square fabric is laid on the ground and the items placed in the center. One corner of the fabric is

	pulled over the items. Its opposite corner pulled over to cover the items as much as possible. The remaining two corners are used to pick up the bundle and they wrap around the shoulders and tie in front. For men, they slide one corner under an armpit before tying them in front.
Q'oa	Quechua. A ceremony to bond people together spiritually.
Que le vaya bien	Spanish. Travel well.
Reaganomics	English. U.S. slang for a foreign policy that made the rich richer and the poor poorer.
Reeboks	English. Brand name of an expensive sports shoe.
Sagarnaga	Spanish. Name of a street in La Paz, Bolivia.
San Miguel	Spanish. Saint Michael. Archangel Michael.
Sartañani	Aymara. We lift ourselves up.
Segundo	Spanish. Literally, second. The main course of a meal.
Señor	Spanish. Mister.
Señora	Spanish. Missus.
Sensei	Japanese. Teacher.
Serpentina	Spanish. Paper streamers wide as fettuccini noodles.
SGI	Soka Gakkai International. Lay Buddhist organization. www.sgi.org
Shoten zenjin	Japanese. Nichiren Buddhist term. Heavenly gods and benevolent deities. Also, Buddhist gods, protective gods, tutelary gods, guardian deities, etc. The gods that protect the correct Buddhist teaching and its practitioners. Gods who function to protect the people and their land and bring good fortune to both. They are the inherent functions of nature and society that protect those who uphold Mystic Law.
Si	Spanish. Yes.
Siku	Aymara. Panpipes. Usually two rows of bamboo tubes, graduated in length. One row of six tubes. The other row of seven tubes.
Sikuri	Aymara. Person who plays the panpipes.

Soles	Spanish. Plural of "sol" or sun. Name of monetary units in Peru.
Sonqoy	Quechua. My heart.
Super Squirters	English. Brand name that has come to mean any large plastic squirt gun that resembles an automatic weapon and shoots a stream of water long distances. Super Squirters are not used by participants in Carnaval - that is the musicians and dancers. Super Squirters are used by boys who do not participate in the cultural event, but attack the participants and observers, emulating the Western style aggressors they learn about through TV, video games and the internet.
Suti	Aymara and Quechua. Name.
SUV	English. Slang for "sports utility vehicle".
Tari	Aymara. Small square aguayo (see llijllay).
Tener es mejor que ser	Spanish. To have is better than to be. (Father Gregorio Iriarte's synopsis of Western values).
TEVAs	English. Brand name of expensive synthetic sandals.
Tia	Spanish. Aunt.
Tio	Spanish. Literally, uncle. Also the name of the earth spirits that live in the mines. The Spanish depicted these earth spirits as demons or devils.
Todos Santos	Spanish. All Saints. Specifically November 2, when the spirits of the deceased ancestors wake up. The living go to the cemetery to visit with them.
Toro	Spanish. Bull.
Tortora	Quechua. botanical: Scirpus californicus. Reed that grows in marshlands of South America. Grows three to nine feet tall, according to the species. Used in construction of roofs, walls and boats. Tortora boats traditionally are used to navigate Lake Titicaca and the sea along part of the coast of Peru.
Toyo	Aymara. Name of the largest size panpipes.

Tranquilo	Spanish. Tranquil. Mellow.
Tu	Spanish. You (informal relationship)
Una(o)	Spanish. One. (-a feminine, -o masculine)
Usted	Spanish. You (the most formal and respectful relationship)
Valerian	English. Name of flowering herb, native to the Americas, that grows in sunny rocky places. Its chemical properties form the base of the tranquilizer Valium.
Valium	English. Brand name of a tranquilizing drug widely used in the U.S.
Vibe	English. U.S. slang for "vibration".
Vicuña	Quechua. (Vicugna vicugna), South American camelid that lives in the Andean high plain in the South of Peru, part of Bolivia, the North of Chile and the Northeast of Argentina. Known for its fine soft hair. It has not been domesticated, unlike its cousins the llama and the alpaca.
Virgencita	Spanish. Literally, little Virgin. A term of endearment referring to the Holy Virgin.
Vos	Spanish. You (the most intimate and familiar relationship).
Wai	Aymara and Quechua. Vocalization sung in some songs.
Waka	Aymara and Quechua. Indigenous pronunciation of the Spanish word for cow, vaca.
Walejlla	Quechua. I am fine.
Wawaycha	Quechua. My dear child.
Wayño	Quechua. Genre of Andean music and dance. Danced by couples or in a circle.
Wayra	Quechua. Wind.
Wiphala	Aymara and Quechua. A flag. Has come to refer specifically to the rainbow colored flag that represents the indigenous peoples of the Andes.
Xerox	English. Brand name that has come to generically mean "to photocopy".
Yo Yo Ma	Japanese. Name of world-renowned cellist noted for the joy with which he plays.

APPENDIX C
ENDNOTES

Chapter 11

[i] Christopher Small, "Musicking", Wesleyen University Press, 1998

Chapter 16

[ii] Jim Schultz, "Lecciones de Sangre y Fuego; El Fondo Monetario Internacional y el 'Febrero Negro' Boliviano" (Deadly Consequences: The International Monetary Fund and Bolivia's 'Black February'), The Democracy Center; San Franciso, California, 2005

Breinigsville, PA USA
09 September 2010
245059BV00001B/6/P